Resolute Love

The Vision of Love Series
Book 4

Dionne Grace

Resolute Love: The Vision of Love series
Copyright © 2017 Dionne Grace

Published by: Dionne Grace
Visit the author's website at; **www.dionnegrace.com**

Acknowledgements

Congratulations to Niki and Sam who won the *Committed to Love* competition and made an appearance as characters in this story.

To Jacquie Sinclair, for donating the words to her new release; "*Without Your Love.*"
If you would like to download this track for free, please contact me at my website; www.dionnegrace.com

Dedication

To my Heavenly Father, Jehovah–Ahavah - The Lord of love; he is and will always be the ultimate and perfect expression of love.

To my readers, thank you for your support.

Chapter 1

Daniel turned off the ignition, his heart racing at the thought of seeing Sara again as he reached for the flowers on the seat. He'd stayed away for three weeks—*three long weeks*. He was frustrated, nervous, and a little overwhelmed. He was adult enough to admit that he missed Sara—needed her. No matter how much he tried to stay away, he found himself drawn back to her yet again.

They'd tried it for a while, and things went back to how it was—home-cooked dinners, quiet evenings in, comfortably working together.

Problem was, it was no longer comfortable for him.

He wanted more.

But honestly, *did* he want more? He wanted her—being with her had become a necessity, something from which he could no longer hide. Nevertheless, a commitment was something else entirely and it was something he wasn't sure he had inside him to give.

He'd met Sara through his sister-in-law, Rachel. Sara and Rachel were close friends and he'd been drawn to her from the very first time they'd met. They became friends, although he'd made it clear to her he wanted more—she made it clear she was a Christian, and there would be no relationship unless he committed to her, which wasn't ever going to happen as far as he was concerned. He was a bachelor and he intended on staying that way, but as time went on, their *relationship*—so to speak—became more emotionally involved. Then there was Negril at his brother's wedding. They became

5

close, and he discovered that she loved him, and everything changed for him.

Women tended to fall in love with him with the expectation that he would fall in love with them and when that happened and they became clingy, he ended the relationship. He had no time or the inclination for love or commitments.

But with Sara it was different; he had an innate possessiveness for her that he couldn't seem to control. The attraction between them tore at him, it was strong—a pull that never left, and that had him fighting his needs which had never been an issue before. He never denied himself the pleasure of a woman, and now he was a Christian. He had to make some steep adjustments which hadn't been easy.

As far as he was concerned, Sara was his. His dilemma was, because he wouldn't commit, that didn't stop other men wanting to step in and take what belonged to him. Which had caused a few arguments between them. He didn't trust her and that was the crux of the matter; he trusted no women, and Sara needed to understand that.

Then there was that night. They'd gone out for dinner at The Langham, and they were waiting in the foyer for the valet to collect his car. A man approached Sara, pulling her into his arms. Instead of the sharp slap Daniel had expected her to administer to the unknown man's face, she'd flung her arms around him as if they were lovers, with a huge smile on her face. The man even closed his eyes as he drew her closer.

Jealousy, rage and a possessiveness rose within him. He wanted to flatten the man.

"Barry, it's been an age," she said, drawing away, still smiling. "I can't believe it's you!"

"You're looking good," Barry said, giving her a slow perusal, a smile on his lips.

Daniel felt his throat constrict. He wanted to do damage. "Aren't you going to introduce me?"

They both looked at him as if they'd forgotten he was there, which angered him even more.

"Barry and I went to university together. We're old friends," she said, her eyes returning to Barry.

Then *Barry* caressed her face, totally ignoring Daniel—*and she let him!* He resisted the urge to punch Barry out and shoved his hands in his pockets.

"Call me, I haven't heard from you in a while." And then Barry walked away, heading inside the hotel.

Daniel said nothing as they waited for his car to pull up and they got in. He was *fuming*, trying his best to calm down. "Who was that?"

"A friend from uni. I told you that."

"You seemed a lot closer than friends." He glanced over at her; she was staring out the window and didn't respond, which riled him. "Do you talk to him often?"

"Sometimes."

Sometimes? She didn't offer anything more in response and he took in a deep breath and tried to remain calm.

Taking out his anger on his Jaguar F-Type, using the power behind the car to drive fast, he swerved round corners, zipping in and out of lanes and put all his concentration on dropping her home as quickly as possible.

He didn't trust women, and Sara was no exception. He'd been wasting his time with her; it was time to take a step back.

He shut her out, driving at speed, his mind in a zone. It was only after a long moment that he realised that she'd said something.

"…wrong, Daniel?"

If she didn't know what was wrong, then he certainly wasn't going to enlighten her.

"Daniel…will you slow down, please?"

He sighed and eased his foot off the gas, bringing the car to a slower pace. It wasn't too long after that he pulled up outside her house. Still, he said nothing as he got out and opened her door for her.

She searched his face. "Daniel?"

"Good night, Sara," he said, and got back in the car. He waited until she opened her door and went in before he drove away.

That was the last time he'd seen her. After he'd calmed down, he tried to rationalise the situation, but it still boiled down to trust for him, which was the reason he'd stayed single all these years. Yet he was here again, and he didn't know what he planned to say to her.

It was late, but he knew Sara would still be up. He was about to get out, when he noticed a man walking along the path to her door. He waited and watched when her door opened; she came out and embraced the man in a fierce hug.

Daniel felt a sharp pain in his chest as he looked on.

She caught the man's hand, pulled him in, and closed the door.

He blinked, not quite believing what he'd just seen. *She's seeing someone else? At this hour?*

Suddenly feeling as if someone was choking him, he threw the flowers on the seat beside him.

He'd stayed away too long, and now it was too late.

*   *   *

Sara walked out the building along with several co-workers in a hurry to get home. She looked at her watch. It was four o'clock—she needed to collect Arianna from school and she was later than usual. Her five-year-old daughter would not be happy if she kept her waiting too long.

She'd had a day of back-to-back meetings, which had overrun and she wasn't convinced she'd achieved anything.

She stepped out of the glass doors to the ground floor reception and noted a familiar figure leaning against a parked car.

Joshua? What is he doing here?

His face lit up with a dimpled smile.

She couldn't help but smile back as she walked over to him. "Hi Joshua, what are you doing here?"

"I'm still waiting for you to call. I guess I couldn't wait any longer."

"I'd like to say I'm flattered, but I think I made things clear at your aunt's barbeque."

He gave a wry smile. "I know. It isn't the real reason I'm here."

She quirked a brow.

"I need to get in touch with Samyra."

"She didn't give you her number?"

"No. After she left David and Rachel's wedding, she promised to call, but never did."

Sara assessed the attractive man before her. He was casually dressed in trousers and a shirt. *Nice shoes*, she thought. She had a about men's shoes. She was turned off by men with scuffed, dirty or ill-thought-out colour-coordinated shoes. It was the first thing she noticed when giving a man an appraisal. He certainly passed with flying colours.

Joshua had a quiet presence; he did not command your attention, as Daniel did. But there was something about him which made you want to get to know him. Maybe it was the distinctive Anderson green eyes that drew her. She could see the resemblance to Daniel; they were very much alike, and could easily be mistaken for brothers instead of cousins.

Without talking to Samyra, she didn't want to make assumptions and just give him her number. Her sister may not want her to. "I can take your number and give it to her."

"She already has my number, Sara. As do you." He gave her a knowing glance. "Daniel made it very clear that you were off-limits. But she isn't."

Daniel told him I was off-limits? When?

She hadn't heard from Daniel since that night at the hotel. He'd been angry and possessive, she'd figured it was over between them—whatever *over* meant, as they hardly had a relationship. "Maybe she's not interested, Joshua..."

He gave a winning smile, exposing his dimples. "Oh, she's definitely interested. I have no qualms about that."

There was a look in his eyes that said something had happened between him and Samyra. Her baby sister was holding back on her. "So, Daniel told you I was off-limits?"

"Yes, you've been seeing him, haven't you?" His eyes darkened. "Or am I wrong?"

She saw the change in his eyes. She wasn't about to clarify things with him. She didn't want further problems with Daniel. "Yes, I have been." She averted her gaze.

"Can I give you a lift somewhere?"

She looked at her watch again. She was running late; at least if she got a lift, she would be on time to collect Arianna. "Yes please, thanks."

He smiled and opened the car door for her and helped her in. He walked around to the driver's side and got in. "Where to?"

She gave him the address and they chatted easily on the way. He told her he was a graphic designer, and they discussed design concepts. As this was her field—being the media relations manager at David and Daniel's company—they had a lot in common.

She liked him, but it was clear he was taken by Samyra as conversations kept returning to her. It was obvious that they had become quite close the night of the wedding, and then she remembered Samyra telling her she'd done something she shouldn't have—too much wine and becoming tipsy, not a good sign. She didn't delve any deeper into what might have happened between them; no doubt Bradley would definitely have something to say. Her brother would not be happy.

As she'd parked her car nearby, she asked Joshua to drop her off at the train station. She smiled and turned to him. "Thanks for the lift, really appreciate it. I was worried I was going to be late for Arianna."

"No problem. Do you mind giving me Samyra's number? I really need to talk to her. I should have handled things better than I did, and I need to talk to her, please?"

There was something in his eyes, a softening…something that told her he cared about Samyra, she could see that. She relented and gave him the number.

She couldn't shake the uncertainty that came over her. Whatever happened between them, she would certainly have to find out.

What had her sister been up to?

*   *   *

"Oooh, ooh…Lord, I adore you. Love you, worship you, in you I'm free, and you've given me so much grace…"

Sara worshipped God, bobbing her head, and rocking her shoulders to the upbeat song, singing and connecting with God as she drove. She pulled up at the traffic lights, singing loudly. Her eyes caught those of the driver beside her, he smiled and she smiled back, continuing to sing. The whole world could see her, but she didn't care; she loved her Lord and wanted to send a praise of thanksgiving to Him for all He had given her. She was ever so grateful for His grace upon her life. She felt tears come to her eyes and they rolled down her cheeks. She loved Him so much and was so thankful to Him. She wondered every day at His mercy upon her life.

Music blared from her car, her worship powerful and adoring— the blessings released into the earth's atmosphere. She was aware of the powerful anointing upon her life and what happened when she sang. Although her worship was to give thanks to her Lord Jesus for all He had done for her, she also sang with a purpose. Knowing from the moment she connected with God in worship, the anointing upon her life touched every person she passed on the street, every home, every car, every town. When she sang, the anointing impacted upon all.

Then she heard the Holy Spirit's voice whisper within her spirit.

"When you sing it brings me great joy, as you touch everyone. Every time you sing, demons flee. They cannot cope with your anointing and have to flee. As you drive, they scatter, leaving an opening for me to touch people, to send my angels, releasing the anointing upon their lives and draw them closer to me. Through your voice, your song, your worship, you are doing a great work. Please do not stop, do not let a day go by without worshiping me, it changes the atmosphere, creates a catalyst that is so profound. If only people knew how through your song of worship, you have protected people, lifted their spirits, changed the course in their life. Made a difference…"

Sara felt elated at the newfound knowledge that God revealed to her. At least she knew that she was doing something right—something worthwhile.

Sara continued to sing, taking in the joy and peace that always enveloped her when she worshipped. She poured out her heart and God poured out his presence, which filled the car. She felt lifted, content, and so in love with her Heavenly Father, and grateful He was in her life.

She was meeting Rachel for their weekly work lunch. It was convenient for her as she lived nearby, and it was easier when she had to leave to collect Arianna from school.

As she pulled into David and Rachel's gated mansion and made her way up the long drive, her mind drifted to Daniel as it always did these days. She missed him so much that her heart ached, but she needed to expand her options. She couldn't continue waiting on Daniel's call, wishing he would visit her. She hated having to cope with the hurt she felt when she dropped Arianna off at his mother's home and he displayed his total indifference to her.

Arianna and Daniel had become close and Arianna naturally wanted Daniel to be her father. Sara couldn't blame her; Daniel showered her with attention, and was part of the reason she fell so deeply in love with him. So Daniel had become the next best thing—Arianna's surrogate uncle, which meant weekends spent with Katherine and her grandchildren, and Arianna becoming part of the family.

Arianna was everything to her, a gift from God, given to her at a difficult time in her life and Sara was fiercely protective of her. Adam, her ex-husband, didn't care, and the hurt of that had never left. So when Daniel had suggested becoming Arianna's surrogate uncle, her love for Daniel had grown even deeper.

But now things were strained between them, to the point where she hadn't felt comfortable staying at his mother's anymore, so she would give some excuse and leave. Then by the time she arrived back in the evening to collect Arianna, Daniel would have already left.

Daniel was a contradiction. She was confused by his jealousy and possessiveness when men showed an interest in her. It made her wonder at his feelings toward her. Did he care? Or was he just as controlling as her ex-husband had been throughout her loveless marriage? Adam only saw her as a possession, just like the many paintings and rare antique pieces he continually added to his collection and displayed proudly around the mansion.

Adam only wanted to show her off and put *her* on display for his friends and business associates, but he was never interested in spending time with her and loving her as a husband should.

Having another man show interest was out of the question. She had numerous arguments with Adam over his lack of interest in her, and over other men when they were out who would talk to her. He would often fly into a jealous rage over a conversation, a smile, or any interest men might have in her. Being a natural conversationalist who loved to interact with people—men and women alike—Adam would make things difficult when she spoke to men and would embarrass her. In the end, it was easier to keep her conversations with the opposite sex to a minimum.

She always had to conform to his word, his lifestyle—business functions and events, organising lunches and dinners at the club— primarily interacting with women. He did not want her to work and felt she should give up her career. He definitely did not want children, and saw anything to do with Arianna to be an inconvenience and an irritation.

His control became unbearable, he felt a woman's place as a wife was in the home serving her husband. She shouldn't think for herself and should do as she was told. Along with that, she should accept that he travelled constantly and she hardly saw him.

To him, she was a disobedient wife. "Difficult" was the word he often used. She insisted on working and progressing her career, not having an abortion when he wanted her to, and then giving birth to Arianna. And to top it off, she became a Christian. Their marriage, as a result, came to an end.

The quandary she couldn't get out of her mind was, Daniel had similarities to Adam. His life was comprised of a great deal of travel, and he was a workaholic. But what had become more and more evident recently was his display of possessiveness. Thankfully, that was where their similarities ended.

Daniel was fun-loving and interesting, so diverse in his character—interested in anything and everything. He was like a big kid at times. He was so sweet and generous, and he made her laugh, which was always a plus point for her.

She smiled as she remembered one night when he'd come over with the excuse of work, when all they did was talk, had heated debates about politics, work, friends—everything. They'd laughed and teased each other.

They were on the sofa munching tortilla chips with a chilli tomato dip. At some point during their debate, he'd shifted close to her, his thigh against hers, his arm curled loosely around her waist, his upper body tucked in close so she had no choice but to lean against him.

"On my travels back from Los Angeles one afternoon," Daniel began, "I was waiting in the reception area of the hotel. I was tired and it was hot, and this woman approached me. She looked glamorous, and could have stepped out of the cover of *Vogue*. She came over to me and handed me her luggage, her handbag, everything. I looked at her, flabbergasted, wondering why—then she said in a crisp British accent, '*Come on, man, chop chop, I'm in a hurry...*' and proceeded to hand me a dollar. I couldn't believe it, the audacity! I was dressed in jeans and a T-shirt, but I didn't look as though I should even be considered as a taxi man—one dollar!" He rolled his eyes.

Sara burst out laughing.

"She headed out of the foyer, expecting me to follow. I was irritated and feeling mischievous that day, and she was rude. So I approached the porter who had brought her luggage down and asked him to take the luggage back to her room. I gave him a generous tip and was satisfied I had done a good deed for the day."

Sara gasped. "You didn't!"

"I did. And it felt good to inconvenience her for that mistake…"

Sara laughed. "You're joking—I can't believe you did that!"

Daniel smiled. "Well I did, anyway, I was in between meetings and on my way to meet a potential client, an influential politician who I had been trying to get on our books for a while, and had a number of conference calls over his requirements. A couple of days later I was sitting in his office, going through the contracts, and there was a knock at the door. *I'd like you to meet my wife,* he said, and who should walk through the door…"

"Who?" She was intrigued.

"Come on, Sara, keep up. The luggage woman in Los Angeles! She literally pointed her finger at me and shouted, *You!* Apparently she missed her flight because of me…"

Daniel trailed off as she was laughing so much, tears came to her eyes.

Daniel laughed with her. "Suffice to say, her husband did not sign on the dotted line and I lost out big-time."

She was still laughing, her tummy hurting. She wiped at her tears. "That is so bizarre, that never happens." She giggled.

"Tell me about it." He paused watching her intently. "You enjoy laughing at my misfortune, don't you?" He raised an eyebrow, pulling her closer.

She sobered quickly at his nearness. She shook her head slowly, a half smile played on her lips.

"Yes, you do," he whispered before his lips brushed hers, drawing her against him and taking her to another place of wonder as he kissed her.

Sara sighed, pondering her thoughts as she stepped out of the car and cast a lingering gaze over the beautiful landscaped gardens—picture postcard—perfect with colourful bushes and evergreens, some with red and yellow berries, quite a contrast to the trees that were bare, a testament to the cold wintery season, yet an inviting display that made you want to go and get lost, and take in God's presence.

Maybe it was for the best that they hadn't developed their relationship any further. The ache that she felt at missing him was becoming unbearable.

Rachel greeted her at the door, ushering her in. Sara was surprised to see David there. He appeared from his office looking strikingly handsome—just like his brother.

"Hi Sara, how are you?"

He came over and kissed her on the cheek, hugging her close, and she ached some more. She missed Daniel and it didn't help that David looked just like his twin brother.

No doubt about it—she needed to get over Daniel.

"I'm good. You're not working today?"

"Working from home," David replied.

He and Rachel shared a look; one that couples shared when they were in love that told of an intimate moment of which only they were aware. The look proceeded to remind her about her own situation—alone, with no life partner. Doubts filled her. She was beginning to wonder if she would ever find someone and she wasn't sure she believed that Daniel was the one.

She headed through the open plan room to the kitchen table and rummaged in her briefcase, taking out four reports. She wanted to get stuck into work and leave, there was too much love going on here.

She didn't want to seem resentful, but Rachel had everything Sara wanted and it wasn't too long ago that Rachel had been fighting marriage, not wanting anything to do with it. Yet Sara wanted it more than anything, and she was still waiting. The thought of it made her ache—for something that was out of her reach and seemingly out of her control. "I wanted to start on the Harrison contract—"

"Are you in a hurry?" Rachel asked. "Let's have lunch first." She walked over to the fridge. "I'm ravenous. I keep eating, I'm going to look like a blimp if I keep this up."

Pregnancy… The other topic I don't want to be reminded of. "I've got a few errands I need to run, so I wanted to finish up early."

Rachel looked over at her and narrowed her eyes. "Something's up—what's wrong?"

Sara averted her eyes. "Nothing's wrong. Honestly, I do have some things to do."

Sara glanced around the vast open-plan room—white, lavish, and immaculate. Black leather sofas graced the living area, with white marble floors. It was masculine, yet the décor suited Rachel's taste and decided she didn't want to redecorate when she married David.

Ahead were floor-to-ceiling expanding glass doors, which opened out into the gardens. The views were beautiful.

Over the fireplace hung a large framed photograph of their wedding—it was the one taken on the beach in Jamaica. Rachel and David looked so in love.

Sara had hired Samyra, to be the wedding photographer as her present to them both. Not many had Samyra's skill to capture a moment that literally could be felt. Crystal blue sea and white sands in the distance—Rachel looking deep into David's eyes, touching his face. David holding her close, the soft smile that played on his lips and the love that he felt could clearly be seen in his eyes.

Such a beautiful photograph—a dream Sara hoped for, too.

Along the mantelpiece there were other photos; Keira and Sophie, David's twins from his first marriage, and Rebecca and Matthew, Rachel's children from her first marriage. Now Rachel was pregnant with twins, bringing their brood to a grand total of six—Rachel had it all.

Rachel had secured a buyer for her house quickly. She'd hesitated about selling at first; she told David she'd decided to keep the property and rent it out, thereby securing an income. David saw through that straight away, knowing she wanted to keep the property because she was being cautious. He wanted her to commit to him fully and reminded her that what was his was hers—they were one. There would no longer be his and hers, only theirs.

"Well, I'm pulling rank. We're having lunch first, plus we haven't spoken much over the last few weeks and I think you're still upset with me after what happened at the barbeque." Rachel closed the fridge door after removing a few items.

The barbeque—Rachel made it sound like some great event, even though it had been grand. Katherine knew how to put on a shindig. Rachel and Sara's friendship had been tested, due to Rachel's loyalties to David. Now that she was married, the dynamics had changed between them. Before, they told each other everything— they were like sisters. Now Rachel was holding back and not being totally honest with her, making Sara feel like an outsider, and it hurt.

"I wasn't upset with you," Sara lied, and internally said a prayer of forgiveness. "It was Daniel I was upset with."

"How is Daniel?" Rachel asked as she began preparing their meal.

David entered the room again, looking as if he was searching for something, then stopped to kiss Rachel. Rachel gazed lovingly into David's eyes and caressed his cheek.

Oh, this is way too much for me to bear today. Sara looked away. "I haven't heard from him."

Two pairs of eyes stared at her. "What do you mean, you haven't heard from him?" Rachel asked. David stood behind Rachel pulling her back against his chest into his arms, his hands resting on her tummy.

Sara shrugged. "We don't talk as we used to. I haven't really seen him."

There must have been a look in her eyes or a tone in her voice that she wasn't able to hide, because David said, "He misses you."

"I don't really believe he does. We used to be closer, but I think his attentions are elsewhere. It is as it should be—I stipulated we should remain friends."

"No, he misses you," David reiterated.

"Did he tell you that?"

"He didn't have to."

"What do you mean?"

Rachel and David shared a look.

"We're twins, we share a connection."

"Meaning?"

"Meaning, we pick up on each other. I know he misses you, I feel it within my spirit."

Sara looked at him, contemplating what he'd said, not sure she fully understood how the 'twin thing' worked between the brothers. "Oh well, it doesn't really matter. We're not in a relationship and he's free to be with who he wants, and so am I."

David looked concerned. "He wants to be with you."

"No, he doesn't. I'm not under any misconceptions there."

"He's been hurt in the past, which makes it difficult for him." David paused as if contemplating what he should reveal. His hand moved slowly over his wife's tummy. "Amy hurt him, which means he doesn't trust easily. He was in love with her."

So Daniel was in love. But he'd always said he didn't know what love was. "What happened?"

"He'll have to tell you himself. Just don't write him off just yet."

"I haven't written him off as such. He's a good friend and I'm coming to the realisation that is all we will ever be."

David's eyes darkened. "He doesn't want friendship, Sara."

"Then what does he want? Can you answer that question? I need a commitment and he is unable to give me that. Anyway, I believe his heart is elsewhere."

David and Rachel shared another look and Sara decided she no longer wanted to continue this conversation.

"Rachel, we need to discuss the Harrison contract." Sara pulled out a report. "His requirements have changed."

Noting the swift subject change, David kissed Rachel once more, releasing her, and then enveloped Sara in a bear hug. The warm embrace felt so good that contracts and Mr Harrison flew out of her head. She figured she must be desperate. Or maybe it was because David looked just like Daniel, it was difficult to differentiate between them. Her tension eased away.

He looked at her, his gorgeous green eyes holding hers captive. "You need to talk to him."

David disappeared into his office after that, leaving her contemplating what he said.

"He got you, huh? There's nothing like David's arms."

Sara smiled wryly. "Yes, there is…Daniel's arms."

"There is that, they are both captivating men, Daniel especially, women can't stay away from him."

"Which is why he doesn't want a commitment."

"Talk to him, Sara."

They'd already been over this. She wanted a commitment, he didn't. They had nothing further to discuss and it was time she moved on with her life. They both wanted different things and she had to see his distance from her as a blessing, it would allow her to build her resolve.

Truthfully, her heart ached for him. She couldn't stop thinking about him and the resolve she'd tried hard to hold strong, waivered whenever he came near or called her.

So who am I trying to kid?

She recalled the day she decided to leave the beautiful Caribbean island of Negril. As it says in the Bible when temptation confronts you, you should flee. Well, she tried, and had been trying ever since.

His mouth found hers and she was unable to resist, kissing him eagerly— passionately. She moaned, feeling herself slip out of control, wrapping her arms around his neck. She was barely aware as he began to walk her backward toward the bed. Then reality struck her. This man was dangerous. She couldn't be alone with Daniel; she was so weak to him. She pulled away, her breathing ragged, resting her forehead against his. She slipped one hand lovingly to his face and leaned back so she could look at him.

"I can't, Daniel," she whispered. She wanted to tell him how much she loved him, but she couldn't and stifled the words in her heart.

"I want you, Sara."

"I know. I want you, too." She gently caressed his face. Reaching up, she ran her hands through the soft curls of his hair. She pulled away reluctantly, wishing she could stay in his arms, praying for something more. He had her heart—if only she had his.

She said a silent prayer: Lord, please give me the strength to walk away from Daniel. I want to do what's right. Please help me.

Sara walked over to the bed to finish packing.

"Come on, Sara. We're in glorious Jamaica. I'll back off. Let's do something together."

She looked up at him and smiled wistfully. She would love to stay with him, because with him was where she wanted to be. But her only option was to leave. If she stayed, she would end up giving in and Daniel was a temptation she couldn't afford to entertain.

"It's glorious, isn't it? When I get married again, I want a honeymoon here."

He stared at her for moment. She wondered what he was thinking and wished inside that they would marry, that Daniel would fall in love with her and want her to be his wife. But it was a fantasy, one which she needed to get out of her heart and mind.

"I already have a flight booked for four o'clock. I have to leave now." She sighed. "I wish things could be different between us, Daniel. But they can't. We need to accept that. I want marriage. You don't."

"Sara, I always get what I want. You and I both know if I wanted to take this thing any further between us I could, so why fight it?"

She looked at him, her love for him betrayed in her eyes. She didn't answer; afraid he would do as he said.

But what she didn't expect after he left her room and she'd made her way to the airport, was to find him waiting in the queue about to check in with her.

"What are you doing here?"

"Something came up, so I decided to travel back and get stuck into work."

"Oh," she said, not really knowing what to say. Her heart leapt at discovering he was coming with her, but it certainly didn't help her resolve.

Besides, she was travelling economy, and no doubt he would be travelling first-class, so it wouldn't impact upon her a great deal. They worked in different offices across London, so she could handle this.

What she hadn't anticipated was for Daniel to flash his gorgeous smile, which had the lady at the check-in desk blushing, and asked for Sara to be upgraded to first class, too. He didn't care about the cost and pulled out his credit card.

They spent the whole journey talking, laughing, feeding each other, and watching snippets of films. She could easily pretend he was hers, and she was his…

She thought about that day often and how close they'd become. And how she'd lived with the hope that he would fall for her and declare his undying love. But it was not to be, and it was time she moved on with her life.

She needed to stop procrastinating and do it.

What's the worst that could happen?

Chapter 2

Sara put on the finishing touches to her makeup, looking at her reflection in the mirror. She was wearing a black dress, with a fitted lace bodice that accentuated her curves. She'd lost a couple of pounds and the dress fit perfectly now. She slipped on matching heels, just as the doorbell sounded.

She was going on a date.

She'd met Gary at church. They'd gotten chatting and he'd asked, so she thought, *why not?* He wasn't her normal type, but had boyish good looks and seemed nice enough. It wouldn't hurt to have dinner with him. He would take her mind off Daniel.

She still hadn't heard from Daniel since the night he'd taken her to the restaurant at The Langham hotel in London. They'd had a wonderful time over dinner. Daniel had been charming as usual—making her laugh, playfully teasing her. His ever-so-subtle touch lured her, made her wonder how the night would end. That, and the look in his eyes, one of desire and a need that he fought to control; the way the tone of his voice would change, deepening and become husky, hypnotising her with his softly spoken words, making her want to do anything he wanted.

He'd shifted his chair close to hers, his thigh resting against hers and every so often he would touch her arm, hold her hand, or finger her hair. She'd been talking and he rested his arm on the back of her chair, his hand curling into her hair and she saw his eyes change.

"Daniel you're not listening to me…"

His lips curved into a lazy smile, his eyes resting on her lips. "I heard every word. All your friends are getting married and it's depressing." He grinned, leaning back. "Too right it's depressing. All my friends seem to be getting married, too. I met up with Chad the other day for drinks. We were down at the pub for all of five minutes and his mobile was ringing. He didn't answer and I didn't think anything of it until his crazy girlfriend turned up. She came over to us, hugged me, and then whispered something in his ear and that was it. His whole face lit up and he was gone. He hasn't even walked down the aisle yet and already he has a ball and chain. That was blatant manipulation."

She laughed. "What did she say to him?"

He raised a brow, giving her a teasing look. "What do you think she said to him? I would never let a woman manipulate me in that way. Except for you…you could manipulate me very easily." His voice lowered, his eyes darkening.

She smiled. "Oh yeah? How? Tell me more," she teased, playing along. She would love to know how to manipulate Daniel—the man who never let women in.

He leaned in. "You only need to ask and I would give you everything you need…"

Her breath caught when his lips touched hers, but only for a moment. Her eyes closed, expecting more, but he pulled away slightly to look at her. He ran a finger along her jaw. "Ask."

She opened her eyes and gave him a sly smile. "Marry me."

He chuckled. "You're funny, Sara." He gave her another brief kiss and went back to his meal, grinning.

She laughed and the evening continued on with their teasing banter, until Barry made an appearance. They were old friends, and had known each other for years. He was a lovely man, but they'd never connected romantically, as he was always involved with other women and they'd been quite content to remain as friends. Every so often Barry would call to say hi and catch up. It was innocent, but Daniel had made assumptions and had been jealous, and she hadn't seen him since.

He'd promised to back off in that regard and she didn't feel she needed to give an explanation as to who her friends were. In the same respect, he was also under no obligation.

So she decided to start dating again, while keeping well away from Daniel. It hurt too much. It was time to draw a line under any hope of a relationship with him. She didn't believe what David had told her and it was best if things were left well enough alone.

She made her way to the hallway, opening the door, but not expecting to see the figure that filled the door frame.

Daniel. What is he doing here? Don't hear from him in weeks and he turns up when I'm about to go on a date!

"Daniel? I wasn't expecting you..."

As always, Daniel's gorgeous good looks took her breath away. She never tired of looking at him. Strong angular features, square jaw, beautiful green eyes, and dark curly hair that she loved to run her fingers through. He was tall and muscular and when he held her, he made her feel safe and protected. Dressed in a striped navy suit, he looked dashingly handsome. She reluctantly stepped back, allowing him room to enter.

Daniel looked at her, taking in the way her dress clung to her body, with her long dark hair flowing down her back. He didn't think he would ever get over how stunning she was. Her honey brown eyes assessed him, his body responded as it always did with her.

His natural reaction was to draw her into his arms and kiss her—he felt it, the rush, the need—his body ached for her, but he could see the annoyance in her eyes. They hadn't parted on good terms the last time they were together and then he realised something else his foggy brain had just alerted him to.

"Are you going out?"

"Yes, I am. I was just about to leave, actually," Sara said as he headed to the living room, clearly not getting the hint.

He pulled at his tie, slipping it off. "Where are you going?"

What's with the twenty questions? "Out for dinner, so..." She gestured toward the hallway. Gary would arrive soon, and she needed Daniel to leave.

"We need to talk, Sara."

"Well, it will have to be another time. As I said, I'm on my way out."

Daniel studied her. She was annoyed at him. He'd stayed away too long, but he hadn't known what to say to her. And after seeing her with that man, he was sure it was over between them. But David had called and told him he'd spoken to her and she wasn't seeing anyone, so he'd decided to try and talk a few things through.

"Sara, I—"

The doorbell sounded again. Sara groaned inwardly. *Great, this is all I need…* After what happened between Daniel and Jayden at the barbeque—jealousy had reared its ugly head, and Daniel became possessive. Then after, his response to Barry—she hated to think how *this* was going to turn out.

Sara headed to the hallway, with Daniel following behind. She nervously opened the door. "Hi Gary."

"Wow, Sara you look beautiful." Gary entered, closing the door.

Daniel stiffened, becoming angry. *She's going on a date? Seeing another man? How many of them were there?*

Sara reluctantly introduced them. "Gary, this is Daniel, Daniel this is Gary." There was an uncomfortable silence as both men eyed each other. Daniel was at least a foot taller than Gary and also broader, due to his muscular frame.

Daniel turned to her. "I think you had better ask Gary to leave."

"*Daniel…*" she said, her tone incredulous.

"Hey, come on, I didn't come here to cause any problems," Gary said.

Daniel turned to him. "*Then leave,*" he responded, raising his voice.

"Daniel!" Sara looked at Daniel in disbelief. *Why is he doing this?* He was so angry. She needed to stop this before things got out of control.

She took the easier option and ushered Gary toward the door. "Gary, I think you had better go." She was worried Daniel might hit Gary, Daniel looked as if he was about to commit murder.

"I thought you weren't seeing anyone?" Gary asked, confusion crossing his features.

"I'm not."

"Then what is this about then? Who is *he*?" Gary looked hurt.

Now wasn't the time to be asking questions. She tried to usher him out further, but he stood his ground. "Gary, I'll call you."

"No, she won't," Daniel said from behind her. "She's with me. Get the hint and stay away from her!" he snapped.

Sara's heart jolted in panic.

Gary kept his eyes fixed on her. "Is that what you want?"

"I think it's time you left." Daniel began striding toward him, ready to do some bodily damage.

She grabbed Daniel's arm. "Please, Daniel, don't..." She stood between them and ushered Gary out the door. "I'm sorry, Gary," she said, before shutting the door.

She spun toward Daniel. *"How dare you! You embarrassed me!"*

"Embarrassed *you*? What were you doing with him? How long have you been seeing him?"

"It was our first date. I don't see what the problem is." She marched into the living room, folding her arms.

He followed. *"So what am I, chopped liver?!* I can't believe you've been seeing other men behind my back."

Behind his back? What...

She looked at him, seeing hurt and uncertainty in his eyes. She sighed; she hated to see him so angry. "What's wrong, Daniel? I don't understand, what did I do?"

"For goodness' sake, Sara! Do I have to spell it out for you?" He turned away from her, anger permeating from him.

"Maybe you need to, because I don't understand. One minute you want me and the next, I don't see or hear from you. Then I get a macho display of possessiveness."

"Maybe because you keep pushing me away. Don't you think I want to be with you? But every time I get close to you, you put stipulations on me."

Surprised, Sara stared at him for a moment. "But you never said..." She sat down to relieve her trembling legs. "I'm sorry I hurt you," she said simply as realisation dawned. He did care.

He was silent for a moment, eyeing her. "I don't want you seeing other men."

It wasn't a question and he did not ask. As far as he was concerned, it was non-negotiable.

"We've never put stipulations on who we see. You visit occasionally, Daniel, so what we have is hardly a relationship."

"I thought we had an understanding. What I didn't expect was to find you seeing all these other men."

Sara's eyes widened. *All these other men?* "What other men?" she asked in confusion.

Daniel's eyes narrowed. "Gary, Barry, Joshua, and then a few weeks back, another man. You were hugging him and then you spent the night with him."

Sara stared at him, trying to think. *Spent the night with him? With who? Joshua?*

"I've told you," she began patiently. "This was mine and Gary's first date. Barry is an old friend, and we have never been romantically involved. We are just that, friends. And as for Joshua..." *Honestly, Daniel is making me feel as if I'm married again. What is it with men and their possessiveness?* "...he gave me a lift one afternoon. He's not interested in me, he wanted my sister's number. How did you find out? Have you been checking up on me?"

"No, we spoke last week and he told me."

"Did he imply that something was going on between us?"

"No, but there had to be a reason he gave you a lift as he would have had to go out of his way. He works nowhere near your offices."

"It was just a lift, Daniel, why would you suspect something would be going on between us?"

"Because he's interested, and you've had his number since David and Rachel's engagement." He raised a querying brow.

"Don't try to make me feel guilty, Daniel, I'm not interested in Joshua and I've not spent the night with anyone. I don't know what you're talking about."

Daniel contemplated her response. *Is she lying?* "I came to see you a few weeks back, it was late and a man turned up at your door and you hugged. It was clearly obvious you were close. I thought we had an understanding." He eyed her intently. "Did you sleep with him?"

Realisation dawned on Sara's face. "That was my brother, Daniel. He stopped off on his way home."

Daniel stared at her for a moment, relief filling him. "So you're not seeing anyone?"

"No, Daniel, I'm not, but I can't say the same for you."

"I'm not interested in other women. It's you that I want."

"So why have you stayed away?" she asked quietly, almost pleadingly, her voice betraying her need for him.

Daniel looked away for a moment. "I was jealous. I didn't like the way Barry touched you, as if you belonged to him." When he thought about it, it still angered him. The possessiveness he felt was overwhelming; he wanted to possess her in ways he shouldn't be thinking about right now. He wanted to make her his. He felt so insecure—an emotion he wasn't used to feeling. His eyes drifted, finally coming to rest on her long shapely legs. *That is some dress...*

Sara folded her arms defensively. "But you said you would back off in that regard."

"I know, but I can't help it. I didn't like it, and I felt you weren't being open with me. How often do you speak to him?"

"Every couple of months or so. We're just friends, Daniel. You have female friends." She raised a brow, testing his response. He had no defence in that regard; he knew too many women.

"I don't like it. No other man should have that privilege but me, Sara."

"Oh, so it's okay for you to see other women, but it's not okay for me to see other men? You can't have your cake, and eat it too."

"I'm not seeing other women. I want you, Sara."

She searched his face, wondering if he was being honest with her. Not too long ago he'd been seeing Emma. But even as the doubts crossed her mind, she knew he was telling the truth. He'd always been honest with her and she'd never made him feel that he couldn't be. But it was evident he was still angry.

"B–but…we've never defined our relationship. Besides, I want marriage, you don't."

Daniel sighed and took a seat beside her as his anger abated a little. "Sara, why do you have to put restrictions on our relationship, whatever this is? Why can't we just take each day as it comes? I can't make any promises."

Because I'm running out of time. I want another child.

"Daniel, it won't work between us. We want different things from life…"

"Go on," Daniel prompted when she trailed off.

"There are two reasons." Three, really, but it made no sense in dwelling on her need for another child which was top of the list. "One being you're a workaholic—"

He looked at her, incredulous. "And so are you."

She gave a slight shake of her head. "No, I'm not. Adam was a workaholic, always travelling, always thinking about the next big idea. His mind never rested. He only married me to possess me, I was a trophy piece for him, a possession that he could show off to his friends and business associates. I was in awe of him, in awe of his mind, but he rarely touched me. There was no affection—no love…" She looked away for a moment. "You two have similarities. I guess a man with an exceptional mind is an attraction for me and something I have to deal with."

He looked at her with a flicker of amusement in his eyes. "You think I have an exceptional mind?"

She wanted to be honest with him; she didn't like the hurt look he had in his eyes before. "Yes, I enjoy working with you, Daniel. Your mind is full of ideas, your intellect astounds me, and I'm learning so much from you. That's the reason why I work with you. Before I met you, after Arianna was in bed, my evenings were spent curled up on the sofa with a good book." She ran a hand slowly along the arm of the sofa.

Daniel assessed her for moment, wishing she was touching him in that way. "And my work schedule is a problem for you?"

"Daniel, I need a man who wants to be with me, who sees me...the person that I am, and is not constantly distracted by work commitments. I can't be with another man like Adam."

"And you don't like my possessiveness?"

She shook her head. "Adam was controlling. If a man even looked at me too long, there was trouble. Please...I just can't cope with that anymore. He suffocated me."

"That I can't help." His eyes raked over her like a caress. "You're the type of woman that brings that out in a man." His voice lowered and he leaned in close. "You drive me crazy..."

Her pulse rate quickened as he tucked his face into her hair and his lips brushed her neck.

"And you smell so good," he whispered.

She reached up, unable to resist sinking her fingers into his hair. The light brush of his lips and the warmth of his breath were making her weak; she needed to distract him.

"You want me all to yourself, yet you won't commit?"

He slowly leaned back and sighed, taking her hand in his. "I can't promise marriage, Sara."

Sara swallowed the disappointment she felt. Well, he was always honest with her; she couldn't fault him on that.

"And the other reason?"

She held his gaze for a long moment. "You're in love with Rachel." He looked away at her words as he always did when she bought up the topic. "I need you to be honest with me, Daniel. I know you have feelings for her, I feel it every time you're with her. You gravitate toward her like a magnet. Eventually you find yourself with her and you touch her in some way."

Daniel groaned inwardly, trying to think. He wasn't ready for this conversation and hadn't realised it was that obvious. "My feelings for Rachel are complicated."

Sara stared at him, pulling her hand away. *His feelings?* Pain gripped her heart. She expected him to deny it as he always did. *He has feelings for Rachel?*

It's what she'd surmised from the very first day they'd met. They'd gone to see a film at the cinema with Rachel and David. He seemed besotted with Rachel; he was constantly watching her.

But Daniel had charmed Sara that night and soon seemed to lose interest in Rachel and focused on *her*. He made her feel as if she was the most beautiful woman in the world to him, which threw her. It still confused her as months on, his focus on her seemed so intense. But when he was in a room with Rachel, Sara felt inadequate, as if she was second choice to Rachel and it was something she could no longer ignore.

She waited for him to continue, but he did not. "Daniel, I won't be second place to another woman, even if she's my best friend. I deserve better than that."

"Yes, you do." Daniel fell silent again, not sure what to say to her. He didn't know how he was going to begin to explain what he felt about Rachel.

He *did* love Rachel, but not in a romantic way, and he needed to work on guarding that when he was around David and Rachel. He didn't want it to cause a problem between him and Sara.

Frustrated and hurt by his lack of response, Sara stood. "You don't need to explain anything to me. Anyway...those are my reasons. Gary is a nice person, I want to get to know him."

Daniel got up at that and stood in front of her, anger lit his eyes. *"But you're in love with me!"*

Oh, so you had to draw that card. The one they'd been avoiding ever since they returned from the Caribbean. "Yes, I am. But that really doesn't matter if you're in love with Rachel. I'm going to get changed." She tried to step past him, but he stopped her, pulling her into his arms.

One arm still at her waist, Daniel tilted her chin so he could look into her eyes; he hated the hurt he saw there. "I don't love Rachel in that way."

"So you admit you love her?" Sara asked, the words almost a whisper. Her heart hit the floor.

"Yes, but not in the way you think. She's my sister-in-law, she's family."

"So you're saying you love her as a brother would love a sister?" She eyed him sceptically. His hand fell to her shoulder, caressing her there, causing her to lose her focus. She stepped away.

He pulled her back.

"Daniel…" She placed a hand on his chest, to try and keep some distance between them, but touching him only heightened her awareness of him and the needs he evoked within her.

"It's complicated, Sara."

Complicated? What did that mean? Rachel had said the same thing.

Sara felt as if her heart was breaking. It was what she'd suspected—she'd seen it with her own two eyes, so why was this such a shock to her? She figured that, because he denied it for months, she could pretend that he didn't have feelings for Rachel and ignore what was so obvious. She did not respond to Daniel's remark as pain seared her heart.

Daniel sighed as his hands slid lingeringly over her shoulders and along her arms. He took her hand in his and pulled her back to sit with him on the sofa.

"What do you know about twins, Sara?"

She frowned, a little confused by his question. Her mind was still reeling from his revelation that he loved Rachel. "What do you mean?"

He was still holding her hand and laced his fingers between hers. "I have a connection to David. He picks up on my feelings and I pick up on his."

"Okay…" She looked at him, searching his eyes. *What is he saying?*

"I feel what my brother feels, and it's stronger when I'm with him. We often think the same way, want the same things."

"And when you say want the same things, you mean Rachel."

He nodded. "We're attracted to the same women."

"What happened between you and Rachel?"

"Nothing happened between us."

"I'm confused, Daniel, what are you trying to say?"

Daniel released her hand and leaned back against the sofa. Telling her was harder than he'd thought. Maybe he should just let David tell her; this was beyond him.

Sara studied him. He seemed to be finding it difficult to say what he wanted to say. What was so hard? Twins... She'd read the article that Rachel had given her about twins having a connection, that they had the ability to think the same thoughts and could often turn up in the same clothes—colours.

Okay, so she'd noticed that about them. One afternoon David had turned up for a business meeting wearing the exact same suit Daniel was wearing and they'd both rolled their eyes in exasperation. Clearly that was something that happened quite often.

So... They were attracted to the same women; interpretation—they were both attracted to Rachel. Did they both pursue her? Is that why there was tension between them? She'd noted the body language between the brothers at times, especially around Rachel. That had been quite revealing. So Rachel was "the one that got away" in Daniel's eyes and he still had feelings for her. Was that why he kept his distance? Because he was in love with Rachel?

Her heart ached and she felt jealousy crawl up her skin. And Rachel never said a word...

So what was *she* to him then? Why all the affection? Why had he been pursuing her for so long? Was this always only about sex for him?

Daniel had never pretended or lied to her, and he never made excuses. He was a man that loved women and he enjoyed them—no strings attached. She remembered his sombre mood at the wedding and unexpectedly, she felt sorry for him. It can't have been easy for him, secretly loving a woman he couldn't have. Maybe the Rachel topic was something they should park for now; she wanted to know about Amy. "Tell me about Amy."

Daniel blinked. *Great. I'm not ready to talk about her, either.* Amy was a sore subject. She was a woman who had found a place in his heart, then smashed it in two. He would never, ever allow another woman that kind of power over him. She'd sent him into a dark place that he had no intention of ever returning to.

He averted his eyes. "What did you want to know?"

"Was she the woman that hurt you?"

"Yes."

Sara watched him, suddenly feeling protective of him; he had a look of vulnerability in his eyes that she'd never seen before.

Why is this so hard for him, Lord?

31

"He was hurt and has unforgiveness in his heart. He needs to forgive Amy. Help him."

She shifted closer to him and touched his face. "You don't have to tell me. I'm sorry she hurt you." She rested her head on his shoulder and wrapped her arm around his waist.

Daniel's heart warmed. This, right here, was the reason he couldn't get Sara out from under his skin. She was angry at him earlier and upset over her assumptions of his feelings for Rachel. Yet she still showed him unconditional love and affection. Over the months they had known each other, she never demanded of him, and she gave him room to be himself. When she showered him with affirmation and encouragement, she made him feel he could do anything; that's what he loved about her.

Loved?

Did he love her? He slipped his arm around her, caressing her back.

He didn't know what love was, not after what happened with Amy. David said *he* was in love with Sara, but right now it wasn't something he wanted to address. "I planned to marry her."

Surprised, Sara lifted her head to look at him. "Really?"

He nodded. "I was in love with her. She was my world."

Sara shifted a little, wanting to look at him closely. She ran her hand along his chest. "What did she do to you? I hate her already."

Daniel looked at Sara, not expecting that response, then he chuckled.

Sara smiled in response, pleased she got him to laugh. She didn't like the hurt look in his eyes.

"She told me she was pregnant. I was ecstatic, I wanted our babies, the lives we made together. We were planning for twins, until I found out she wasn't pregnant by me." He gave a sardonic laugh. "She played me. She used me for my money, and tried to get as much out of me as she could before the truth came out. And the truth came in the form of her husband turning up at my office, unable to control his wife."

She gasped. "She was married?"

"Yes, obviously I didn't know. She fooled me."

"And pregnant?"

"Yes, she told me the babies were mine and I believed her."

"Daniel, how *awful*—how could she do such a thing to you?" Her heart hurt for him. No wonder he had such an issue with trust—his possessiveness and his view that all women are deceptive. "I don't know what to say…that's unbelievable. Unfortunately there are a lot of women out there that can be deceptive that way. I'm sorry she did that to you, but we aren't all bad, Daniel."

"Women play games, Sara. I've seen it and I've experienced it, time and again. I don't trust women."

She looked down at his chest, idly fingering the fabric of his shirt. "I would never do that to you." She said the words quietly, a little afraid of his reaction to her.

Daniel watched her. Somehow, deep inside, he knew this. Maybe that's why he'd allowed her to get close. He did not respond, trying to control his needs. When she touched him, restraint proved to be very difficult.

Sara met his gaze again. His lack of response was a clear indication that he didn't believe her. "Do you still love her?"

"No, my feelings died a long time ago. She broke my heart and I have never allowed myself to feel again. I won't ever let a woman use me like that again." He said the words with such conviction, making his message clear.

"Maybe it's time to forgive her and give it to God. You won't ever forget what she did, but you need to allow God to heal your scars."

He contemplated her words for a moment. "Maybe I don't want to."

"When you have unforgiveness in your heart, it puts a block between you and God. You need to let it go, Daniel."

"I guess because I'm reminded of her through the women I meet. I've held on to the pain I felt so I can't be hurt again."

"Who are these women that you've been encountering? You're clearly hooking up with the wrong ones."

He gave a derisive laugh. "They seem to seek me out. Vanessa was one of them."

"Vanessa? What happened between you and Vanessa?"

"She's put in an unfair dismissal claim against me."

"Did you dismiss her unfairly? You always said you couldn't fault her on her work."

"Which is the basis of her claim. It's true, I couldn't fault her on her work. It was her behaviour that came into question. And from recent communication, she has added sexual harassment to the claim."

Sara frowned. "Sexual harassment? What happened?"

"One evening I was working late and jet-legged, having returned from New York. I fell asleep on the sofa in my office and awoke to find Vanessa on top of me, trying to kiss me. My automatic reaction was to do what you did to me—I threw her off me. She landed in a heap on the floor, very embarrassed..." Daniel trailed off at the sounds of laughter from Sara.

"You're joking?" she asked in between giggles. "You threw her off you?" She laughed again, tears coming to her eyes. "You're never going to let me forget that, are you?"

"No, I won't." He smiled.

She laughed again; she couldn't help herself. "Ahh, poor Vanessa..."

"Poor Vanessa? Sara, this is not funny." He scowled. "She's taking me to court."

"She wanted your attention and you ignored her. Maybe you just need to give her the acknowledgement that you valued her."

"I did value her."

"Did you tell her that?"

"Yes, well...I praised her when she'd completed a good piece of work. I couldn't give any more than that, as she might have taken it the wrong way."

"What happened after that—what did you say to her?"

"I was annoyed. She'd been coming on to me for months, but I ignored it. In hindsight, I guess I should have told her it was inappropriate. I told her I was unhappy with her behaviour and we couldn't continue working together. She begged me not to terminate her employment, but she'd crossed the line. I gave her a good severance package, I wasn't expecting her to take me to court over something *she* did. And now they want me to consider mediation, like we're married or something."

Sara smiled, wiping her tears. "I'm sorry, Daniel, I guess I can understand the way Vanessa must have felt about you. You are irresistible..." She chuckled, teasing him.

Daniel couldn't resist smiling with her, although it was at his expense. It still angered him that Vanessa was doing this.

"Just give her an acknowledgement, Daniel. I promise you, she will take a different approach."

Rachel had given him the same advice. Daniel wasn't convinced, and conscious that they hadn't discussed the Rachel topic, but Sara wasn't angry at him anymore and he was hungry. "Where's Arianna?"

"She's at my mother's for the night."

"Do you want to go and get something to eat? Or did you want to order something in and we could watch a film?"

Sara wanted to stay in, but maybe that wasn't such a good idea, as they would be alone. Still, she wanted to talk to him some more. He was finally being open with her and if they were to go out, he would clam up again.

"Let's stay in, I feel like Chinese. Let me go and change." She stood, but Daniel caught her arm.

"I don't want you to change. I love the way this dress looks on you." He gave her a slow perusal.

She grinned. "Why, thank you, Daniel. But this is a designer dress and it cost the earth. There's no way I'm sitting on the floor eating Chinese in this!"

Chapter 3

Later on, dressed in olive tapered trousers and a brown vest top, Sara did just that. She sat on the floor beside the sofa, watching *X-Men* with her legs crossed and her plate balanced on her lap.

He was disappointed at her choice of trousers, although they hugged her curves. He loved her legs. Her hair was a mass of curls flowing down her back and around her face, he could easily get lost in her beautiful hazel eyes, and her skin was unblemished and soft to the touch. She had an exotic look that captivated him. He'd dated many beautiful women in the past, but none compared to Sara. There was a refinement, a grace to her that, even if she was wearing jeans and trainers, she would still draw a man's attention.

Daniel shifted closer to her on the sofa, deliberately allowing his leg to touch her back and stole a vegetable spring roll from her plate. She in turn reached up with her fork and took some of the sweet and sour fish off his plate.

"Mmm, that's so nice...I should have ordered this instead," Sara complimented, licking her lips.

"Let me try yours."

Sara lifted her plate toward him allowing him take some of her fish in chilli black bean sauce.

"This is *good*. We've got to share..." They swapped plates, sampling the accompanied onion and bean sprout chow mein.

Daniel eyed her, amused. She was so down to earth; it was one of the things he liked the most about her. When she dressed to impress—looking like a real socialite, elegant and sophisticated— any man would be proud to have her on his arm. Yet she happily sat on the floor, eating takeaway with him, not a care about how it looked, eating with gusto. How many women did he know who would dare to do this in front of him? None. Sara was confident in who she was; she didn't need to pretend.

Chewing slowly, Sara looked up at Daniel as he leaned back against the sofa and groaned, rubbing his stomach. "I'm stuffed."

Sara chuckled. "Me too. Another hour on the cross-trainer for me tomorrow!"

"You don't have to worry about your figure, do you?"

"Only because I exercise."

"You have a beautiful body, Sara."

Sara smiled, her heart skipping a beat at the change in his eyes. "Thank you, Daniel."

"I mean it. I want you, Sara."

"Daniel...I can't give you what you want," she responded quietly.

"I know, it's part of the reason why I've stayed away. Not because I didn't want to be with you, but because of this...because of you."

She blinked, feeling a catalyst of emotions soar through her at his words and felt it prudent to put some distance between them. The intensity in his eyes pulled at her, making her want to be enclosed in his arms. If she gave into her impulse, she knew what would happen next and she didn't trust herself.

She stood, picking up their plates and headed to the kitchen. She placed the dishes in the sink and stood for a moment, trying to regain her composure and slow her racing heart. And when Daniel entered and came up close behind her and placed both hands on either side of her barricading her in, she closed her eyes and said a silent prayer.

Lord help me, please help me to be strong.

"Sara," Daniel whispered, his breath brushing against her neck. "Why do you keep pushing me away?"

She did not respond, her hands gripping the counter, her legs beginning to tremble at his nearness, sensations flooding through her.

He breathed her in, tucking his face into her hair. "I want to kiss you...please? Just for a moment...?"

Why is he asking? He never asked... She didn't know how to answer.

He turned her in his arms, pulling her close. No matter how much she tried, she couldn't say no to him. She loved him too much.

His mouth touched hers tenderly—a sweet kiss that took her breath away. He immobilised her, making her lose all thought, all care. He consumed her, making her want only him. His arm curled around her waist, and his other hand caressed her back. She moaned, wrapping her arms around his neck.

Daniel closed his eyes and deepened the kiss, wanting to possess, make her his forever. He groaned, his heart racing out of control, passion spiralling through him.

"Daniel, are you ready to commit?" Holy Spirit's voice seared his spirit.

A light flashed before his eyes. He saw Sara and two young girls who looked to be at least two years old—identical twins. And Arianna a little older, all three playing in the garden of his home. Sara looked happy, joy filled her, bright sunlight touched them. It was summer. They were his family—his joy...

The vision ended.

He opened his eyes, slowly easing his mouth from hers. He gazed at her for a moment; her eyes were dark with desire for him, sending him a message that told him she was his.

It took all his will, but he stepped away from her, realising in that moment that if he wanted to keep his promise and do what was right, he needed to walk away. He also needed to address the vision he'd just seen.

"I'm sorry...I shouldn't have done that. I think I'd better go."

Sara felt disappointment fill her. Why was he apologising? He never used to before; he would just kiss her senseless, sending her emotions into turmoil. Then it dawned on her that he was a Christian now, realising that sex was no longer an option, and she guessed he felt kissing was something maybe they ought to keep to a minimum, especially with the way he made her feel. But she didn't want him to go; she needed him. "No, please don't go. I miss you, Daniel."

"Sara, I can't stay. If I stay, I'll..." Daniel closed his eyes for a moment, taking a breath. He opened them again, looking at her intently.

"We used to be close. What happened?"

I fell in love with you, that's what happened.

It shook him what he felt about her, he didn't even know when it happened, but it was there, deep within. And he needed to accept it was how he felt. But was he ready to commit? He didn't even know. How could he know, when he didn't know how to trust? When only two hours ago, Sara was on her way out with another man.

He reminded himself of the games women played— of Amy, and the numerous women of his past—and found his resolve.

No, he wasn't ready to commit.

After a long moment of Daniel not saying anything, Sara slipped her hand in his and led him back to the living room. "Please don't go, Daniel," she begged, pulling him down beside her on the sofa. "Let's pray, can we do that? I think in a moment like this we need to invite God in. What do you think?" she asked tentatively.

He nodded his agreement, and they prayed and asked for God's guidance. The atmosphere changed between them, the sexual tension eased away, and God's presence entered in.

"I dreamt about you last night," she said.

Daniel gave her a curious look. "What did you dream?"

"We were about to board a plane, but every time we tried to board, something got in our way. A mob of people separated us at one point, then a wall seemed to erect itself. It was a very short dream."

It was the same dream I had this morning. That was random... But maybe not so random. David had told him how he and Rachel had shared the same dreams before, just as Daniel had shared dreams with David.

"I had the same dream this morning, but it was a little more abstract. You were there, but at a distance."

"Do you know what it means?" she asked.

"No, some dreams are clear, yet others are obscure and confusing. Then some nights I don't dream at all."

"You dream every night—you just don't remember them."

"Really?"

Sara nodded. "Yes. Do you pray when you dream?"

"No. I never thought to do that."

"For every dream, our response should be to pray. Dreams are God's parables and sometimes he hides things from us through symbols."

He frowned. "Why would he hide things from us? And what do you mean by symbols?"

"When God sends us a dream, it's his way of communicating with us. Because we are so busy with the distractions of life we don't notice when God is trying to communicate with us, so he waits until we're asleep and sends us a dream. Through dreams he advises us of our present and our future, sometimes also our past, if it is affecting our future."

"Yes, I get that all the time. Sometimes I dream of someone, and then I meet that person the following day. But the dreams I get about my past, I don't really understand them."

"I can show you how to interpret them. But sometimes the reason you don't understand is often intentional. If God has a plan for us and it's something we don't want or are not ready for, he will make you aware of it through a dream, preparing your spirit for his plans, even if your logical mind may not be ready for it. You may fight what he wants, or change direction away from what he wants for us, so he hides it from your logical mind. Your spirit knows and will begin to prepare you until the time your logical mind catches up, usually at the last minute, sometimes through symbols or by not allowing you to remember the dream at all." She thought for a moment.

"In answer to your question, symbols are metaphors. They are things in a dream that mean something else. Dreams are often not literal. Like the phrase 'the stars are sparkling diamonds' or 'you are my sunshine.' So literally speaking, the stars aren't diamonds and you are not the shining sun, although—" she smiled "—you are *my* sunshine, you do warm my heart, my skin, my body as the sun's rays would warm my skin, and you are my love as the song goes..." Her smile broadened.

He turned his head slightly and looked at her, his gaze curious. Then his eyes darkened. "Why do you tease me?" He ran a finger gently along her arm.

Sara lowered her gaze, having difficultly trying to contain the feelings he evoked in her at his touch. "I don't mean to," she whispered. It wasn't a tease, it was how she felt. Her life was brighter with him in it. He *was* her sunshine.

Daniel watched her. He wanted to kiss her again, but he resisted, taking her hand in his instead. "So our dreams are made up of symbols, which mean something else? Yes, I've found that. Sometimes there are so many symbols, I don't really understand them and then, often I remember a dream when I awake and then it's gone and I can't remember it, no matter how many times I try to recall it." He brushed his thumb across the soft skin of her hand. "But when we were at the conference, I remembered a dream that I had months ago, but I had forgotten it, and it came back to me, crystal-clear. It was about the conference and Preston James. So God had advised me of it before, but I'd forgotten it—or as you say, God obscured it from my memory so I would go. Thinking about it, if I'd remembered the dream, I probably wouldn't have gone." He smiled. "When you think about this, it's amazing. I can't even begin to analyse how powerful this is, that God communicates through our dreams."

"Yes, it's very powerful. It still astounds me, the things I discover—the insight. Take Rachel, for instance. As far as she was concerned, she was sworn off men, didn't ever want anything to do with them, but God had a plan for her to marry David. Months ago, before she met David, she dreamt about him and their marriage, but God hid it through symbols, preparing her spirit for his future plans for her life. She didn't understand the dream— God had used symbols to obscure it from her. If He had revealed it in the beginning, she would have fought it. She would have done everything in her power not to let David get close. Knowing her, she never would have attended his church and maybe they never would have met." She laced her fingers with his. "If we are wise, and have a close relationship with God, you can decipher what he is telling us by interpreting the dream. It is very much the same way Jesus used parables throughout the New Testament."

"I never knew that, this is really interesting. You said you attended a dream interpretation course?"

"Yes, I was taught by Preston James. He is a true prophet of God."

"Wow, I feel like I should be taking notes or something... Go on."

She smiled. "There are a number of symbols in the Bible—in the book of Daniel, for example. Daniel interpreted dreams." Sara's smile broadened. "Maybe there's a reason why you were named Daniel. Maybe it's God's plan for you to interpret dreams..."

Daniel contemplated that for a moment. The thought interested him. "So how do you interpret a dream?"

"It's like pieces of a puzzle that you have to try and fit together." She got up and retrieved a notepad and pen from the coffee table, then returned to sit next to him. "When you dream, it's important that you write your dreams down as they disappear. God communicates with us for a moment and then it's lost, so you must write it down, otherwise, you will forget. Also, you'll find when you try to remember your dreams your memory of it is strongest at the end of the dream, so you have to think backward to recall the whole dream from the beginning. You have to concentrate and have a little quiet time."

Realisation dawned on his face. "Yes, you're right, it does. Sometimes it gets a little jumbled and I only remember parts of it."

"I always lie still for a few moments in bed before I get up just to replay my dreams and get total recall in the correct order and then I assess the dream."

She looked at him for a moment, he seemed to be still interested and she wondered what he might think about the interpretation of his dream. She didn't want him to distance himself again.

"Your dream for instance...there was a plane, people, me, and you. They were the main focuses of the dream." She wrote this on the pad, circling the words, making a mind map.

Daniel leaned in close, looking at her diagram.

"Plane means higher spiritual calling. There was also a wall preventing me from getting to you. You appeared quite content for me to stay behind the wall and you were not in any hurry to get on the plane." She looked at him "Have you worked it out yet?"

He shook his head slowly, still looking down at her notepad. He frowned. "Seems a little complicated to me."

"I have a list of dream symbols and their meanings that I can give you. They're meant to be a guide and may not always help you..." Sara trailed off as she felt him finger her hair. She looked up at him. His eyes had darkened to what seemed like a smouldering blue. "You're not listening to me, Daniel, you're distracted."

"You distract me... I find it difficult to concentrate when I'm around you." He took the notepad from her and looked at it. "So if you can't work out what the symbols mean, what do you do?"

"You pray and ask God to give you the interpretation."

"Okay, I'm lost, what does it mean?"

"God is calling you to a higher spiritual level, one that will impact multitudes of people. However, you have erected a wall of distrust against women—against me—and in order for you to move to that higher level, you need to stop guarding yourself. You need to forgive."

"You got all that just from looking at these symbols?"

She nodded. "And also from discerning with my spirit. I had an understanding as I replayed the dream in my mind, and picked up on the impressions I got."

They went through another dream, one that Daniel had. Again, it was about her. They were walking along a beach—holding hands. A giant crystal blue wave hit them and he let go and stood away from her for a while—distant.

"This is a similar dream, Daniel. Blue means revelation of God, water means the Holy Spirit. God is bringing forth revelation and knowledge of the things of Him as we become closer. But every time we become close, you draw away. Is that what you have been doing? Trying to keep your distance from me?"

"I don't know I..." Daniel didn't know what to think about the situation—about any of this. He was fascinated about the insight to his dreams. Amazed, really, and he wanted to learn more, although it exposed things he'd kept hidden. He wasn't so sure he wanted Sara to know how he felt, as recently most of his dreams were about her.

"Did you know that one third of the Bible is devoted to dreams and visions—the prophetic? Therefore, it's important to God. When we begin to write our dreams down and show him that we value what he is communicating to us, then he will give us more, allowing us to develop a relationship with him. God has shown me so much, I'm not a seer as Rachel is, but God gives me insight through my dreams."

"I see things sometimes..." Daniel began, not sure what he should reveal. "I seem to be seeing more and more recently, when I'm around you and Rachel. So that dream is confirmation of what has been happening."

She smiled. "Isn't God amazing? What do you see?"

"Angels... when you sang, I saw my father and he confirmed what you told me." Tears came to his eyes. "He said he was proud of me, I never knew..."

God had given her insight to his past with his father—the years of pain and unforgiveness through misunderstandings and lack of communication.

She'd prophesied, giving him a word of knowledge.

Allowing him to finally forgive.

Sara shifted closer to him and touched his chest. "Oh, Daniel, he loved you. I felt it when I prophesied, you were his pride and joy."

"I don't know what to feel anymore...I've had so much anger and resentment inside, I..."

She reached up and caressed his jaw. "Let it go, Daniel. Give it to God, he loves you too." *As do I, so very much...*

She tucked in close to him, resting her head on his shoulder and wrapped her arms around his waist. She closed her eyes when his arms closed around her.

They hadn't resolved their issues, but deep down, within her spirit, she knew there was a change between them. She said a silent prayer of hope that he would finally let her in.

Chapter 4

Sara looked over at her mother and Samyra, deep in discussion about Samyra's return to the UK, which was planned imminently. Samyra had not said what the reason was for her return; she loved Los Angeles, and had been living there for the last three years, so Sara was confused as to why she wanted to move back. Samyra was at the height of her career, travelling the world, enjoying life. Why the rush to come back home now? She needed to talk to her—there was something going on, she could feel it. And she sensed it had everything to do with Joshua.

Sara eyed Samyra suspiciously. Samyra was what men would call beautiful—perfect features crowned with shoulder-length curly hair. She had the same family genes—amber coloured eyes—and had started her career as a model, but her love had been photography. Samyra soon gave up the life of "no food" as she often joked, preferring to be behind the camera rather than in front. Although she was still very slim, Sara always felt she could do with putting on a few extra pounds.

They both got their good looks from their mother and father. Her father died when they were young, and he was just a distant memory now, but she remembered his light brown eyes and dark curly hair. His heritage was a mix of South American and European. Her mother didn't know whereabouts in Europe he'd descended from, and her own parentage was also a little fuzzy as her parents died young. Her mother was also of mixed heritage—Guyanese and European. She assumed it was British, but did not dwell on it, the UK was her home now, people often wondered at her heritage. Dark shoulder-length hair, straight nose, angular jaw line, high cheekbones and full lips—she was often mistaken as being of Indian descent, so between her father and mother's genes, Samyra's and Sara's looks were deemed as exotic.

Ava had been strict in their upbringing and would not allow them to be infatuated with their outward appearance, knowing that others would do that for them—especially men. Sara had also been strict in her stance until she met Adam, who became obsessed with her looks.

Samyra looked up as if sensing her sister's stare. "What?"

"Oh, nothing. Just wondering why you're returning to the UK."

Samyra shrugged. "England is my home. I want to settle down here. I've done my time in Los Angeles."

"Fed up of the glorious weather and miss the rain?" Sara responded, grinning cheekily.

Samyra smiled, but there was something in her eyes; Sara couldn't quite work it out, and her mother was talking then, so she missed the moment.

"... said he was coming. I miss him," Ava said.

"You know what Bradley's job is like. Things change at the drop of a hat," Samyra responded.

"I know but he should be here." Ava sighed dejectedly.

Bradley had promised to spend Christmas with them, but at the last minute, his plans had changed. That happened too many times to mention. Her family was comprised of individuals sharing the same mother, but who never really saw much of each other, due to the demands of their careers.

"I saw Joshua a few weeks back. He asked for your number..." Sara paused, waiting for a response from Samyra.

Samyra gave her a pointed look that said, *keep your mouth shut.*

"I gave it to him. I hope you don't mind?"

"No, that's fine. He called, thanks." Samyra turned to their mother. "Mum, this turkey is really succulent. Did you do something different this year?"

The turkey is really succulent? Sara thought it was dry as always.

What is Samyra up to? She's hiding something.

The swift subject change was evident enough—*but turkey?* Her remark led Ava to go into a detailed explanation of how she'd prepared the turkey.

46

Sara wanted to laugh. Samyra caught Sara's gaze and she saw the amusement dancing in Samyra's eyes. Sara smirked, shaking her head. There was one thing that was guaranteed—her sister knew how to steer people down a path, anything to avoid subjects she didn't want to talk about. She was a skilled deflector; she could put Daniel to shame.

Sara sighed. As always, too much food was spread out across the dining table. The amount on display could easily feed a third-world country. Thank God she was only spending one night; turkey leftovers for the next two weeks was an awful thought.

Arianna was quiet, missing her now-extended family and so was Sara; one man in particular—Daniel. She longed to hear his voice, she missed him terribly. It was Christmas Day and she wanted to be with him.

Daniel had resumed his regular visits for a while, stopping for dinner and working together until late. She was finding it more and more difficult being away from him. Some nights she would just curl up on the sofa with him, listening to him negotiate over the phone or rest her head on his shoulder, wrapping her arms around his waist as he worked at his laptop, and every so often he would stop to kiss her. She had it bad—totally besotted with him.

She wondered what he was doing. From what he'd told her, his family had a big extravagant affair at Christmas. Daniel hadn't asked her to join them and she assumed he would attending on his own. Or maybe it was because he'd taken another woman to the dinner party. She had no right to expect anything less, she guessed, but she still ached at the thought.

As was her tradition, Christmas was always spent with Rachel, Matthew, and Rebecca. Rachel would either spend Christmas here with her mother, or Sara would spend Christmas with Rachel's parents; they had always spent it with either family. Now Rachel was married, so that was no longer an option. It forced her to look at her life; something needed to change, she couldn't continue on like this. She was discontent and tried her hardest not to let it affect her, but it did.

She missed Rachel. She was going out of her mind with boredom. She picked up her mobile, tapping out a message. *What are you doing?*

Watching the kids open their presents. This is large-scale extravagance. Wish you were here.

I wish you were here—turkey and Brussels sprouts, my favourite!

Ha ha! How could I forget—that is one meal I will not miss!

Sara chuckled. *I certainly will not be leaving with a leftover dish—unless you want some?*

I'm laughing—no thanks!

Sara smiled and looked over at Arianna, who was pushing her Brussels sprouts around her plate. Her long dark hair loose down her back, she was wearing one of her favourite party dresses, pale blue with frills.

"Aren't you going to eat your baby cabbages, Arianna?"

Arianna frowned, looking affronted at her suggestion that they were cabbages, Arianna would not be fooled. "They're Brussels sprouts, Mummy—I don't like Brussels sprouts."

"They're good for you, Arianna. Try and eat one."

Arianna looked at Sara's plate. "But you haven't eaten yours, Mummy."

Sara chuckled. So much for leading by example. "When Grandma is not looking, slip them on my plate," she whispered conspiratorially in her daughter's ear.

Arianna giggled and surreptitiously tossed the Brussels sprouts onto Sara's plate. "Can I watch TV now?"

Sara nodded, but before Arianna left the table, she asked, "Is Uncle Daniel coming, Mummy?"

Her heart ached for Arianna; she'd been asking for three days now. "I'm not sure, baby."

"I miss him, Mummy."

Hiding her feelings behind a smile, Sara caressed her cheek. "Yes, I miss him too."

"He promised to get me a present," Arianna pouted despondently.

"If he promised to get you a present, then he will get it for you. Remember, he is very busy and often travels a lot. He hasn't forgotten."

"Okay. But I want to give him my presents."

They had gone out especially to buy Daniel a Christmas present. Arianna had saved her pocket money and brought him a personalised cup, with a picture of herself with the words, "I Love Uncle Daniel." Knowing his love for sports cars, she'd also bought a model Aston Martin DB9, and a Jaguar F-Type which looked just like his cars so he could keep them in his office on his desk. Arianna carefully wrapped them and was eager to give them to him.

Sara bought him gold cufflinks, engraved with his initials, which she knew would suit his style. They were extravagant pieces— which hit her bank balance heavily—but wanted him to have something nice, as he'd always been generous with her.

She gave Arianna a gentle smile. "I'm sure he'll call soon, but if not, a little later on you can send him a text, okay?"

Seeming to be satisfied with that response, Arianna hugged Sara, then made her way over to the sofa to watch TV.

Sara looked around the room, religious paraphernalia scattered about. Haphazard Christmas decorations hung in places. The room was small, cluttered with a large oak dining table and a bookcase at the far end of the room, a small sofa and a TV in the corner. At the other end stood her beloved upright piano; which she practiced on growing up, and endured hours of piano lessons. It was old now and needed tuning. She hadn't played it in years.

Maybe she should play a piece to liven things up. Samyra wasn't herself, her mother kept fussing about Bradley, and Arianna had zoned out, focused on a programme she was watching.

Sara stood and began clearing the table, suddenly feeling low. It was Christmas Day and they should be celebrating Jesus' birth—a joyous occasion. But she felt far from joyous.

She headed to the kitchen and returned to collect some more dishes. The sound of her mobile—Daniel's ringtone—had her hurtling across the room for it, ignoring the looks from Samyra and her mother.

"Hi," she answered breathlessly, with a huge smile on her face.

"Merry Christmas, Sara."

"Merry Christmas, Daniel." *I miss you*, she wanted to say. Recently she hadn't felt able to be as open as she used to be. Although she'd seen a little more of him recently, he'd been different with her, more considered, not as expressive as he used to, seeming to be a little distant at times.

"What are you doing?"

She could hear sounds of music, and people talking and laughing in the background. "I was about to wash up, we've just finished Christmas dinner."

"You and Arianna should be here. I'm coming to get you."

Sara's heart leapt. She looked over at her mother and sister, still in conversation and Arianna alone, watching a film. Arianna was used to spending Christmas with Rachel's children, she missed their company. It didn't take much convincing. She promptly washed up the dishes, after all, it was the least she could do to ease the guilt she felt.

When Daniel arrived, she introduced him to her mother and Samyra. Seeing the appreciation cross both their faces, Sara smiled watching the scene. They were full of smiles by the time Sara said her goodbyes, Daniel charmed both women, but she ignored the disappointed looks they gave her and headed home with Daniel to change.

*   *   *

Daniel was nervous and he didn't know why.

Sara and Arianna had already headed in. He retrieved two Christmas presents from the car, placed them under the Christmas tree in the living room, and paced. Maybe it was Sara's present that was making him nervous. It was a declaration, wasn't it? A declaration of how he felt about her, the words he couldn't say.

He'd met her mother and sister, which made him nervous, too. He didn't do mothers, or bring girlfriends to Christmas dinners.

Girlfriend? Was Sara a girlfriend? He really didn't know what to call their relationship. It wasn't what you would call a traditional relationship, he visited infrequently, but nothing had ever been defined and he'd been content with that before. Now, it was no longer enough.

He couldn't stop the possessiveness he felt about her—it was an emotion he'd only ever felt for Sara and one he couldn't control. He hadn't even felt this way with Amy. He'd wanted to marry Amy, but she was never his from the beginning, and it never came up. It was different with Sara, *she* was different—and she loved him. He held that close within, maybe that was why he felt so possessive of her—she was *his*. There was no way he would let another man take what belonged to him.

His heart raced at the thought. He recalled how he'd felt when she'd got all dressed up for Gary. He'd been sick with jealousy; he wanted to pummel the man. His chest grew tight; he took in a calming breath. He felt uneasy and...*insecure*.

He could admit that to himself, because if he didn't, he'd probably do something he shouldn't. Sara could leave at any time, just as Amy did, and where would that leave him? Maybe deep down he expected her to, maybe that was why he held back. But every time she'd taken a step in that direction, he'd shut it down straight away, hadn't he? The thought of her with another man was not even a consideration. But what if there was another Gary waiting in the wings?

He didn't know if he could trust her and that was his problem.

He loved her, he accepted that now, and as far as he was concerned she was his…but a girlfriend? A relationship—*a commitment?* He wasn't so sure.

He felt guilty; he should have collected them earlier for dinner as his mother had invited them. But he wanted to downplay their relationship. It seemed too much like a promise of things to come—a commitment he wasn't ready for. But as the evening wore on, he felt devoid somehow, watching the family—Leah and Susanna, James and Carl and their children. David and Rachel and their children. Fun and laughter was had by all, and he'd missed Sara and Arianna, regretting not having invited them. It forced him to see things with greater clarity.

When they entered the living room—Sara dressed in an elegant maroon Bardot slip dress. Arianna in pink, looking like a princess with a pink ribbon in her hair—Daniel smiled, they looked stylish in their party dresses, a mother and daughter duo. "You are both very beautiful, I will be proud to have you both on my arms tonight." His gaze drifted over Sara appreciatively. He was captivated and couldn't keep his eyes off her.

"Thank you, Daniel, I'm always proud when I'm with you."

A sweet seductive play formed on her lips, which did not help Daniel's resolve. He was distracted. Distracted by Sara in that dress... The unease gone in an instant; the way the dress skimmed her curves, moving with her body, her hair in waves to her waist, the smoothness of her skin. He took in a breath. He ached with a need that was becoming overwhelming, which he seemed to battle with daily. Celibacy was new to him; to wait with a woman was something he'd never had to do before, and to involve God in prayer regarding it was also new, he didn't think he could do one without the other.

Sara watched the scene. Arianna giggled and gave a twirl, then ran over to Daniel, hugging him tightly as he lifted her into his arms. Just seeing the shear excitement on Arianna's face was enough to ease the guilt Sara felt at abandoning her mother and sister on Christmas day. Arianna loved Daniel, and so did she, so very much.

Sara met his gaze, there was something in his green eyes, and she couldn't quite read what it was. They had darkened and looked almost blue. She loved the way his eyes changed colour—so beautiful. She sighed wistfully.

He must have gone to the car while they were upstairs as two presents had appeared under the Christmas tree in the corner by the TV. When he released Arianna, she shrieked and rushed over to the huge present with her name on it and ripped into it to reveal a laptop.

Arianna beamed. "Mummy, look!" she exclaimed excitedly, and then she threw herself into Daniel's arms again. "Thank you, Uncle Daniel! I love you."

She gave him a big kiss, then rushed over the tree, scooped up Daniel's presents, and handed them to him to open. "I saved up all my pocket money," Arianna announced proudly.

Daniel was surprised. "I wasn't expecting anything, Arianna, thank you." Touched, he excitedly ripped the packages open, to Arianna's delight. He smiled. "I love them. Thank you, Arianna, they're beautiful presents. I shall put them in my office."

Arianna grinned in response as he drew her into a hug. "Open Mummy's present," she said, eagerly.

Sara went over and sat next to him on the sofa, handing him her gift.

He frowned, not used to women giving him gifts; the expectation was always for him to give. "I wasn't expecting anything from you either..."

"It's only a small thing." She smiled as he tore into the wrapping.

Daniel smiled, pleased with his gift. "These are exceptional, thank you."

He hugged her close, then promptly released the cufflinks he was wearing and replaced them with hers. "They remind me of my father's, his cufflinks were always engraved with his initials, I remember once when I was young, I asked him if it was because he was afraid of losing them." Daniel laughed, remembering.

Sara chuckled. "I can just see you asking that. I bet you were so mischievous growing up."

He grinned. "Yes, I was. David and I both were. Now open yours."

Arianna enjoying the exchanges, went over to the tree again and returned handing the small square box to Sara.

Sara looked down at her present that was professionally wrapped, with a silver ribbon and bow. She ripped into the gold paper, and uncovered a small jewellery box. She nervously opened it, not knowing what to expect. She didn't want to make assumptions, as she'd done before when he'd given her the ring.

The ring that never left her finger since the day he'd bought it for her.

She was speechless, looking at him wide-eyed as she saw what was revealed. A masonry screw, placed neatly in the box, with a red ribbon tied around it.

Daniel laughed.

Sara couldn't believe it. She hit him playfully, joining in with his laughter. "So much for the romantic moment, Daniel."

Daniel continued to laugh at her expense, tears coming to his eyes. She affected a sigh. "I'm offended," and then grinned; she couldn't help herself as he kept laughing. "You're something else, Daniel." She stood, grinning. "Let's go. I want to show off this dress."

He stood next to her, grinning widely. "I'm sorry, I couldn't resist a cheap laugh. You won't ever forget our first Christmas together, and I hope you won't forget this." He handed her a Cartier box.

She smiled, excitement filling her. She opened it to reveal a beautiful round diamond graduated V-necklace, with matching drop earrings. Her breath caught.

"Oh, Daniel, they're so beautiful...you bought this for me? Oh my..." She flung her arms around his neck and kissed him. "I love them! Thank you."

She pulled away, fingering the extravagant pieces that must have set him back thousands. Tears came to her eyes.

"Hey..." He tilted her chin so she would look at him. "It wasn't meant to bring tears."

Overwhelmed, more tears rolled down her cheeks. "I'm sorry, it's been a very long time since anyone has done anything like this for me."

Daniel wondered what that meant. Before he could query her, she handed him the necklace and turned, lifting her hair out of the way so he could fasten it around her neck.

He'd wanted to do this. It was a need inside him to declare his love through this gift. She was the type of woman that deserved to be adorned, and he yearned to make her feel special with beautiful jewellery. She'd been married to a wealthy entrepreneur, and he remembered what she'd told him; *"...he would take me out to exclusive restaurants, buy me expensive gifts, clothes, jewellery, anything I wanted, he made me feel like a queen..."* He noted that he'd never seen the jewellery that he expected a woman of her stature to possess. She owned the clothes, the car, the poise; but she was devoid of jewellery and only wore the pieces he'd given her. There had to be a reason; her reaction was very telling.

His heart constricted at her unexpected tears. He wanted to pull her in his arms and comfort her, to make whatever had upset her right again.

Sara went over to the mirror in the room and looked at her reflection as she touched the necklace; it was an exquisite piece. She put on the earrings, they reminded her of her past.

Adam used to shower her with gifts just like these at the beginning of their relationship and marriage. And then it stopped, and so did his affection. When she divorced him, he took all her jewellery back, telling her it was a clause in the prenup she'd signed. Some of the pieces he'd given her had held great sentiment to her at the time. It hurt so much that he took them back. They were gifts he'd given to her, not a family heirloom—which suggested he must have had them in mind for someone else.

This was literally the first time a man—anyone—had given her anything of this value in years.

She made an excuse of wanting to fix her makeup and went upstairs to her bedroom to compose herself.

She never expected anything like this. Daniel was always generous, but this was different. Cartier diamonds were not something you gave to a woman that meant nothing to you.

She touched the Cartier love bracelet she wore tonight, that Daniel had given to her for her birthday, and the ring which had never left her finger. She'd wondered if it was love; that he was somehow showing her through his gifts, but the way he distanced himself from her was contradictory to his actions. It confused her—but then she'd discovered the reason why he fought what he felt, hadn't she?

Amy. She'd broken his heart, making it difficult for him to trust. While he still had his trust issues, to a certain extent he trusted her. He'd partly let her in with his family, not many women—if any— could say they had that privilege. And after he distanced himself from her, fighting what she hoped he would one day see, he always came back.

I must mean something to him, Sara thought, *a lot more than I'd ever realised.*

Her heart began to pound. He *did* care about her. She hoped and prayed deep down that his care and affection would turn into love, and not be a farce as it had with Adam.

When they arrived at Katherine's home, the drive was filled with cars, luxurious ones. Clearly this was a popular annual event. Sounds of music could be heard from outside, along with the hum of hundreds of people talking and laughing.

Daniel held her hand as they weaved their way through the crowd. Arianna had already disappeared to play with her friends. He pulled her into the main room where everyone was dancing to the music.

"Shouldn't I go and say hello to your mother?" Sara asked.

"Later. I want to dance with you." He pulled her close then, his arms curling around her waist. "I want to hold you all night," he whispered.

She slipped her arms around his neck, remembering their time in Negril where they'd danced the night away. Neither of them wanted the night to end. And here she was again in his arms. It was a dream, a wonderful dream that she didn't want to wake up from. She closed her eyes as he tucked his face into her hair, his cheek brushing against hers.

"I want to be with you, Sara." He kissed her cheek. "I've tried to stay away, but I can't anymore."

Could this mean that he would finally commit? Her heart skipped a beat and she waited for him to continue, but he didn't.

"What are you saying, Daniel?" she asked tentatively.

Just at that moment, a woman tapped on Daniel's shoulder. She was tall, attractive, and wore a fuchsia dress that clung to everything. "Daniel, you promised to dance with me."

Irritated, Daniel paused and introduced them. Janice was the daughter of a friend of the family. She'd hoped they would become an item but that would never be the case. They'd had a brief affair years ago and he discovered that she was way too clingy and controlling. "As you can see, Janice, I already have a dance partner."

"You don't mind, do you, hon?" Janice asked Sara.

Sara raised an eyebrow and stared at her for a moment. *What is this? The cheek of the woman!* She swallowed the retort that came to her lips and pulled away from Daniel's arms.

Daniel tried to pull her back, but Sara dodged him, stepping aside, not wanting to have any part in haggling over a man, regardless of how she felt about it. Women never failed to flock to him, and it was irritating. Still, she was confident that Daniel wanted to be with *her*, and that was all that mattered.

She walked away and went over to the buffet table where the service staff were at hand, ready to serve. She looked at the selection.

The thought of more turkey was definitely a no-no, although she'd never tried turkey roulade with cider sauce or tandoori turkey, turkey jalfrezi, turkey meat balls, smothered in parmesan, even turkey samosas.

Rachel approached. "I thought I saw you sneak in." She gestured to the table. "Not more turkey..."

"No way—not after Mother's delights!" Sara laughed and hugged Rachel. "You look fantastic. Your mother would be proud. Is she here?"

Rachel rolled her eyes. "No, thank God. My loving parents are travelling again, so we won't see them for a while."

Rachel had a tumultuous relationship with her parents. Rachel's mother had high standards—to the extreme sometimes, but they seemed to have accepted David into the fold, which Sara knew, deep down, Rachel was grateful.

"You look really nice, and those pieces you're wearing are exquisite." Rachel widened her eyes. "Wow, did Daniel give them to you?"

Sara smiled. "Yes." She felt tears come to her eyes again. "I couldn't believe it, Rachel. They go with the love bracelet he gave me and the ring." She lifted her wrist, wriggling her fingers for effect. "What do you think it means?"

"You know what I think, Sara. He loves you, without a doubt, he just needs to deal with his inner demons—give him time."

That was the problem; she didn't have time.

Rachel gestured to Daniel. "Who's the starlet? And why is she with Daniel?"

Sara raised a brow. "I was wondering the same thing." David appeared at Sara's side before she could contemplate it any further.

"We missed you at dinner. You should have come, you're family," David pointed out.

I wasn't invited, Sara wanted to say, but held her tongue. He enveloped her into a bear hug. *Oh Lord, being in his arms is so divine...* She noted he wore the same aftershave as Daniel, and for a second, she got lost in the scent. The moment was brief as he whisked Rachel away, resuming his focus totally on her. He pulled Rachel close against him for a dance, leaving Sara alone again.

Her mind drifted and she wondered what Daniel was about to say to her before they were rudely interrupted.

She headed to the far end of the room, weaving her way through the crowds where the huge Christmas tree stood twinkling proudly and presents were laid out below for decoration—or so she thought, until she noticed two presents: one with her name and the other with Arianna's. She frowned, looking down and wondering if Daniel had put them there, but he'd already given them their presents. She absently fingered the necklace he'd bought. Then she turned to see if Daniel was dancing with Janice, and collided with his chest.

"Why did you leave?" Daniel asked impatiently. He looked annoyed.

"She said you promised her a dance, I didn't want to get involved in a lover's tiff," she teased.

"Lover's tiff?" Daniel scoffed. "I did not promise her a dance and she shouldn't have come over to us like that. I brought you here because I want to be with *you*, not anyone else."

He'd told Janice in no uncertain terms to back off. She knew the score, but he guessed this was the first time he'd ever brought a woman to a family function like this, so jealousy was rearing its ugly head. That and the fact that Sara being here with him made it clear to everyone that they were together and he needed to make that right. It was what the Holy Spirit had been telling him and he couldn't fight it any longer.

"Well, I'm happy to take a back seat to an old girlfriend."

"She was never a girlfriend." He looked at her intently, ensuring his message was clear, and then looked down at the presents under the tree. "Those are from my mother."

She looked up in surprise. "Why would she do that? She didn't have to... I feel so bad, I didn't get her anything."

"She considers you family, Sara."

She looked deep into his eyes. "Do you consider me family?"

"Yes, I do," he said simply. Then he took her hand and led her back to the dance floor and pulled her into his arms. "So where was I...?"

"You tried to stay away, but you can't anymore..." She smiled sweetly at him.

Daniel smiled in response. He'd stayed away for a number of reasons, reasons that had everything to do with the dreams he'd been having lately, and ironically, she was the one who could interpret them for him. "I think we should try at a relationship...I want to."

"I want everything, Daniel. Are you willing to give me that?"

Daniel swallowed the unease that rose up in his chest. "I don't know, Sara. Can't we just take each day as it comes?"

Sara considered his response for a moment. "I don't think we can, Daniel."

It was the Holy Spirit's whispered words within that halted her; *"Trust me, Sara."*

She wanted to—she did. Only she was running out of time, she wasn't getting any younger and Daniel was in no hurry, nor had the inclination to walk her down the aisle. She was at a loss about what to do, but knew in that moment she could trust her Lord and Saviour without a doubt.

She needed to be patient—she only hoped she could.

Chapter 5

Daniel looked over at Vanessa. She averted her eyes, looking down. No doubt she was feeling guilty over the lies she'd told about him.

Annoyance and disgust filled him. He'd been a good employer to her and always treated her with respect. And what good did that do him? Now he was having to endure this legal battle. He should never have hired a woman to be his assistant—his mistake, and a steep learning curve for him.

He looked across the gleaming, polished mahogany conference table that dominated the room. Sunlight poured in through huge floor-to-ceiling windows overlooking London's landscape. In the distance, he could see St Paul's Cathedral, Tower Bridge, Westminster Abbey, the Houses of Parliament, and Big Ben. The River Thames flowed through dividing the capital. He'd always loved London's architecture, and the views from his offices on the nineteenth floor were spectacular, especially on an unusually bright winter day such as this.

Seated across from him were Vanessa and her lawyer. Another female; he was surrounded by them, which did not bode well for him, and he wondered again whether he should have opted for a male colleague from his legal team.

Sharon sat beside him, looking no-nonsense in her dark-blue business suit, her blonde hair in a neat bun. He'd had several meetings with her over the last few weeks and had discovered she was quite a nice person, pleasant to speak with, and very easy on the eye. Five months ago, given the interest that was clearly evident from her, he would have jumped at and easily formed a connection by now, but with this thing hanging over his head he'd kept things professional between them. Well, that, and the fact he was a Christian now. There was no point in complicating things.

"So what were you hoping to achieve from this suit?" Sharon addressed Vanessa's lawyer. She was dark-haired with her long hair tied into a loose bun, also clad in a dark suit.

Niki Greer's eyes drifted to him, seeming to assess him shrewdly. She was pretty and well endowed, exotic looking—very attractive in fact, possibly from a Greek heritage. Manicured nails tapped on a wad of papers she'd placed on the table in front of her. She met his gaze, her big brown eyes asking a question—one of interest. Daniel looked away, refocusing his mind. He certainly didn't need any distractions right now.

"The claimant would like her job back. She feels she was unfairly dismissed. Mr Anderson could not fault her on her work, which he has confirmed. This is outright harassment and discrimination, and she is a defenceless young woman," Niki responded, looking directly at him.

"*Pardon?*" Daniel was outraged. "*Harassment and discrimination?* I have never treated Vanessa that way and she knows it." Daniel was angry; it was one thing seeing the allegations in black and white, but to have them slung in his face was too much to stomach. *This is ridiculous.*

Sharon placed a hand on Daniel's arm, as if to calm him. "What do you say in response, Miss Banton?" Sharon began softly. "In what way do you feel that Mr Anderson has harassed you?"

Vanessa looked over at Niki.

In response, Niki nodded reassuringly.

"Well...he didn't...he..." Tears came to Vanessa's eyes and spilled over.

Exasperated, Daniel rolled his eyes.

"I don't care about all that...I just want my job back." Vanessa's eyes met his for a brief moment, then she looked away again.

"So, Mr Anderson did not harass you?"

"Do not lead the claimant, Sharon," Niki jumped in and gave Sharon a hard stare.

"Miss Banton just said Mr Anderson did not harass her." Sharon gave Niki a smug look and raised a brow.

"That is not exactly what she said. Let us only address the facts," Niki replied, making some notes on her papers.

"If you wish. What are the facts, then? You have made a sexual harassment claim, and under what basis does this allegation hold any merit?" She turned to Vanessa. "Miss Banton, did Mr Anderson sexually harass you? And if so, can you give me an example of when this happened?"

Daniel watched Vanessa. She fidgeted in her seat, her head down, brushing her tears away. "I...he didn't harass me, exactly..." she trailed off again as tears streamed down her face.

Daniel sighed, his anger abating a little, but still irritated at having to go through this on the whim of this woman. The cost to the business was unnecessary.

He assessed whether he should have handled this differently. Vanessa was clearly upset. Then he thought about Sara and Rachel's words, and what they'd said about Vanessa needing affirmation from him.

He rose from his seat; he'd had enough of this nonsense. He walked around the long table, making his way over to Vanessa.

"Mr Anderson, I do not think it is wise to—"

Daniel held up his hand to silence Sharon and sat next to Vanessa. He pulled out a handkerchief and handed it to her.

Vanessa looked at him with her big sorrowful brown eyes, and his anger dissipated. "Vanessa, what is all this about? You and I both know I never harassed you. Neither did I discriminate. I've always valued your work—in fact, you were the best assistant I have ever had. But you know the reason I had to let you go—I had no choice. What do you want from me?" He spoke gently with the hope that she would finally be honest about what was really behind all of this.

"I know...you didn't harass me or discriminate. You were the best employer I have ever had and I'm sorry—" more tears spilled over, "—please, can I have my job back? I love my job...I never intended for things to go this far. My brother is a lawyer, and he pushed me...I'm sorry...please, can I have my job back?" She grabbed his arm desperately. "I'm sorry about what I did and I promise it won't ever happen again. I just...you just don't understand the affect you have on a woman. Men always find me attractive, but you never once even acknowledged me in that way, and I guess I was a little frustrated. I'm sorry for that."

Daniel stared at her for a moment, not quite believing what she'd just revealed. So all this time, if he'd complimented her, he wouldn't be in this position? Whatever happened to equality and feminism? He was confused. He had no words...

Daniel eased away from her grasp, feeling uncomfortable as the three women in the room stared at him expectantly. This was a first—that a woman would take him to a tribunal over a sexual harassment claim; reason being that he *hadn't* sexually harassed her, this was bizarre. And one of those rare moments that he would love to take a picture of and frame so he could laugh about it.

He sighed, wanting this to be over already. "Vanessa, I'll give you your job back, but you will not work for me. After what has happened between us, I do not feel it is appropriate. I'll let you know the department you will be moved to."

Her face lit up and she smiled. "Thank you, Daniel. I won't ever let you down again."

He rose to his feet and addressed the two lawyers in the room, who were now assessing him with renewed respect. "I trust this situation is now resolved."

He made his way to the door. "Sharon, I'll leave the details to you. I have another meeting I have to attend." With that, he left the room, wondering at women and their wiles. They were complicated souls that he would never, ever understand.

*   *   *

"Well, that was a turn-up for the books."

Daniel looked across at Sharon, his legal rep. She was cutting into a very large steak that filled her plate. He liked a woman who had a healthy appetite and did not shy away from it. "Yes, one which was unexpected. I got the distinct impression that you believed her story."

"I wondered...but I can understand the way she feels, though..." She smiled and filled her mouth, chewing slowly.

Daniel opted for fish, wanting to keep his lunch light. "Why?" He raised a querying brow.

"Sometimes an attractive woman, who wants the attention of a man she likes and he seems not to be interested in her, can find this a little frustrating."

Daniel chewed slowly, quietly assessing her, noting the change in her tone. "Enough to put in a sexual harassment claim?"

"Oh I wouldn't put in a sexual harassment claim. I would handle the situation in a totally different way..."

He held her gaze. It was a pity. Under different circumstances, he would have loved to take this where she clearly wanted it to go, but he would have to pass. Sara was very much at the forefront of his mind and the only woman he wanted right now. "Sharon, you are a very attractive woman, but I'm seeing someone at the moment."

"From what I understand, your pursuits don't last long-term, so..."

"So...?"

"So, you have my number, call me..."

Daniel smiled.

Sharon reminded him of another woman; Samantha, his PR and Social Media manager. She was one woman he'd often wondered about. His mind drifted to this afternoon and his discussion with her. She was attractive; light caramel skin, her long dark hair swept up in a ponytail, softly brushing the shoulders of her tailored business suit that fit her body perfectly. Long manicured nails, always well-dressed. A woman who looked after herself—driven and very much his type, but she'd made things clear that they should keep their relationship professional.

Samantha was a Christian. He didn't stand a chance and at the time, he wasn't prepared to attend church with her every Sunday. At one point when he'd taken her out, she'd whipped out her Bible for a night of Bible study and prayer. He'd been rendered wide-eyed and speechless that day, and it had been a running joke between them ever since. After that they'd decided by mutual consent to have a platonic relationship.

"I don't have a place for her."

"Vanessa is a good worker, and she won't disappoint you."

Samantha raised an eyebrow. "I have five men on my team, Daniel, I would have a riot on my hands—no way, the way she dresses..." Samantha leaned back in her chair, assessing him.

"Well, I have all confidence that you will rectify that."

"So what's the reason she stopped working for you?"

"I felt she would be best placed in a department that will stretch her."

Samantha smiled knowingly. "She fell for you, didn't she?"

Daniel chose not to respond to that comment. "She's a good worker, Sam."

"What is it with you? You only need to look at a woman and they're throwing themselves at you."

"Didn't work with you, did it?"

She eyed him mischievously. "You didn't try hard enough..."

He laughed. "So if I'd tried that little bit harder, you're saying you would have thrown yourself at me, too?"

She chuckled. "Maybe..."

Grinning, Daniel replied, "The fact that you only have eyes for your very rich fiancé would have been a factor in that never happening."

"Well, there is that." She affected a sigh. "I am in love."

Daniel continued to smile, enjoying the banter they always had with each other. "Vanessa starts with you on Monday," he said, as he walked out the door. "Make her feel welcome."

He came across many women in his field—a wide choice of women, so he never got bored, his mind always on his next conquest. Could he be happy with just one woman? He didn't know if he could.

But then, when he was with Sara, boredom was far from what he felt. He liked her before he loved her. She was fun to be with and the attraction between them was potent, a compelling force, not something he'd ever come across before. With Amy, it had also been strong, but not like this.

Setting his emotions aside, he liked who Sara was, just as he liked Sam and Sharon. They were strong, intelligent women that kept his mind active, but there was something about Sara.

He had an innate need to protect her—a possessiveness that he found difficult to control. The thought of losing her to another man was too much for him to even contemplate. And with that in mind, where did it leave him?

A life with her or a life without her—he knew there could be no in-between.

Chapter 6

"Oh, Sara, I dreamt about you last night." Rachel turned, opened the fridge door and looked inside.

"Tell me, don't leave me hanging." Sara smiled, switching on the tap and washed lettuce leaves and cherry tomatoes.

"Holy Spirit just reminded me." Rachel handed Sara a cabbage and some carrots.

Sara placed them on the counter impatiently. "And? What was the dream about?"

Rachel checked the fish fillets that were simmering on the cooker, then placed sweet peppers on the chopping board and began slicing. "Dreamt you got married again, but this time I saw the groom..."

Sara waited.

Rachel continued to chop with a smirk on her face.

Impatient, Sara placed a stilling hand over Rachel's. "Will you tell me?"

Rachel laughed. "Well, he's wealthy and very attractive..."

"Rachel!"

Rachel giggled, a mischievous glint in her eyes. "It's Daniel. But you knew that."

Sara sighed. "It's what I want, but *he* doesn't. I think God will have to work a miracle for Daniel to walk me down the aisle." Sara sliced the cabbage into fine shreds.

"Have faith, Sara. When you met Daniel he wasn't a Christian, now he is, I don't foresee you'll have to wait for much longer."

"Did God give you timescales at all? Was it summer or winter when we got married?"

"I don't know. Ask Holy Spirit, He will reveal it to you."

"Reveal what to you?" David asked as the brothers sauntered into the room. "The dining table is set."

Sara resumed slicing the cabbage, hoping David didn't really want his question answered and that Rachel wouldn't say anything.

Rachel and David had invited Sara and Daniel to dinner, and they were preparing this in the kitchen.

Sara moved with ease around the spacious white open-plan kitchen that looked like something out of *Home & Gardens* magazine; modern and sleek, island in the centre, breakfast bar overlooking the gardens, which set off picturesque views through floor-to-ceiling walls of glass that opened out to bring the outdoors in. The tastefully laid white marble floors gleamed in the sunlight. In fact, the entirety of David's home was impressive and reminded her of the home she'd shared with Adam.

She was loathe to call it her home, even though that was what it had been for ten years. It had also been her responsibility to take over the care and maintenance of the mansion when she moved in, including management of the staff. She was subsequently relieved of her duties when she divorced Adam.

Truthfully, she missed this—the lifestyle. It was everything she'd become, the wealth—the prestige. All her clothes were designer labels—her car; a Mercedes, although she was seriously thinking of selling it, as maintaining it was becoming too much for her current budget.

Signing the prenup when she married Adam, meant when she divorced him, she'd ended up with very little to show for the years she'd been his dutiful wife. He paid the mortgage on her small three-bedroom house and Arianna's school fees. He also paid monthly maintenance and she had to provide receipts for expenses, giving an account for everything.

She'd chosen not to take spousal maintenance payments, as Adam would have tried to control her and she wanted to be free of his control over her life. Changing her lifestyle had been a steep adjustment for her; she could no longer have shopping sprees in Bond Street at London's exclusive designer boutiques, just because she could. Or travel to the Caribbean or the US, because she wanted the feel of the sun on her skin. She missed the freedom of having wealth, but she did not miss the life. She'd become resentful of Adam—she'd been a kept woman, showered with money that, in the end, meant nothing.

David slipped his arms around his wife's waist, kissing her neck. He whispered something in her ear and she giggled in response. Rachel was indeed a blessed woman.

Sara's gaze rested on Daniel, who was sitting in the living area with the children, a game on Matthew's console keeping him occupied. However, at David's display of affection, Daniel turned and watched them for a moment, his eyes focused on Rachel.

More and more she noticed how much Daniel watched Rachel. He seemed unable to help himself and she couldn't help the jealousy that sneaked its way inside her heart.

They didn't even have a relationship, per se; he came to see her occasionally, and less frequently of late—Arianna saw more of him nowadays than Sara did. She missed him, missed being with him. He'd stipulated that he did not want her seeing other men, but they hadn't defined their relationship, and she was frustrated by his seemingly overall lack of interest in her.

The last time she saw him was Christmas Day. He'd said he wanted a relationship and she'd mistakenly thought she would see much more of him, but it wasn't to be. She wondered if he just wanted to ensure she didn't see anyone else, or that this was a control tactic. She was used to men's attention, and if she wanted to, she could use it to her advantage. He seemed not to be affected by her at all, and right now, the only woman he seemed to be interested in was Rachel.

At some point the brothers headed to David's office to discuss business, while Sara and Rachel continued preparation of their evening meal.

"So...how do you feel about you and Daniel marrying?"

"I don't really see it happening, to be honest, but I guess I should have faith."

"My dreams always come true, Sara. If God said it's going to happen, then it will."

"Daniel is the one that needs convincing."

"He already knows, Sara."

Sara looked up, surprised. "He knows?"

"Yes, God has sent him many dreams about your marriage, but he's fighting it. He doesn't want to get married."

It hurt to hear her say that Daniel didn't want to marry her. "Maybe he just doesn't want to be with *me*. He's not exclusive to me, he still sees other women."

Rachel frowned. "What makes you say that?"

"I've seen him. Last week I stopped by at his home. I guess I missed him, so I'd cooked dinner and brought some for him. I saw him leaving his house with a woman. So clearly they had been together."

"I'm not sure that's correct, Sara."

"It's what I saw."

"Well, that's not what Daniel's told me."

"What's he told you?"

Rachel looked toward the office to check the door was closed and the men were not going to suddenly appear as they had before. She lowered her voice so the children couldn't overhear. "He told me that he hasn't been with anyone else for over five months and that's not usual for him. By now, he would have sought the attention of a willing female, but he can't keep his mind off you."

Sara blinked. "He actually said that?"

Rachel nodded, turning the gas off the pots. "Dinner is ready. Can you let David and Daniel know?"

"But he was seeing that Emma woman."

"I asked him about that, and he said they were old friends. They had a couple of dinners together and nothing else. In normal circumstances, he said he would have slipped into his old ways, but since meeting you, he hasn't wanted to, and obviously he's a Christian now, so it wouldn't have been a consideration."

Sara continued to stare at Rachel, trying to digest what she'd told her. "So he isn't seeing anyone else?" Sara asked, not sure she actually believed her.

"No, Sara. He has no interest in anyone else. He wants you. God clearly wants you to be together, so you need to focus your prayers in that direction."

Rachel dismissed her, turning to serve their meal into dishes.

Sara gave Rachel one last glance. She had so many questions and felt insecure.

She made her way to David's office. The door was ajar and she could hear the brothers having a heated discussion. Sara halted in her tracks, listening intently.

"...are you going to hold that against me forever? It was one kiss, David."

"One kiss that could have ended my marriage."

"Maybe you should have ended it, the fact that she allowed the kiss to happen said enough."

Sara held her breath. *What is going on?*

"She thought you were me, you made her believe that. She was my wife, Daniel, you had no right!"

Daniel looked at his brother, hesitating before responding. "You might not want to hear this, but she wanted it."

"So that relieves you of all guilt, does it?"

"No, it doesn't, and I'm sorry for what happened. I shouldn't have allowed it to continue." *If you knew the truth, we wouldn't be having this conversation.*

"You keep well away from Rachel," David warned.

Daniel sighed, eyeing his brother. "It's difficult with Rachel..."

"Daniel—"

"Do I have to remind you of what happened with you and Amy?"

David sighed, seeming to calm down a little.

"You nearly found yourself in the same situation I found myself in with Karen."

"Yes, all the more reason to stay away from Rachel. I'm not really happy with the Bible study evenings when I'm not here, Daniel. I'm content for it to happen when I'm home, but I don't want you here, alone. I know you still feel for her, but she's my wife now."

Daniel smiled. "Yes, the one that got away." He couldn't resist winding David up.

"She was never yours."

"No, but I can't help what I feel, David. The love between you is sometimes overwhelming and this has nothing to do with Rachel..."

Rachel and David's shared emotion was so overwhelming that all it did was heighten his feelings for Sara. He tried to fight it, but when he was with them it was impossible, their love was strong, it changed the atmosphere—pushing his thoughts to Sara, again and again.

Lately, all he thought about was her—no, ever since he'd met her in fact—being with Sara, kissing her, holding her, thinking of when he could next spend time with her. No matter how much he tried to fight it, the force remained within him. She was making him soft—vulnerable to her and he couldn't have that, so he'd stayed away, keeping his distance. Just hearing her voice, seeing her smile, hearing her laugh, seeing the light in her beautiful honey-coloured eyes had his heart racing in his chest. Any resolve he had fell away, and he needed to touch her somehow, connect with her.

He was a besotted fool and that just would not do. He needed to get a handle on what he was feeling. He felt as if he was out of control and it was easier to suppress it and not to analyse what his heart and mind told him. Then it was made all the more intense when he was around David and Rachel, bringing all his feelings for Sara to the surface.

"I know...your feelings for Sara are exposed."

Not wanting to discuss his feelings, Daniel countered. "It's noted that you have been a little more...shall we say, amenable toward Sara."

"Because I can feel the love you have for her, I can block you to a certain extent, but when you suppress it, it makes what I feel stronger. Why are you fighting what you're feeling?"

Daniel loves me? Sara gripped the door frame, taking a breath.

"Because...I don't understand what I feel yet."

"But you understand what God has been showing you."

Daniel looked at his brother stubbornly; he wasn't going to have this conversation right now. It had all become a little overwhelming.

Stop now. Daniel held his gaze for a long moment, waiting for David to get the message Daniel communicated to him.

"Okay, but you can't bury your head in the sand forever. You will have to address this."

Daniel chose not to respond and swiftly changed the subject back to work matters.

Sara stood motionless for a moment, her mind whirling with questions. *Lord, I really don't understand any of this...*

"Discern with your spirit, Sara."

But before she could assess what the Holy Spirit had said, Daniel turned and noticed her at the door. "Dinner's ready," she said, lowering her gaze and made a hasty retreat.

Over dinner, seated around the large dining table—the children occupied at the head, a debate being had about whether they should eat their salad—Sara watched Daniel, Rachel, and David share in their banter. Rachel laughed at something Daniel had said and she could see the love which was always in Daniel's eyes when he looked at Rachel. He'd confirmed it and she'd overheard the confirmation again today, although she didn't understand it.

Watching Daniel and his reaction to Rachel, Sara was made to feel as if he was being disloyal to *her*. He belonged to her and should be giving *her* the attention, not Rachel. But truthfully, when he did focus his attention on her, what did she do? She pushed him away. Stating they could only be friends. So really this was her own fault, wasn't it? All three were close, she could see that, and she felt very much an outsider, as if she was intruding on something she was not allowed to be a part of.

Suddenly resentful, she looked down at her half eaten meal. She felt sick inside and so confused. She didn't understand any of what she'd overheard today; did Daniel love her? Or did he love Rachel? And what had happened between David and Amy? Daniel and Karen, even? And what were David's feelings about *her*? Then as if David could hear her thoughts, he looked over at her and met her gaze. He smiled at her and she looked away.

Abruptly, she rose from the table. "I'm just going to make myself a drink," she said and made her way to the kitchen. She scraped the contents of her plate in the bin.

She wanted to cry and she didn't know why. She hated what she was feeling; this jealousy she had for Rachel. Rachel was a like a sister to her, and she shouldn't be feeling this way. It was wrong, but she couldn't help it.

"Sara..."

Startled at the sound of David's voice, she nearly dropped the plate in her hands. She placed it on the counter and turned to look at him. He was just as beautiful as his brother. Both in jeans and a white shirt, which was confusing. They were identical, so how did she know this was David? She didn't even know. Daniel had shaved his beard recently, so there was nothing to distinguish between them. Even their voices sounded the same.

But there was something about Daniel; it was the way he looked at her. There was a desire for her behind his eyes—an awareness, and his presence was also different. If Daniel was standing before her, by now he would have found a way to be near her or touch her in some way.

"Are you okay?"

"Yes, I'm fine." She looked away from his intense green eyes.

"He loves you, Sara."

"Does he?"

"Yes, he does."

"Or does he love Rachel?" She watched him, he hesitated at her question, she wanted to provoke a response, she needed to get to the bottom of this as Daniel had not been forthcoming with the truth.

"In a way, yes. I think he does, but not in the way you think."

Sara was alarmed by this and David could see the reaction on her face.

"Let's go for a walk," he held out his hand. She hesitated thinking maybe she shouldn't, as to hold his hand was an intimate gesture, but she thought better of it and slipped her hand into his.

Amazingly, she didn't feel the same way she felt when she touched Daniel, or when he touched her. She didn't know what she expected to feel. She'd been attracted to David from the very first day she met him, but it was a subtle awareness of him. It was no way as intense as she felt when she was with Daniel. When they touched, she felt the rush of electricity.

Hand in hand, they walked through the landscaped gardens, which were very beautiful. There was a chill in the air, but it was sunny and bright, allowing the presence of wild flowers to remain, blossoming red, yellow and purple with splashes of white. The lawn was cut low and very neat and divided into sections; flowers were neatly placed, with evergreen plants of differing shades of green and with colourful shrubs and bushes.

David watched her. Feeling self-conscious, she looked away. He released her hand, but came and stood before her.

"Sara."

She looked up at him.

"He's in love with you."

"So why doesn't it feel that way?"

He thought about that for a moment. "Because of what *you* think he feels for Rachel?"

"Yes."

"Has Daniel told you about Amy?"

"Yes, but he didn't go into great detail about her."

"She broke his heart, and it was when he was going through a difficult time with my father, and I also wanted my own individuality."

"What do you mean?"

"Hasn't Daniel told you about us?"

"He tried to, but I didn't understand." She chose not to reveal that she'd overheard their conversation back at the house. She wanted to hear what he had to say first.

"My brother and I shared everything. We had the same friends, went to the same schools—university. We sometimes shared our girlfriends."

Sara raised a brow. "You shared your girlfriends?" She gave a nervous laugh.

"Yes." He gave a wry smile. "Daniel can feel what I feel for Rachel, and because of this, things can become confusing. Part of the love he feels for Rachel, is what he picks up on through me. In the same respect, when he was seeing Amy, I picked up on what he felt for her. I nearly fell in love with her, too, but I learned how to block my feelings. Daniel is unable to block what he feels." He paused for a moment.

Okay that made sense. Even she could feel the love between Rachel and David when they were together; the atmosphere changed. But she couldn't get past the fact that they shared girlfriends. She touched his arm to stop him from continuing. "You and Daniel shared girlfriends?"

David gave a wry smile. "Yes."

She raised a questioning brow. "Explain."

"We are always attracted to the same women, and in the past, some women didn't mind the fact that we were twins."

Sara couldn't even begin to think how they worked that one out and she didn't want to know. "And you and Daniel were attracted to Rachel, am I right?"

"Yes."

Sara felt uneasy, again confirmation that Daniel was in love with Rachel. Which was why David didn't want Daniel left alone with Rachel. So then why was David trying to protect Daniel? It didn't make sense.

"Don't get the wrong idea, Sara. I know what he feels for you."

"Do you?" she responded sceptically.

"Yes, Sara, I do."

"So are you saying that you can feel what he feels about me, in the same way you nearly fell in love with Amy?"

"Yes, Sara, that's why I know that he loves you." He gave her a knowing look. "But I can block what I feel, he can't."

Well that answers two questions; David can feel what Daniel feels and vice versa, but David can block it—so David doesn't have feelings for her. She was relieved about that. But what really warmed her heart was the confirmation that Daniel loves her—but how much? What about Daniel's feelings for Rachel? If Daniel can't block what he feels through David, then where does that leave her? Could David be mistaken about this? "Okay, go on. So Daniel is unable to block what he feels. You were saying..."

"When the truth about Amy was revealed, Daniel was devastated. He cried for days—totally broken. It was hard for me, because I felt what he felt. He went into a deep depression, and when he came out of it, he cut all his emotions. He no longer allowed himself to feel..."

Her heart tugged. Now she understood why Daniel was so guarded with her.

"...He never let another woman close, he became hard and cynical. He uses women, just as they use him. Although he would never take advantage of a woman and is only interested in women that fully understand that he cannot offer them a commitment—love of any kind, and as long as they understand that, he will show them a good time, but when they become clingy, as invariably they do, he cuts all ties with them."

He looked at her. "That's why he tries to keep his distance. He won't take advantage of you, he respects you. I'm not so sure he respects the women he sees."

"Why can't he block his feelings, just as you can?"

"Because God will not allow him to."

"I'm not getting this, David, what are you saying?"

"After what happened with Amy, Daniel became dead inside. He cut himself off emotionally, and he felt nothing. God left the channel open for him to feel through me. He can't stop what he feels through me and because of that, it has softened his heart and allowed him to fall in love with you."

Sara stared at him for a moment digesting what he'd just revealed. "How do you know he has fallen in love with me? He has never said."

"Because I can feel it, Sara. I can feel the love he has for you."

"If he loves me, why are *you* out here and he is not? Why is he with Rachel—yet again? I'm not sure I believe you, David."

"He wants to be. I told him I wanted to speak to you. He's agitated right now. He wants to come out. It's not Rachel he's thinking about right now..." he trailed off for a moment, then smiled. "He's coming..."

How did he know that? Clearly the spiritual connection between the brothers allowed them this knowledge, and she of all people should understand this as she picked up on things about people when she discerned with her spirit and God gave her spiritual insight. But she wasn't sure she believed what he told her, or maybe she just didn't want to believe it because it would mean that Daniel had feelings for Rachel which, even David didn't seem to understand himself, and Daniel hadn't been able to fathom either. But no sooner than David said the words, Daniel appeared by the house walking determinedly toward them.

"I think I'll take over from here, David." Daniel slipped a possessive arm around Sara's waist.

David smiled. "Sure. Go easy on him, Sara," he said, before walking back to the house.

She let Daniel pull her into his arms for a moment, then eased away from him. "So you have a twin thing...?"

"You could say that, yes. What did David tell you?"

"More than you told me." Then the question—the same question she'd asked him before, which she hadn't been able to get off her mind since—was out of her mouth before she even thought about it. "Are you in love with Rachel?"

Daniel looked away.

"Are you? You told me before you had feelings for her. I need you to be honest with me..."

Daniel remained silent, shoving his hands into his pockets defensively. "It's complicated."

At that, Sara spun on her heel and began making her way back to the house, but Daniel caught her arm and pulled her against him. "Don't."

She flattened her hands against his chest to push him away, but the feel of his hands on her waist and back, made her lose all thought. Her response to his touch was immediate, the familiar rush of feelings that sent her body into overdrive. Every time he came near she had to cope with a riot of feelings that she couldn't control.

He rested his forehead against hers and whispered, "Don't be angry with me, I'll try to explain..."

She shifted slightly so she could look at him. "I don't understand..." She felt tears threaten. The thought of Daniel loving Rachel was too much to bear.

Daniel reached up and caressed her cheek. Guilt hit him. He wanted to tell her how he felt, but *he* didn't even know how he felt, and he still wasn't sure he could trust her. But the look of vulnerability and hurt in her eyes tore at him.

His lips brushed hers and her lips parted expectantly, but he only lingered there and kissed her cheek, drawing her closer, one hand slipping into her hair. He felt the change in her straight away; she melted against him. He tucked into her neck, taking in her perfume.

"It's you, Sara... You're all I think about... you're all I dream about..." he whispered, he nuzzled into her hair; a hint of cherry shampoo teased his senses combined with her perfume.

He held her firmly at the waist and his other hand caressed her back. Sara felt weak; he hadn't even kissed her and she was turning into mush. What was wrong with her? Why did he have such an effect on her? And what did he mean by that? She couldn't even think straight to analyse what he was saying. *What is he saying...?*

He kissed the nape of her neck. "God, you smell so good..." his voice was barely a whisper.

Sara closed her eyes.

"From the very first moment I laid eyes on you, I wanted you...you have never left my mind. *You* are who I want...Sara..." His lips brushed her neck. "*Sara...*"

He said her name as though it were a caress, and she felt her legs begin to tremble. She held on, her arms sliding around his waist as she rested her head against his chest. This was all very overwhelming, she couldn't think when he held her, touched her and spoke to her like this, his words, his whispered tone all the more seducing than any kiss or touch. Daniel was so intense, he mesmerised her and if he asked for anything right now, she would give it to him, not caring about the consequences.

"Sweetheart..." Daniel closed his eyes and felt an overwhelming need to pray; it bubbled up in his spirit and came forth in tongues.

He prayed for a least a full minute, then he stopped as abruptly as he started. He opened eyes again, a little perplexed.

Sara lifted her head and looked at him and felt the interpretation of his prayer come forth within her. She touched a hand to his chest and spoke. "Daniel it is time to take hold of what I have shown you—what I have told you. The healing you require is right there where you are, it's time to trust again..."

As she spoke the word that God was speaking through her, the Holy Spirit was talking to her at the same time. *"Sara, I am with you, I will always be with you. Daniel loves you. You only need to feel it, trust it, do not doubt it. Give him the love he needs..."*

A vision appeared before them then. A bright light flashed in her eyes, it wasn't apparent what she was seeing at first, then it became clear as if a cloud lifted and she could see... *Daniel was sleeping in bed and he was dreaming. There was an angel in the room who suddenly appeared. He had a white glow around him of God's glory. He did not have wings but had a notebook in his hands. He pointed to Daniel and she could somehow see what he was dreaming...*

Daniel held out his hand toward Sara; she took his hand, their fingers interlaced and an angel wrapped what looked like twine around their wrists, binding them together. Daniel awoke from his dream a little confused.

Revelation of the dream dropped in Sara's spirit, her gaze returning to the angel. He smiled at her, closed his notebook and disappeared, and the vision ended.

Sara looked at Daniel.

Daniel looked at Sara.

Then they laughed in delight at what had just happened.

"I saw an angel!" She shrieked in delight. "I've never seen an angel before, wow! That was amazing!"

"Yes, it was." He grinned. "I'm still astounded by the things God shows me, I've only ever shared that with Rachel."

"I've never shared anything with anyone, because I normally don't see anything. It must be you...." She looked at him in awe, and then looked to the heavens. "Oh Lord, thank you so very much!" Tears came to her eyes. "Oh Daniel, I've been praying for so long to see something—an angel. Rachel sees them all the time, I thought God had forgotten me..." Her tears spilled over.

Concerned, Daniel touched her arm. "Are you okay?"

She nodded, still overwhelmed. "They're happy tears."

Daniel took her hand and they walked toward the lake and took a seat on the bench overlooking it. The sun shone across the water, making it look like sparkling diamonds; it was beautiful.

Sara brushed at her tears and grinned, turning to him. "So what was that? A dream within a vision?"

"A dream I had this morning."

"Really?"

He nodded and held her gaze.

She looked away as realisation touched her at the message God had sent, and what it meant to them both. "When you had the dream, did you understand what it meant?"

"No, as you know, they often don't make any sense at all."

"God is showing you that we are spiritually tied, hence the twine."

He frowned. "It's that simple?"

"I wouldn't say it was simple. God sent an angel, a vision with the interpretation of a dream he sent this morning and an interpretation of tongues. I think he feels it's important."

"I guess. I wasn't trying to trivialise it, but what does it mean?"

"Maybe he is showing us that we now have a connection that we never had before."

He held her gaze. "So..."

"So...maybe we need to work at it."

Daniel was silent, contemplating her response.

"Why don't you share your dreams with me if you don't understand them?" Sara asked, watching him closely.

"Maybe because I won't like what God is telling me."

"Don't you want to know?"

"Maybe deep down I already know."

What am I supposed to say in response to that? "Maybe we need to define our relationship..."

"From *friendship,* you mean?"

She picked up the note of irritation and the emphasis he put on friendship. "That was all I could offer, Daniel."

"And now?"

"I still want the same things. I need a commitment, has that changed for you?"

He sighed. "I don't know. I don't know what I'm feeling right now."

They were silent for a moment, watching the ducks and geese at play on the lake.

Sara felt a subject change was needed, afraid of what his response would be. He still hadn't explained his feelings for Rachel, but the Holy Spirit said he loved *her*, so she had to trust that and be patient.

"What happened between you and David's ex-wife?"

Daniel eyed her, not wanting to delve into his unpleasant past. He'd hurt his brother and he regretted it. Besides, he didn't want Sara to think badly of him or get the wrong impression—although what other impression could she have?

It was bad. He couldn't fancy that one up. "Why? What has Rachel said?"

"She hasn't said anything." Sara decided to be truthful. "I overheard you and David earlier."

Great. Daniel tried to assess what she might have overheard, realising he had no choice but to be honest with her.

"One night, I stopped by to see David. He hadn't arrived home as yet, but Karen was home. She kissed me, and made it clear she wanted things to progress between us."

Sara gave him a disapproving look.

He held up his hands defensively. "Listen, I was the innocent party in this. I made an attempt to try and stop what happened, but she wouldn't stop."

"So she knew it was you?"

"Yes, she knew. She told me she wanted both of us. *She* kissed *me.* The only thing I did wrong was to not to be a little more forceful when I tried to push her away and David came home, got the wrong idea and he was understandably angry." He paused thinking back. "Karen told David I pretended to be him. She begged me not to tell him the truth, knowing their marriage would be over. She made me out to be the ogre. David refused to talk to me for months over it."

No wonder there were issues between them.

"Why have you never told him the truth?"

"What good would it do to make him feel worse about his wife, who was supposed to hold their marriage sacred, who was lusting after me the whole time. I couldn't do that to my brother. It would serve no purpose other than to hurt him and their kids."

She nodded in agreement. "But maybe the truth would have eased the tension between you."

Daniel shrugged. "It wasn't the first time she'd done this. She was very suggestive. But I kept my distance. Maybe I should have told David about his wayward wife, but the problem was, it happened before David married her. We kissed then, and David had been so angry. At the time if I'd told him, he wouldn't have welcomed any truths about Karen and I'm not sure he would have believed me. I didn't want to cause any problems, we already had a rivalry between us and this would have been something else. So I kept my distance. That day she kissed me, I tried to push her off me, but she kept on. And that was what David saw. Maybe I could have tried harder to push her off me. Maybe I should have done what you did to me and pushed her to the floor." He raised a brow, amusement flickering in his eyes.

Sara smiled in response, she couldn't help herself, "She sounds like a nightmare, poor David..." She trailed off. She still wasn't sure about his feelings regarding Rachel and she needed to be clear. She swiftly moved the topic back to Rachel. "So, you could easily find yourself in the same situation with Rachel?"

He shook his head. "No."

"What do you mean, no? That's what David believes."

"Because he believes what Karen told him, which is not the truth, and because of our rivalry." He took her hand in his. "I'm not in love with Rachel. I love her as a sister. I feel close to her because of our spirituality. She sees what I see and I gravitate toward her. I still find it all so astounding and it's good to talk to someone about it. And when Rachel and David are together I can pick up on what he feels for her, but they are David's feelings, not mine. I can't deny I was attracted to Rachel at the beginning, but when I met you, you blew me away. The feelings I have for you far surpasses anything I feel for Rachel. But what I do feel for you, I don't even fully understand yet, and I can't make any promises, Sara."

Her heart leapt. At least he was acknowledging he felt something for her. "So where does that leave me? You told me you don't want me to see anyone else, and I can't wait forever."

"I'm asking for a little time. I don't want to make promises to you I can't keep. I've been a bachelor my whole adult life, I know nothing else. I don't even have women over to my home, Sara. This would be a huge adjustment for me."

Well that isn't the truth, I've seen you with a woman. "I've been to your home."

"You're different."

"And I've seen you leaving your home with a blonde." She raised a querying brow.

"Blonde..."

"Last week."

Realisation dawned as he remembered. "Oh, that was Bella— she works on my graphics team. You saw us? What were you doing there?"

"So you *do* have women over?"

"No, Sara, she was dropping off some paperwork that I needed urgently. She didn't even come in."

"Oh, I thought..."

"Yes, I know what you thought."

A little ashamed, she changed the subject. "Why am I different?"

"There's no hidden agenda with you. You told me from the beginning what you wanted from me and I'm not going to suddenly find you undressed in my bed or have your clothes magically appear in my wardrobe without my permission."

Sara grinned. "I would love to meet some of these women you've seen. They sound horrendous."

Daniel smiled. "Indeed, always trying some way to get their claws into me. So, you came to see me?"

She nodded. "I missed you, so I cooked dinner, and I bought you some."

His heart warmed. He loved the way she was so open with him. She freely expressed what she felt without expecting anything back from him. "I would have loved that. Why didn't you call me?"

She shrugged.

"Because you thought that Bella had just left my bed..." He gave her a disapproving look. "Bella is happily married with two young kids, so no, not a possibility."

Sara smiled, relieved.

"So, are we going to try at this thing?" Daniel asked.

"Okay, let's try."

Later, just before Daniel drifted to sleep, thinking about their conversation, knowing that God would send him yet another dream about Sara, he hoped she would be patient. He needed to be sure he could trust her. Trust didn't come easy to him.

Still, he would park his feelings for now, as tomorrow would be another day.

Chapter 7

"*I can't live without your love...Jesus, oh I can't live without your love...my Lord...*" Sara sang, rejoicing to her creator, lost in worship. Tears came to her eyes as she thought about Him.

She looked down at the music sheets she held in her hands. She had eight songs to learn and, having been so busy with work, she hadn't had the time to rehearse. She was singing in the choir on Sunday and needed to get it right. But this particular song was special to her. She'd written it herself. The words came to her one night, flowing out of her spirit like a prayer, and she wanted to sing it in church for the first time. It had been on her heart for so long. She wanted to develop it and maybe do the one thing that she'd always wanted to do, but didn't have the courage to do—which was to record it in a studio and release it as a single.

She worshipped best when seated at her white baby grand piano. She missed it, missed the feel and sound of her fingers flowing across the polished keyboard. She sighed with regret. During her divorce, the piano was one of her assets she was unable to bring with her, as it was too large for her home.

She eyed the small keyboard she was forced to use in the corner of the room. She hated it. It wasn't the same, but she had no choice.

She sat down and played, enjoying the music, allowing the notes and the sound to touch her spirit, and then she sang—the words flowed through her and around her.

Arianna came over and stood beside her. "Come and sing with me, baby." She held out an arm for Arianna to join her on the bench. She and Arianna had been singing since Arianna was old enough to make sounds with her mouth. Arianna was gifted to sing and had the most beautiful voice, more so than Sara had at that age.

When Arianna was three years old, Sara realised that God had given Arianna a powerful gift. Arianna would sing and God's presence would enter in, so powerful and so profound it would reduce Sara to tears. She'd known then that it would be Arianna's ministry, her calling—just as Sara had discovered late in life that it was also hers.

"Can I sing with you on Sunday, Mummy?"

Arianna had on two occasions sang with her at church and God's presence had been so strong, the whole congregation had been touched and remarked on the anointing on her voice. "Yes, of course. But you'll have to learn this song. Do you think you can?"

"Yes, Mummy, I like this song." Arianna paused and began to sing. *"I can't live without your love...Jesus, oh I can't live without your love...my Lord..."*

Sara smiled as she felt the change in the atmosphere as Arianna sang. She closed her eyes and listened to the perfect, soulful sounds that came from her daughter. God's presence filled the room.

Sara began to pray in tongues for a moment, taking in his presence and allowing it to wash over her. Tears came to her eyes, and her spirit filled with joy and a sudden peace. Then she sang with her daughter and the atmosphere changed again. She felt the spirit flow through her and God's voice was so loud and clear as it entered in.

"It is time now, Daniel. It is time to take hold of the life I had always planned for you. You will no longer dictate your will, my will must come first in your life. I have shown you in dreams and visions, you cannot run from it. Your life with me is preordained. It is time."

Stunned into silence for a moment, Sara's fingers stilled on the keyboard, digesting what the Holy Spirit had said. She hadn't asked about Daniel, although she'd prayed for him. She wondered what this would mean for their relationship. Daniel never really left her thoughts, so she guessed God would speak directly to her about him.

"Pray for Daniel, Sara."

Yes, Lord I will.

She hadn't seen Daniel in a while. At first, when he'd been away on business, he called sporadically in between meetings or about to board a plane. But she was afraid now she'd scared him off, and figured eventually she wouldn't hear from him again.

New Year's came and went without seeing him. He rang, though, a few minutes before midnight, to wish the new year in.

When the clock struck twelve, loud bangs could be heard as fireworks went off outside from her neighbour's home, and London's landscape could be seen on the TV of flashing lights of colour as fireworks were set off there.

"Happy New Year, Sara."

"Happy New Year, Daniel."

"Where's Arianna? I want to wish the new year in with her, too."

She smiled. "She's in bed. She tried to stay up, but only made it to ten o'clock."

"I'll give her a call later on. I wish I was there with you, but I had to attend this event. It will put my client in the public arena. I couldn't get out of it."

"I know. I miss you, Daniel."

"I miss you, too."

They were silent for a moment, neither wanting to say what they really felt. It was left unspoken, but they knew.

"Any New Year's resolutions?" Sara asked.

"Yes, this year I plan to delegate to my staff more. I really don't want to be here. I have a good team of people. They need to do more of the hands-on work. I need to take a backseat from now on. I guess I'm fed up with the constant travel and living out of suitcases, and my mother wants me to get involved in the family business."

He never said, but she wondered if his change in approach had anything to do with her. She smiled, hope filling her. She hated it when he travelled.

"What about you?"

"I plan to be married this year."

Daniel was silent for a moment before he responded. "To who? To anyone that just happens along?"

He sounded annoyed. And before she even thought about it, the words were out of her mouth; "No, Daniel, I was hoping to be married to you."

The silence at the end of the phone was deafening. But she couldn't take the words back. She waited a few moments more, until she heard him sigh.

"Sara...is that a marriage proposal?" he asked, trying to make light of the moment. "Well, it wasn't a very good one."

She didn't know what possessed her to ask him, and over the phone when he was a million miles away. But she did and held her breath, then asked again; "Will you marry me, Daniel?"

Another long pause. "Sara...I don't ever want to get married. It was never a part of my plans. I've always been honest with you in that regard."

Her heart hit the floor. She knew it was a gamble, but she couldn't pretend anymore. "So where does that leave us?"

He sighed again. Then she could hear someone was speaking to him in the background and he had to go, disconnecting the call. They hadn't spoken since and neither had he been back. She'd scared him off.

At the weekends, he still included Arianna in his family visits; he did not renege on his promise in the role of surrogate uncle and she was grateful for that. But he'd been avoiding her—she hadn't seen him at all, and she didn't know what to do about it. She couldn't stop thinking about him, so she guessed it wasn't surprising that the Holy Spirit would give her a word of knowledge for him. She wasn't so sure how he would take it, though, since he'd given his heart to God, he hadn't really talked to her about it.

She missed him and she longed to be with him, but he'd made it clear he didn't want to be with her, and it hurt. She loved him so much. She couldn't help the doubts that plagued her mind that what she'd heard from the Holy Spirit might not happen. He had told her Daniel would be her husband. Rachel had also told her, but she was afraid—and where there was fear, there could be no faith. It was something she was conscious of, her confidence in herself and what she assumed Daniel felt about her had been knocked. She needed to pray to build her faith, but the doubts just would not go away.

She knew he had an issue with trust—Amy had hurt him, more than he'd let on. David had touched on it, saying Daniel had gone into a deep depression. Clearly, his scars ran deep. She reasoned that her womanly attributes were not enough for him to reconsider his stance. She was no fool; she was well aware of her appearance and her physical features that men regarded as exotic. In the past, she'd become bored with men tripping over themselves to be with her. Try as she might to downplay her looks, it was always what drew men first.

Professionally, she refused to allow men to make this their focus, partially because she'd been married, but also because she wanted to be taken seriously. She had a brain and hated to be treated the way Adam had always treated her—as his plaything, a beautiful trophy wife who was not allowed to think for herself—a Barbie doll that should be seen and not heard.

Part of the reason she'd fallen in love with Daniel was because he didn't just see her looks—he wasn't so infatuated with her as some men she'd dated. They'd behaved like fools, just wanting to be with her. Daniel saw her intelligence and drew on that and often challenged her thinking. Maybe because he was used to beautiful women, she was amongst a long list of beautiful women he could easily choose from. She was in no way unique in that regard, and she liked that. Although she knew, and he'd made her very much aware, that he found her to be beautiful and told her this often, but it wasn't all that attracted him. In the same respect, that wasn't all that attracted her to him.

So, it begged the question—did he love her? As she suspected and had seen in his eyes—the Holy Spirit had also confirmed it to her. But did he love her enough to want to spend the rest of his life with her? That was the ultimate question that hung in the balance.

Unfortunately for her, Daniel didn't want to.

She suppressed the stab of pain in her chest. It was ironic. Adam wanted her, but didn't love her, and Daniel loved her, but didn't want her. She felt as if someone was playing a trick on her.

After praying on it, she decided to accept her fate, take a step back, and leave it to God. He would make a way for her—he always did, without fail.

When Daniel called after so long and announced that he was coming for dinner, she'd been surprised. When he arrived looking gorgeous as ever in jeans and a black T-shirt, she sighed wistfully as her eyes raked over him with appreciation. His T-shirt accentuated his muscular upper body, making her want to do nothing else but step into his arms.

His eyes seemed to mirror hers, as he gazed at her with the same longing and need.

"How have you been?"

Missing you.

"I've been okay, it's been busy at work. Since Rachel and I joined your company. It's been crazy. We're fighting fire at the moment. Soon we may need to recruit more staff."

Daniel watched her, trying his hardest to keep his emotions and his body under control at the sight of her. She was stunning today in a cream short-sleeved cropped top and a matching skirt, her hair in waves around her shoulders and back. He wanted to pull her into his arms and kiss her. *Why did I stay away?*

"Yes, you both warned me that things would take off like this once Rachel's proposals were in place. It's been manic at my end too."

Rachel had put together a marketing strategy that had virtually propelled the business into the international heights. He was struggling to keep on top of it and needed to put some plans into place to mitigate the impact.

He told himself that was the reason he'd stayed away, but truthfully, he hadn't known how to respond to Sara's proposal. Ever since their New Year's Eve conversation, God had sent him dream after dream of their marriage and he realised that he couldn't run from it anymore.

"I was expecting you to be coming from work—Friday night and all that. Are you taking a break?" Sara wasn't used to seeing him in casual clothes. She also wasn't used to him being so distant with her. By now, in normal circumstances he would have pulled her into his arms and kissed her. It felt awkward that he didn't do it. They both stood in the hallway making pleasantries while she ached to be in his arms.

"I'm working tomorrow, then flying out to New York in the evening, so I won't see Arianna this weekend."

"So you didn't come to see *me* then?" she teased. She knew she shouldn't entertain this type of conversation, especially after his knock back, and he probably thought she was just like all the other women he encountered who were too clingy and tried to get their hooks into him. But she couldn't help herself.

Daniel looked at her intently. "Of course I've come to see you, too." He'd missed her, ached for her. An ache that kept him awake most nights.

Sara's heart skipped a beat at his words and the way he looked at her. But he was teasing; there was amusement in his eyes. She wanted to be honest with him about her feelings.

But how can I when he was so guarded and cannot trust?

They headed into the living room and as soon as Arianna saw Daniel, she hopped off the bench and ran into his arms.

"Uncle Daniel!"

Daniel scooped her up and playfully staggered backward. "Arianna, you're getting heavy." He made a face and she giggled.

Sara smiled at the scene. He was so good with her—he was everything Arianna needed in a father. Then her heart filled with regret at the impossible situation. She said a silent prayer.

Daniel pulled out a small box.

Arianna beamed, her face lighting up with excitement. He always brought her a gift of some sort when he travelled. Even when he saw her at his mother's, he would pull her aside, away from the others, and give her a present. He would say it was just between them and her mum. Daniel was always careful to let Sara know what he'd given Arianna.

"What is it?"

His eyes widened expressively. "Well, open it and find out."

She opened it and there was a beautiful necklace with a dolphin pendant.

"I love it, Uncle Daniel!" She hugged him tightly and gave him loud kisses on his cheek. "Look, Mummy!" Daniel released her, and she bounded over to Sara to show her.

Sara smiled. "Oh wow, it's beautiful, Arianna—let me put it on for you."

She met Daniel's gaze as she clasped the necklace around Arianna's neck, and mouthed a thank-you.

Daniel smiled and nodded his acknowledgement. He looked up then and noticed for the first time that there were angels in the room, or maybe they had just appeared, he wasn't sure. He'd felt God's presence as he entered, but he hadn't noticed the angels before. There were two of them and they had what looked like a type of instrument in their hands.

"Uncle Daniel, will you listen to this song? I'm singing with Mummy at church on Sunday. I have to learn this song," Arianna announced proudly as if it was of great responsibility, and in a way, it was.

He'd heard them sing at the barbecue. They had touched everyone there. His mother's life had been changed by it. When Sara and Arianna sang, a vision had appeared—an open heaven—of his father, and he had a message for them all. His mother no longer held the burden of worry inside, knowing that he'd made it to heaven. He later discovered that David had seen his father, too, and he had given David a different message, telling him he had done well, that he was pleased.

Because of Sara and Arianna, Daniel had finally accepted his father was proud of him and had let it all go—the unforgiveness and resentment. He regretted the years he'd wasted and he no longer wanted to waste time and needless energy on internal issues he could not change. He gave everything to God. He'd finally turned a page in his life.

"You sing in the choir at church?" he asked Sara, surprised. She'd never mentioned it.

"Yes, not all the time, only when they have a particular event or a guest speaker."

There was still so much he didn't even know about her. He'd briefly met her mother and sister on Christmas Day. Both very beautiful women, he'd seen Samyra at David's wedding and noted the resemblance between the sisters. Sara had told him that Samyra used to be a model; he could believe that, as both Sara and Samyra were stunning. He wondered if Sara had ever considered modelling.

When he'd asked, he'd received a very forceful *no thanks,* followed by rolled eyes. *"You think because of my looks my only option should be to model? I did go to school you know—I do have a brain..."*

He knew better than to bring up *that* topic again. She'd made it clear from the beginning that she did not like the emphasis put on her looks. Even though he respected her wishes, he couldn't deny that her beauty captivated him, as it did all men she encountered, which he admitted was part of the reason he was so possessive of her.

She'd told him her father had died when she was young and didn't remember much about him. She also had a brother that she didn't see much of—the man he'd mistakenly thought she was seeing. They hadn't discussed meeting him yet.

They talked a lot about life—about everything. But her spirituality she'd only touched on, and he'd not allowed her to be totally open about it the few times she'd broached the subject. But *he* hadn't been open with her. Now it was important that he knew; he wanted to know everything.

"Okay, go ahead, I would love to hear your song."

Daniel sat on the sofa opposite them, fascinated. He understood now why there was an angelic presence in the room.

He watched as they sat at a keyboard that he'd never noticed before. Sara began to play. She sang first, taking the lead, and it was the most beautiful sound. The two angels began to play their instruments, producing a sound he'd never heard before that could only be described as holy.

He took in a breath as God's presence hit him—it filled the room. And when Arianna joined in and sang with her mother, his eyes filled with tears. It was amazing—*they were amazing*. It ripped at him; there was no defence against this, it touched him, touched his spirit. The beautiful sounds that came from both mother and daughter were so powerful and astounding.

Part of him wanted to run, to put some distance between them, to hide. But hide where? This was where he wanted to be, where he *needed* to be. And as they continued to sing, another two angels appeared, making the atmosphere in the room stronger, more tangible.

And then it stopped. All too soon.

"It is time, Daniel," Holy Spirit said.

But I'm not ready.

"It is time."

Can I trust her?

"Yes, Daniel. You need to ask her."

Arianna turned to face him. "Was I good?"

She waited expectantly for a response, so unaware of the anointing on her life. Any response he could give would be inadequate. "It was wonderful, Arianna. You have a special gift." He looked up at Sara. "And so does your mother."

Sara smiled in response.

"Come here, Arianna." She walked over to him and he enveloped her in a bear hug. "You did good and you'll do really well on Sunday. Everyone will love you, just like I do."

She nodded and looked into his eyes, then touched his face at seeing his tears. "What's wrong, Uncle Daniel?"

"I just loved your singing so much that it filled my heart with joy, and made tears come to my eyes."

"Are they happy tears?"

"Yes, they are."

She wrapped her arms around his neck, hugging him tightly. "Jesus loves you and he said it's time."

Daniel blinked. Not sure he'd heard her correctly. In his dream only that morning, Sara had told him the exact same thing.

He looked over at Sara, questioning what he'd just heard from Arianna.

"Sometimes God speaks through her," Sara confirmed. "He also gave me a word for you." She told him what God had told her. "I think he's trying to tell you something."

"Yes, I guess he is."

Sara studied him. He seemed to be contemplating something, but he said nothing further in response so she didn't push.

"Let's go and get dinner ready," she told him heading for the kitchen.

"I know that song now, Mummy, can I go and watch TV?"

"Yes, hon, you can."

She looked back at Daniel and smiled. He had tears in his eyes. She wanted to step into his arms and hold him, but she held back, afraid he might reject her.

Although the way he'd been looking at her since he arrived, she doubted he would.

He followed and took a seat at the table. "I didn't know you could sing like that—your voice is captivating," he said in a wistful way. "I've dreamt this...I've dreamt you...singing. I didn't understand it before. I've heard you..." Daniel trailed off, frowning as he remembered something.

"What have you dreamt?"

"You. It's always you..."

Sara didn't know what to say to that, the way he said it, he was clearly confused by it. She held his gaze, wondering when he would finally make a commitment to her. She sighed inwardly and began preparation of their meal.

Daniel watched as she moved around the kitchen, sometimes bending down to get pots and pans from the cupboard or reaching up for dishes as she prepared their meal. This right here was the reason he stayed away. He couldn't keep his eyes off her. He wanted her badly and it was becoming unbearable.

Sara turned to look at him. She could feel him staring at her; she felt a shiver go through her, suddenly acutely aware of him.

"You okay?"

No. Daniel held her gaze. "Yes. You look nice today." She smiled, that beautiful smile that lit up her whole face and he loved the look in her honey brown eyes.

"Don't I normally look nice?" she teased.

"Yes, you do, and that's the problem..."

Sara didn't ask for him to clarify what he meant. She knew exactly where he was coming from; she felt exactly the same way about him. She felt the yearning—the need.

After dinner, Daniel helped her pack the dishwasher and as was his way, he would come close; setting off butterflies in her stomach. Occasionally their fingers would brush as he passed her plates and cutlery, and she wondered if it would always be this way between them—the electricity, the heat that came whenever they were together.

She set the dishwasher to start and turned, almost colliding into him as he was standing so close. She met his intense gaze, his green eyes darkening as they rested on her lips. She didn't want to pretend anymore; she didn't know how to. She'd missed him so much. She touched his face and allowed him to kiss her, so thankful when he pulled her close, wrapping his arms around her. She closed her eyes and wound her arms around his neck and gave in to the waves of passion that flowed through her.

She loved him so.

She slid her fingers into his hair, loving the feel of him, the intimacy. The kiss was slow and lingering and sent shudders within.

Daniel eased away, gazing at her, too overwhelmed by the emotions he felt to speak for a moment. He just wanted to hold her. He'd been a fool to stay away.

Sara opened her eyes and held his gaze. Her heart pounding, she said simply, "I missed you."

"I missed you, too. You know how I feel about you, Sara."

"Do I? That's just it—I don't know how you feel, Daniel. You know how I feel about you, God confirmed that to you. Do you feel the same?" She sighed deeply. "I know you want me physically, but is that all you want?"

Daniel didn't say anything for a moment, not sure what he wanted to reveal. He wasn't sure he knew what he felt himself. He loved her—that much he'd finally came to terms with—but it was everything else that came with that acceptance that gave him pause for thought. If he told her, he would be at a disadvantage, and he couldn't have that.

He would never allow himself to be vulnerable to a woman again, no matter how he felt about her.

"I've missed our friendship, Daniel. Was it only ever about sex for you?" Sara asked quietly, tentatively, afraid of his avoidance, afraid that nothing could ever happen between them. And when he didn't respond and glanced away, she continued.

"Were you only happy to spend time with me as friends as long as there was the hope of sex at the end of it, and now because you know that cannot be a possibility, you're not interested in seeing me anymore?" She hadn't realised how much Daniel distancing himself from her had affected her and she couldn't stop the flow of words. She needed to get it out in the open, as she hadn't really spoken to him in months. They had gone from being so close to nothing.

"No, that's not the reason I've stayed away."

"Then why, Daniel? You said I kept pushing you away, so I accepted that and agreed to try with you, but you've distanced yourself even further. Is it because I asked you to marry me?"

"Partly."

"I'm sorry..." She looked down, embarrassed and disappointed.

He reached up and tilted her chin so she would meet his gaze again. "Don't be."

"I don't understand, Daniel."

"Don't you think I want to be here with you?" He caressed her cheek. "Sara, you're all I think about, you're all I dream about, but when I'm alone with you, all I want to do is make love to you and I'm not equipped to know how to turn off what I feel. I'm really trying to do what's right and respect the situation, but sometimes I just can't be here."

Sara was stunned into silence for a moment. He'd touched on this before, but he still didn't call. But he hadn't been totally honest with her. She knew, for him, it all boiled down to trust. He was afraid she would hurt him like Amy hurt him, and she didn't know how to reassure him anymore than she already had.

"So what do we do?"

Daniel pulled her close; his lips touched hers briefly, but he was careful not to prolong the kiss. He kissed her cheek, then buried his face in her hair.

"Ask her, Daniel," Holy Spirit insisted.

Why was this so hard? He wanted to; he wanted her to be his wife—didn't he? He hated being away from her. She was everything to him and he wanted a life with her. But his doubts held him back, afraid she would hurt him the way Amy did.

He sighed, he wanted to be honest with her finally, maybe he could consider marriage. Maybe it wouldn't be so bad. As the Holy Spirit said, it was time.

"Sara, I—"

The doorbell rang.

Sara looked up, puzzled; she wasn't expecting anyone. "Let me go and see who that is," she said, lingering for a moment and touched his face before heading for the hallway.

She opened the door and standing on her doorstep was her ex-husband. *Oh no! Why today? This is not going to be good...*

"Hello, Sara," Adam said. When she said nothing in response, he continued, "I came to see Arianna and give her a gift."

Tension filled her. "You're supposed to call before you come here. You can't just turn up."

"I pay the mortgage on this house, so I can turn up here to see my daughter whenever I please."

Irritated, Sara squared her shoulders. He'd totally missed Christmas—not so much as a card for Arianna—and turns up now, unannounced, demanding as always.

"I am not saying you can't see your daughter. I'm saying you can't just turn up without letting me know. I have a friend here, you'll have to come back another time."

His eyes narrowed. She could see he was becoming annoyed that she'd challenged him.

"Well, that's not convenient for me. I'm flying out again tomorrow, so let me in, and stop being difficult."

Annoyed herself, Sara gave an exasperated sigh and allowed him room to enter. His aftershave wafted under her nose, bringing back memories of their past together—*his control.*

She felt apprehension rise within her. *This is all I need.* Adam was not going to be happy at Daniel being here, and she she was afraid of what the repercussions were going to be. She followed behind him and watched the scene unfold.

The two men eyed each other, weighing each other up. She sensed the difference in Adam straight away. He was tense—the square set of his shoulders, his stance one of quiet anger.

"Daniel, this is Adam, Arianna's father."

Both men nodded their acknowledgements. She chose not to introduce Daniel; as far as she was concerned, Daniel was none of Adam's business.

"Arianna, come and say hello. I've brought you something," Adam called to Arianna.

Arianna slid off the sofa, and stood before her father. "Hello, Daddy."

"How are you, Arianna?" Adam asked.

"I'm fine," Arianna replied.

Daniel watched, taking in the awkward scene. He'd wondered about the elusive ex-husband and was surprised. He was well dressed in an Armani suit, good-looking, younger than he'd thought he would be, and he was of a similar age to him. Adam wasn't what he'd expected, not that Sara had really said much about him. She'd made him sound like a sugar daddy; seeming older somehow. But there was a dark presence about him. Daniel could feel it as he entered.

Arianna was clearly uncomfortable with her father, and he was just as uncomfortable with her. He watched as Arianna took the gift from him, seeming not to be overly interested in what was inside, and only at her father's insistence did she open the package.

Daniel looked over at Sara. He tried to catch her gaze, but she kept her eyes on Arianna and Adam. Her arms were folded, and her body language displayed annoyance.

Arianna unwrapped a jewellery box. She appeared not to be particularly enamoured by the gift and gave her father a polite kiss on the cheek. She returned to the sofa, placing the box on the coffee table.

There was definitely something wrong here. Arianna never reacted that way to anyone, and as this was her father, Daniel was very much surprised.

"Sara, can I talk to you a moment?" Adam asked, making his way to the kitchen.

Sara followed. Of course he asked the question, but did she have a choice? No. It wasn't a negotiation as far as he was concerned. His tone held the underlying thread of control, but she could tell he was angry. And she hated to think what Daniel must be thinking.

She avoided Daniel's eyes as she walked by him. He had questions, she would have to answer those once Adam left.

"*Are you seeing him?*" Adam spat out angrily.

"Daniel is a friend."

"Are you seeing him?" he asked again, his eyes narrowing. "Is he the reason you don't want to get back with me?"

"It's none of your business who I see, Adam."

He loomed, menacingly close, to her. "It damn well is my business when I pay the mortgage on this house!"

She backed away from him, leaning against the counter. "No, I am not seeing him," she blurted. It wasn't exactly the truth, but she could hardly say she was seeing Daniel. She hadn't seen him at all over the last month.

"So what is he doing here, then?"

"I'm not going to keep repeating myself to you, Adam." She folded her arms defensively.

"I've been talking to your mother, and we both feel it's about time that you come back home."

Sara said nothing for a moment, becoming angrier by the minute. How dare he make plans for her life with her mother! And her mother had seriously overstepped the mark. It was time he left.

"You have no right to be discussing me with my mother!" she flung at him angrily. "*I want you to leave.*"

"I can give you everything you need, more than *he* ever could. I can look after you and Arianna. You don't have to live this way."

Typical Adam, making an assessment of Daniel's clothes and assuming he wasn't wealthy, when Daniel was probably just as wealthy—if not more so—than Adam. "You think that's all that is important? There's more to life than things."

"It used to be important to you. You're my wife, Sara."

"Well I grew up and it's not the life I want anymore. And I'm not your wife," she reminded him disdainfully. "We have been over this before, and I am not going to change my mind." Her eyes flashed angrily at him. "Adam, please leave."

"You are my wife." His eyes were dark, a possessive gleam filling them. "I want you back, and I want you back in my bed."

He grabbed her, pulling her against him, his arm holding her tight around the waist, making it impossible for her to move.

"Adam! Will you let me go!" She pushed against his chest, but he was too strong for her. He went to kiss her, but she turned away. "*Don't...let me go!*" She struggled in his arms, trying to get away from him, which he seemed to relish as he smiled mockingly at her.

* * *

Daniel felt uneasy, tension filling him. What were they talking about in there? He'd seen the possessive gleam in Adam's eyes as he looked at Sara and the way he demanded she speak to him. Sara didn't even bat an eyelid, she followed obediently like a dutiful wife.

What am I doing here?

He looked over at Arianna.

What am I doing playing the father role to a child that isn't mine?

He never did this. He never stuck around a woman who had baggage, he didn't do ex-husbands and the drama *that* involved. He did not want to be a part of some love triangle and Sara deciding she wanted to go back with her ex. He'd been down that road before, and he was the one that lost out.

Maybe he should leave. He'd virtually told her he didn't want to get married, so he was no longer a viable option for her, while all along, she was probably still in love with her ex. He felt sudden anger at the thought; jealousy hit him hard. He began to pace.

"Daniel, Sara needs your help." Holy Spirit's voice was insistent.

Daniel needed to know once and for all. Frustrated, he asked, *does she want to be with her ex-husband?*

"No, Sara's heart belongs to you, Daniel."

Daniel didn't waste any further time.

He headed for the kitchen.

Chapter 8

"Stop fighting this, Sara. I will look after you and Arianna."

"I will never go back to you!" she said tersely, eyeing him defiantly.

He shoved her hard against the counter, pressing himself against her. She winced as pain hit her spine. He grabbed her arms tightly, hurting her.

Fear filled her then, tears stinging her eyes. She needed to get away from him. *Lord, please help me*, she prayed silently.

"You belong to me," he whispered in her ear. "I'm going to enjoy every moment of taking *everything* that I should have as a husband, everything that you've denied me for so long." His fingers gripped her harder, biting into her flesh. "You will not deny me any longer."

Sara's heart pounded hard in her chest. *"Let go of me!"* His fingers tightened as she tried—to no avail—to get away from him. "You're hurting me!"

"Is everything okay in here?" Daniel asked as he appeared in the kitchen doorway.

Sara sagged with relief at the sight of Daniel.

"It's none of your business. This is between me and my wife," Adam responded defensively.

"Well, I'm making it my business and you need to leave."

Daniel stalked over to him, ready to do damage. Adam released Sara as he approached and backed off.

"All right, I'm leaving." Adam turned to Sara. "We're not finished with this," he warned and walked out.

Daniel followed, making sure he actually left. Thankfully, Arianna was still engrossed in the TV.

When he returned, he wasn't prepared for the anger that consumed him at the bruising he could see beginning to appear on Sara's arms.

"Sara...why didn't you call me?"

Overwhelmed, Sara couldn't speak. She tried to hold on to her resolve, but couldn't stop the tears that came to her eyes.

Daniel pulled her gently against him as she burst into tears. He held her close, feeling fiercely protective and wishing he'd stopped it sooner, instead of debating like a fool whether he should leave. He stroked her hair and offered words of comfort.

As he held her, Sara clung to him as if her life depended upon it.

In that moment, Daniel finally admitted what he'd been fighting for months—the love he felt for her and the need to be with her. And the sight of her ex-husband with his hands all over her, filled him with so much rage, he wanted to tear Adam apart.

"Does he have keys to this house?"

Sara nodded.

"I'm going to arrange for your locks to be changed, okay?"

She nodded, not wanting to move from the security of his arms.

"Who pays the mortgage?"

"He does. He could pay it off, but he won't. He uses it as a form of control."

"Can you take over the mortgage?"

She shook her head. "No, I couldn't afford it on my own."

"I'll buy it then, and have it put in your name."

She pulled away then and looked at him in shock. "I couldn't ask you to do that."

"You didn't ask. I offered."

She shook her head and took a seat, taking a tissue from the box on the table and wiped her tears away. "I would never be able to pay you back, Daniel. Thank you for offering. I really appreciate it, but I've got to try and somehow sort out this situation myself."

He sighed and sat next to her. "As long as he pays the mortgage on your home, he will use that as an excuse to turn up here whenever he feels like it, Sara. Is that what you want?"

"No." She looked away, not knowing what to do.

Daniel studied her, wanting to protect her. What he'd seen and the threat Adam had made, caused adrenaline to rush through his veins. He took in a deep breath, trying to calm his anger. "You need to consider going to the police, Sara."

Sara's eyes flew to his. She hadn't considered the implications of this.

"Sara..."

"I don't want to blow this out of proportion."

"Sara. He assaulted you. What would he have done if I wasn't here? Have you considered that?"

She frowned. She didn't want to consider it. He was scaring her.

"Report it to the police, Sara, please."

She didn't respond. It was all too much to take in.

Daniel was quiet for a moment and considered again if she still had feelings for her ex. Why else wouldn't she want to report it to the police? "Move in to my place for a while. I'm going away tomorrow. I don't want you here on your own."

Sara didn't know what to do—she needed to think.

Daniel studied her. *She doesn't trust me.* "Why won't you let me help you? I'm going away for a week so I won't be there. Only tonight."

She didn't want to be alone tonight. And Daniel was right, Adam could come back and he'd already threatened her, which she couldn't ignore. Fear gripped her. Daniel was trying to help her, she needed to accept his help and then think about her options.

"Okay. We'll stay with you."

*　　*　　*

Sara thought about staying with Rachel and David, but she didn't want to disturb them. They were newlyweds; she wouldn't want to impose upon them. And then there was her mother, the one person who she should have been able to go to, but was part of the problem. Her mother had been encouraging Adam, making him believe that they had a chance, so going to stay with her was not an option. Samyra would blow things into epic proportions; she'd already warned her and would tell her "*I told you so.*" She would also remind her of how foolish she'd been, and Sara didn't need that right now.

She hadn't spoken to her brother in a while, but she knew if she was ever to tell him what happened, he'd be so angry he would get on the next flight over here. Always protective of his younger sister, he'd turn up at Adam's door and cause a riot—and she didn't want any trouble.

She had other family and friends but she wasn't close enough to burden them with her problems. Besides, it was embarrassing.

After the locksmith left, she packed a suitcase for her and Arianna, and went with Daniel to his home. She'd been there a few times before, and felt it was missing something. A woman's touch—a family. It appeared far from lived in, and was very modern and immaculate. She doubted he spent his nights here. With the amount of travelling he did, and the willing females who would gladly share their beds with him, there really was no need for him to spend much time there.

Not wanting to alarm Arianna, they told her they were going on a holiday break to Uncle Daniel's house. She chattered excitedly all the way there. Sara was quiet and Daniel was worried. He was seriously considering cancelling his flight, he didn't want to leave her on her own.

After Arianna fell asleep in the king-sized bed in one of the first-floor guest bedrooms, Daniel made them both hot drinks, placing them on the huge glass kitchen table. He sat close to Sara, studying her.

"Are you hungry, do you want me to make you something?"

"No, I'm okay. Just tired, I guess. What time is your flight tomorrow?"

"Eight-thirty."

Sara avoided his eyes, not wanting to reveal how she felt. She didn't want him to go. "Is it PR work?"

"No, it's some potential investments I plan to make." He looked at her for a moment. "Are you still in love with him?"

"No, I've told you. I don't feel that way any longer."

"Then why are you protecting him?"

"I'm not. I—he's Arianna's father."

"*And?* What am I missing here?"

She didn't respond, looking away.

"He tried to force himself on you. What would you have done if I hadn't been there? He assaulted you, Sara." Daniel was still very angry and her nonchalance about the situation angered him even more.

"Please, Daniel, I don't want to talk about it anymore. I think I might go to bed." She rose stiffly from the chair.

"Are you okay?" He stood too, concern filling him. "He hurt you somewhere else, didn't he?"

"It's all right—it's nothing."

"Sara, let me see."

"It's okay, Daniel, really."

"Sara..." He placed a hand to the small of her back. "Let me see?" he asked again, his voice gentling.

Embarrassed, Sara turned, facing away from him.

He touched her first, sliding his hands under her top. His hands were warm and inviting, and sensations flooded through her at his touch. She held her breath for a moment as he lifted her top, exposing her lower back, and he cursed. He touched her gently, easing his hand to her lower back where she assumed it was badly bruised.

"What did he do to you? Sara, why didn't you call me?" he asked, annoyance filling his tone.

"He shoved me against the counter. Is it bad?"

"Give me your phone."

She handed it to him and he took a few photographs, then handed it back to her.

She stared at her phone, at what Adam had done to her; she was black and blue across her lower back. She felt tears sting her eyes.

"We're going to report this tomorrow and I'm coming with you."

Daniel waited for a response, but none came as he watched her, and he could see she was becoming upset again. He was angry and felt guilty for not stopping this sooner. He'd been right there, he could have stopped it. Thank God he decided to see her tonight. He'd overheard what her ex had told her and there was no way he would allow him to hurt Sara again.

"Where does he live?"

Sara didn't respond. She didn't want any trouble—she wanted it all to go away.

"If you won't go to the police, then I'll deal with him."

She turned in his arms and touched his chest. "Okay, I'll go with you to the police station tomorrow. I'll be all right, please don't go there." She touched his face, and to lighten the moment, she said. "I don't want you to damage this beautiful face."

"Sara, he had no right to hurt you that way."

"I know. I'm just so glad you're here... I need you to hold me."

He pulled her into his arms and held her for a long moment, one hand in her hair, neither wanting to move. Daniel closed his eyes, he could feel her warm breath against his skin, her arms around his neck, clinging to him.

Thoughts he shouldn't be having began to filter into his mind and he wondered how his brother had managed to remain celibate for over two years after his divorce.

Deciding he wasn't strong enough, he pulled away after what seemed like an eternity, conscious that his wants—*his needs*—were beginning to cloud his mind. He needed some distance; it felt too good holding her in his arms. He wanted to kiss her and that just wasn't what she needed right now. She was upset and vulnerable and he should remember that. "Let's go to bed, okay?"

Sara nodded and let him lead her by the hand upstairs to the guest room next door to Arianna's. She barely took notice of the décor all she wanted was to be in Daniel's arms, she didn't want to be alone.

"My bedroom is on the second floor if you need me, okay?"

Sara nodded, not wanting him to leave, and avoided his eyes. "Goodnight, Daniel," she said quietly, then busied herself with her suitcase that Daniel had brought up earlier.

"Goodnight, Sara," Daniel responded, walking away.

Sara slumped on the bed the moment he closed the door. What must Daniel be thinking? He did not do dramas and this was definitely a drama, one which she was ill-equipped to avoid. Even Samyra had warned her, and what had she done about it?

Nothing.

She hadn't even prayed. But she knew God would protect her—he sent Daniel this evening. If Daniel hadn't have been there, she was afraid of what the outcome would have been.

Daniel had been so sweet to her. He'd protected her, he'd gathered her into his arms and looked after her and brought her here to his home—the place he never brought women. That should count for something, shouldn't it?

The Holy Spirit had told her that Daniel loved her. She hoped so. She longed for it, and his actions showed her that he did, but he was fighting it. She guessed she had to give him the time he needed to come to the realisation himself.

Her mind drifted to Adam again. Why hadn't she seen this coming? It had been two years since they divorced. He knew she dated, didn't he? Why all the anger and aggression now? Okay, so she hadn't been forthcoming with information about her dates, because, deep down, she'd been afraid at his reaction. But she'd never expected anything like this.

Yes, he wanted her back, but she never took that seriously. She knew he only saw her as his possession. He never really loved her. And now she had to report him to the police. He was Arianna's father she wasn't sure it was the right thing to do.

"You belong to me...I'm going to enjoy every moment of taking everything that I should have as a husband, everything that you've denied me for so long."

His words played around and around in her mind, fear filling her. It was a threat she was afraid he might try to fulfil. She'd been terrified tonight—powerless. Adam had been too strong for her. She would never be able to stop him if he came back and tried again.

She used to love that man; now all she felt was disdain and a sickening feeling within as she replayed the scene over and over in her mind. He hurt her—it had been deliberate. Why would he want to hurt her that way? Did he hate her that much?

As she unpacked her suitcase she was barely aware as tears came to her eyes and spilled over. The pain was too great to bear.

*   *   *

Daniel wanted to stay. He felt protective of Sara and hated the look of vulnerability and fear in her eyes. It pulled at him. But how could he stay? It would cross boundaries he'd never traversed with a woman. Just having Sara here invading his space, his home, had already spanned several boundaries he'd set for himself. And this was one step too far. He never allowed a woman into his home, not even for coffee. He'd had a number of bad experiences with women and he wouldn't allow any woman the room to use situations such as allowing them in his home to their advantage. His home was his domain, his sanctuary, not for conniving females.

But Sara was far from conniving, she was open and giving—and honest, because of this he'd allowed Sara into his home a few times. They'd worked together. He told himself it was semantics, that his home was nearer to his offices, but in essence he was testing her and she never failed his tests. She never imposed upon him, allowing him room to be. She never demanded of him; even though she loved him, and she'd somehow put her life on hold when he'd asked her not to see other men.

He was discovering more and more, and with his newfound spirituality, there wasn't much that was hidden. His feelings, and hers, were transparent—exposed. She seemed to be waiting on him; she never said, but he got the distinct impression that she was waiting on him to accept their fate together and commit.

Their fate being marriage, which he never promised her.

After his shower, he pulled on pyjama bottoms and began to pace, his mind still whirling. He couldn't sleep—he was still angry at the way Sara's ex had hurt her—and he was worried. What if Adam tried it again and he wasn't there to intervene, what then? The thought of her ex assaulting her again—or worse—made his blood boil with rage.

Before he even thought about what he was doing, he made his way downstairs to her room—to check on her, he told himself. It was because she was upset, he had to be sure she didn't need anything.

Not because he just wanted to be with her, and needed to hold her.

When he stopped outside her door, the sounds of her sobs tore at him. He knocked tentatively, unsure she would want him there. "Sara, can I come in?"

"Yes."

Her response sounded muffled. He opened the door.

She was laying across the bed on her front and her head in the pillow. She sat up on the bed, dressed in cream silk pyjamas, her hair damp from her shower. She looked glamorous, even going to bed.

"Are you okay, Sara?" *Stupid question, she clearly wasn't.*

"I'm all right," Sara replied, brushing at her tears. "Things just got on top of me, that's all. I'll be fine...really." In nothing but pyjama bottoms, Daniel was gloriously made, rock-hard abs and muscle. She blinked, lost in the moment.

Daniel said nothing further and sat beside her on the bed, leaned back against the pillows and pulled her into his arms.

Sara rested her head on his shoulder and nuzzled into his neck, wrapping her arms around him gratefully. She closed her eyes when he pulled her closer. "Stay with me." she whispered.

Daniel caressed her back comfortingly and she relaxed against him. She was warm and responsive, and she smelled good too—citrusy. His body was on instant alert.

He closed his eyes against the onslaught of emotions that rushed through him and then she whispered the words that were unexpected and hit him to the core, "I love you, Daniel." Then she drifted off to sleep.

Chapter 9

She awoke to the sound of Daniel's breathing as he slept, which she found comforting, his warm, solid chest and body beside her. They had moved in the night and her body was tucked up close beside his. Her arm was around his waist, and his arm around her shoulders. He was a beautiful man. She'd only ever seen him dressed in suits, long-sleeved shirts and on rare occasions, T-shirts, where it was clear his body was hard, lean and muscular. His biceps were sculpted perfectly, but seeing him beside her, topless, was enough to set her heart aflutter. He was magnificent, like a Greek god, not a smidgen of fat on him.

She sighed wistfully, then her dream flashed through her mind...

There was a spider in her living room; it was black and ominous— lurking. She was afraid at first, but then she began to sing. She sought God's presence and the spider disappeared, gone in an instant.

She was still for a moment, running the dream through her mind, contemplating what it could mean. She knew spiders meant an attack was coming. Or was it a confirmation of what had just happened with Adam? Unsure and a little worried, she prayed for God's protection.

What does my dream mean, Lord?

Silence.

She thought about the dream further and realised that God was showing her that she was triumphant; that she'd used the anointing God had placed upon her life through the gift of her voice in worship to him. This was, in fact, a good dream.

Sara somehow managed to ease off the bed without waking Daniel, and headed for the shower. She still felt sore where Adam had shoved her against the counter and a little worried that something further would come and God was warning her. She said a prayer, asking God for guidance and wisdom, and began to sing. One thing she'd learnt in her walk with God was to rejoice always, through trials, pray continually and to give thanks in all circumstances. She sang adoringly to her Lord, worshipping him and giving thanks.

After her shower, she stood in front of the mirror a little more awake, but her mood had changed and she was concerned by the bruising developing on her arms and back. They were worse than yesterday, but she was grateful they could be kept hidden.

After moisturising and blow-drying her hair, she slipped on a skirt and vest top—conscious that the police would want to see evidence of what Adam had done to her. She finished the look with a long-sleeved cropped cardigan, which easily hid her black and blue bruises from the outside world, and fastened the top button.

She wasn't looking forward to this day; she felt low. She hummed a tune to lift her spirits, but it didn't help. She didn't want to go to the police station and re-live what happened with Adam, explaining to a bunch of strangers how she felt and have them look at her with pity.

She sat on the toilet seat, and put her head in her hands. *Oh, Lord, please help me make it through this day.*

She felt apprehensive and didn't want to do this on her own. Daniel would be leaving in a few hours and she didn't want him to go. She thought back to how good it had felt in his arms and waking up beside him. She wished they were married, that she could be with him every day. But in reality, it wouldn't be that way; he would always be travelling and she would be in the same situation she'd found herself with Adam. Alone in an empty home, awaiting his return.

She looked at the bathroom door and decided that sitting in here hiding from the world would not do, she had to face the music.

Daniel was awake when she returned, sitting up in bed and tapping on his mobile. She was again astounded by his beauty—a body that was enough to make any woman drool. It was no wonder women lost their minds around him and wanted to happily move in. She was just as bad, she'd already proposed to him. How cliché was that?—*and desperate*. She should be ashamed of herself, but she wasn't.

He looked at her, his eyes drifting slowly over her. "Why didn't you wake me?" He sounded annoyed.

"I didn't want to disturb you."

"You wouldn't have disturbed me, wake me next time."

Next time? Would there be a next time? He was leaving in a few hours.

"How are you feeling? Are you still sore?"

"It's okay." She looked away.

"It's not okay. It's worse, isn't it?"

"I'm all right, really." His concern over her made tears prick her eyes, she kept her eyes averted, she didn't want him to see.

Daniel stood and made his way over to her, gently pulling her close and rested his hands on her shoulders. Her heart skipped a beat at his nearness—his touch. Did he even know how good he smelled?

He was studying her with his gorgeous green eyes and she was tempted to touch his bare chest as she'd done as they slept together. His body was warm, smooth, and solid—pleasure at her fingertips. He caressed her cheek, then his hand slipped lower. She looked up at him, her gaze locked with his. She suddenly became breathless as he undid the top button to her cardigan that was fastened. "It's not cold in here, let me see, Sara." His tone was deep and husky.

She didn't stop him when he slowly lowered the cardigan down her arms. Her breath caught and her pulse rate quickened as a warmth flooded through her at his touch. Sara inwardly stifled a moan. The effect he had on her was crazy. No man had ever made her feel this way.

Her eyes drifted again, taking in the cut to his chiselled chest and then on down to his rock-hard abs. But the reality of the situation swiftly returned when she saw his expression as he looked down at her arms.

"Sara, has he done this before?"

She slowly shook her head. She didn't want to be reminded of what Adam had done, she'd cried enough—it was depressing.

"Once when I was pregnant with Arianna, he tried to, but God stopped him."

He frowned and looked at her quizzically.

"He was blinded and I hid—"

"Pardon?"

"I can't really explain what happened, all I know is that God was with me, and he protected me. Adam went to hit me and suddenly, he couldn't see. I didn't waste any time, I got out of dodge quick and locked myself in the bathroom until he left. You would have been proud at how fast I moved." She smiled trying to make light of the moment.

"This isn't funny, Sara," he chided. "He's an abuser, why didn't you tell me this before? I wouldn't have allowed him to be alone with you. I should have protected you."

Her smile faded. "I know it's not funny, but if I don't laugh, I'll cry, and I've done too much of that already." She touched his chest. "You did protect me, please don't think that you didn't. He was just so strong..."

She stepped away, slipping her cardigan back on. "Over the years, deep down, I was afraid of him, there was always an undercurrent of anger within him. So I played smart, I never defied him, I ensured I did everything he asked. Being the perfect obedient wife kept his anger at bay. Other than that one time, he has never harmed me. But as the years have gone on, I've felt the difference in him. He's changed—he's not the man I married. I just didn't feel safe with him..."

She trailed off, not wanting to delve any further into her past. It had been a dark period in her life and she just didn't want to focus on that right now. "I'm sorry, Daniel, this is drama that you shouldn't have to deal with."

Daniel felt his anger return, wanting to know more, but didn't want to push. She was clearly upset and frightened. *What did he do to her?* He felt his chest tighten. He would ensure that Adam paid for this. "We'll drop Arianna off at my mother's and then we're going straight to the police station, okay?"

She nodded in response, but he somehow felt it was a reluctant acquiesce, which made him feel uneasy. But the look of vulnerability and fear in her eyes was enough to make him want to take on the world for her and wished he'd dealt with her ex-husband when he had the chance.

Somehow he knew that there would be another occasion that would present itself, and he would then expel the burning anger he felt inside.

*   *   *

Sara stared out the window on the way back from the police station, and tried not to think. She could feel Daniel's anger and tension, but he said nothing, and she didn't know what to say.

She glanced at the clock on the dashboard. It was already after one, he would be leaving soon, and they'd been in the police station all morning.

She hated it. She hadn't ever been to one before, and she could honestly say it was one of the most unpleasant things she'd ever had to endure and she wasn't in a hurry to repeat *that* experience. The looks between the police officers were aloof and uncaring. They had seen it all before and they were even more disinterested when she'd decided not to have Adam arrested.

She felt humiliated and fearful. They asked her a number of questions she hadn't even considered. *Is there easy access to her home? Windows and doors? Did she have an alarm system? Did he have the keys to her home? Did she have a panic room?* Thankfully Daniel had remedied part of her problem with the change of locks, but after that ordeal, she suddenly had visions of Adam jumping out of the bushes at her. Or stalking her and following her home.

But she knew that wasn't Adam's style. Somehow she knew his approach would be a lot more sinister. He was wealthy—powerful, and she didn't have the financial means to fight him. That was the reason she didn't want to rock the boat.

Right now, all she wanted was Daniel's arms, and she wasn't sure he would be offering that comfort anytime soon.

She noticed he was heading in the direction of his home. They'd dropped Arianna off at his mother's on the way to the police station. She'd assumed they would pick her up on the way back. She looked over at him. His face was set in tense lines, and he seemed to be still angry at her. "Aren't we going to collect Arianna?"

Daniel glanced over at her. "No, we need to talk."

He needed to know the truth once and for all, and there was no negotiation as far as he was concerned. What happened at the

112

police station had him tied up in knots. He was angry—*very angry*. He was finding it difficult to contain. She was protecting Adam and that thought did not sit well with him. It meant that she still cared; it also meant that Sara wasn't as honest as he'd thought. It made him uneasy—alarm bells ringing in his head. He wouldn't allow her—or anyone—to hurt him again, and if that meant ending it with her, he would.

Sara didn't want to argue, all she knew was that Daniel would be leaving in a few hours and she didn't want to be left in his mansion all alone. Not that anything could happen; Adam didn't know where Daniel lived and even if he did, he could never get through security. "What time are you leaving?"

"Around five o'clock."

Less than four hours before he left her again. Her heart sank. "Could we stop at my home so I can pick up my car?"

"No."

Did he say no?

She frowned and glanced over at him. His tone was clipped, and he faced straight ahead as he drove. She could see the tension in his hands on the steering wheel.

Were they going to have another argument? Or should she back down as she always did, with a strong, alpha male—as she'd done with Adam for years. She avoided the confrontation, the arguments, and gave in, always the good dutiful wife.

Was Daniel controlling and moody, as Adam often was? She didn't know. They'd known each other seven months now and they had disagreements; of course they weren't exactly arguments. She'd seen him angry and annoyed, but that had always been when other men had sought her attention, and he'd become possessive of her. Then he would back off. He didn't force his will on her. Other than those few times, he'd always been gentle with her, fun-loving, intense...

His presence alone was intense. He walked into a room and he commanded everyone's attention. And when she was his focus, she couldn't help but want to please him; he had a way about him that no matter what she might think, when she was with him, everything flew out of her mind, lost in his beautiful green eyes. She wondered how many women he had this effect on, the power he had to command the way he did. He only needed to look at her and she would do his bidding.

"I just thought I could take you to the airport in my car..." As she uttered the words, she kept her voice soft and reasonable. She'd become an expert at that.

He looked over at her then, and his eyes softened a little. "I'll have your car brought over and I'll take a taxi to the airport. You don't need to do that."

Daniel pulled up at the traffic lights; he glanced at her, his eyes drifting to her hands, her long tapered fingers and manicured nails. She nervously fingered the hem of her skirt. Why was she nervous? Was she hiding something? He couldn't understand why she didn't want to press charges against her ex-husband. It made him wonder at what had happened between them before he entered the kitchen yesterday. Did she still have feelings for her ex? The thought angered him. He didn't know if he could trust her. Was she lying to him? He felt uncertain about the situation, insecure; his old wounds resurfacing.

When they arrived back at his home, Daniel didn't waste any time getting to the point. Sara steeled herself, apprehension filling her.

"Why didn't you have him charged? We spent hours down at the police station for you to decide you didn't want him arrested. I don't understand—*he assaulted you!*"

He was very angry—*at her.* She needed to calm him down. She removed her coat, placing it and her handbag on the sofa, then walked over to him. She placed a hand to his chest, knowing that he softened when she touched him. She didn't want their last few hours spent together arguing.

"Daniel, please don't be angry with me. I'm sorry...I just couldn't do it."

Daniel stepped away from her. "What do you mean, you couldn't do it? The man assaulted you! *What is this?*"

"I lived with him for ten years...I just—he's Arianna's father..."

"So that gives him the right to hurt you the way he did?" Daniel began to pace, frustrated. He should have torn that man limb from limb when he had the chance. He was so angry he wanted to beat him to a pulp!

She looked away, not knowing what to say.

"*Does it?*" he asked again.

"No, it doesn't," she replied, quietly.

"What if he does it again? Have you thought about that?"

"Well, we've reported it, and now they have a log of everything—the photos. Please Daniel, I don't want to blow this out of proportion...I was humiliated, please..." Tears came to her eyes and spilled over. She brushed them away. "I'm sorry, I'm not usually such a crybaby."

At her tears, Daniel's anger abated. He wanted to pull her into his arms, but he held back and asked the same question he'd asked before; it still worried him. He wasn't convinced she was being honest with him.

"Are you still in love with him, Sara?"

"No, Daniel. Why won't you believe me? My love for him died when he demanded I have an abortion. And ironically, part of the reason I fell in love with you was because of your love for Arianna. Adam is cold and heartless, I don't think I ever truly loved him. I was blinded by his wealth, his intelligence—his stature. When I really got to know him, I didn't like what I discovered. So, no, Daniel, I don't love him. I love you."

Daniel went to her then and gathered her in his arms. She clung to him, her arms around him, her face burrowed into his neck. He closed his eyes and steeled himself against the onslaught of emotions that came when he held her, when she responded to him like this. He could feel her soft lips against his neck, her warm breath whispering over his skin. Her hand was stroking the nape of his hair. *God, he loved her.* He wanted to be with her and decided in that moment that he would not leave her—he couldn't.

Sara sought the comfort she needed in his arms and closed her eyes as he slowly caressed her back. She didn't want to let him go; she needed him. *Please stay with me,* she silently begged. Then, as if he'd heard her silent communication, he took his mobile from his pocket and made a call, cancelling his arrangements. Her heart leapt, and he pulled her close, walking her over to the sofa.

They remained there for a good part of the afternoon. Daniel leaned back in the corner of the sofa, Sara next to him, their bodies connected, her head resting on his chest, her arms wrapped around him, his around her. And they talked and every so often she would look up at him and he would kiss her.

He told her about his spirituality, the visions he'd seen, the angels. How he was developing a relationship with the Holy Spirit, and somehow God's presence had always been with him. He'd felt it through David, he would see things, hear things—know things.

"I saw angels at your home yesterday."

Sara looked at him, wide-eyed. "You did?"

He nodded. "There were four, they had musical instruments in their hands, similar to a harp and one had a golden trumpet. When the angel blew on it, no sound came out, but the atmosphere changed and when you and Arianna sang together, the sounds that came from the harps as they played was holy, sweet... It's difficult to describe. God's presence was so strong, I just didn't want you to stop singing."

She smiled. "I feel it. I know they are there, but I never see it. The first time I saw an angel was with you at Rachel and David's home. God is so awesome. I delight in everything to do with Him. I'm so pleased you became a Christian, Daniel."

"Do I meet your standards now?"

"I never had a standard—" he raised a brow at her, "—okay, yes I did but I fell in love with you virtually straight away, Daniel. My heart didn't care..."

His eyes darkened, and he didn't look away. She waited, hoping he would say the words she so longed to hear. But his mobile pealed beside him and the moment was lost.

She sighed and sat up. Heading to the kitchen, she decided to prepare lunch as it sounded as if it was going to be a long call.

As she prepared their meal, her mind drifted to Arianna. She wanted Arianna here with her. She recalled last weekend when she was carrying out her weekend chores of changing the bedding.

"Mummy, I want Uncle Daniel to be my daddy," Arianna announced as she stood beside the bed, watching Sara.

Sara sighed and dragged the bedsheets off the bed. "We spoke about this, Arianna, haven't we?"

Arianna nodded, looking contrite.

Sara wondered what had happened and why she'd brought this subject up again. Arianna was stubborn at times, and often wouldn't let things lie.

"But I want Daniel to be my daddy."

If only it was that simple. "I know, but he has adopted you as his niece, and that's the next best thing." Sara fanned out a clean sheet across the bed, waiting in anticipation of what Arianna would do next.

Arianna proceeded to jump on the bed under the sheet, allowing it to cover her, giggling as Sara fanned the sheet once more so it would float down on top of Arianna again. The sounds of Arianna's laughter made Sara smile.

Sara then poked Arianna in the ribs, tickling her and producing further giggles until Arianna was laughing uncontrollably. Sara pulled the sheet down so she could see Arianna's face, laughing with her. Her face was lit up with joy, her honey brown eyes bright with amusement, the curly waves of her hair framing her face.

She loved Arianna so much—she was the one thing in her life that Sara did right. What saddened her was that she could see some of her father's good looks in her, yet he showed no interest in wanting to develop a relationship with his daughter. He just didn't care and Arianna picked up on that. Sara tried to shield her and give her unconditional love to overcompensate, but Arianna knew. She was a very insightful child, probably as a result of her spirituality; God allowed her to understand things which others didn't.

Yet with the knowledge of her father's indifference, she was still a happy child and Sara understood why Arianna loved Daniel, but she was concerned that Arianna had become too attached to him.

What if things didn't work out between them? What then?

Sara hoped it would, she prayed it would. Daniel was everything she could ever want in a man. She would never have considered him if he hadn't loved Arianna, that was paramount. He'd taken Arianna under his wing, given her the love she needed—which only resulted in Sara loving him even more—Daniel would take time out to help Arianna with her homework, read her a story before bed. Sometimes he would even turn up and take her off somewhere; to an ice-cream parlour, to see his cousins, or when he was doing mundane things such as going to a newsagent to pick up his papers. After, he would drop her back and he would be gone again. Arianna often saw more of Daniel than she did.

He always considered Arianna; bought her gifts, cared about her welfare. Sara had never come across a man that was as attentive as Daniel. And truthfully, he was just as attentive to her, when he wasn't fighting what he felt. When he was with her, she was always his total focus. He did love her, she knew that, he didn't need to say it; he demonstrated it every time he was with her. Not to mention he loved Arianna and that was important to her. He would be a wonderful father to Arianna—he already was. More so than Adam ever had been—or could ever be.

Sara lay down beside Arianna, then kissed her forehead, hugging her close.

"You could get married." Arianna beamed, her eyes lit up as if her suggestion was the solution to everything.

Sara's heart ached for Arianna—she was everything to her. She wished she could give Arianna what she wanted—she wanted it too, so very much.

"Daniel loves you, Arianna, but I'm not sure that he wants to get married."

Arianna looked at her then, as if contemplating something. "He loves you, too, Mummy. He told me." Arianna's face was serious, in that adult way of hers as she told her this information.

"Did he?"

"Yes, he said he loves you. You should get married, Mummy." Arianna reached up and touched her face as if to emphasize the importance of what she was telling her.

Her interest piqued at that, but then she remembered when Daniel responded to Arianna when she'd brought this up before by saying he loved her. Which at the time she'd thought he was joking, but now she realised it was true. "When did he tell you that?" she asked, pulling her closer.

"Mmm...can't remember, after school. I asked him if he was going to marry you and he said yes, one day soon. So when are you getting married, Mummy?"

Sara shifted her weight on her elbows and looked down at her daughter, trying hard to hide her feelings and not burst out in a grin.

"Nanna told me, too. It was our secret." She grinned. "Uncle Daniel will be my daddy then, won't he? Will we live at Uncle Daniel's house? Is his house big like Nanna and Uncle David's...?

Arianna had chatted on as if it was the most trivial of conversations, but to *her* it was momentous. She wondered again why Daniel hadn't said anything, yet he'd told Arianna and what was even more perplexing was the secret. She remembered when Katherine had mentioned that, was it wishful thinking on Katherine's part? But going by Arianna, clearly not.

She looked over at Daniel, he was on his laptop still in discussion with a client on the phone, she was thankful he wasn't travelling tonight. She loved him so much and she wanted more than anything to be with him as his wife.

He looked up, sensing her stare. He winked at her and smiled. Her heart leapt with joy and she smiled in response, saying a silent prayer in the hope that God would give her an answer to her prayers very soon.

Chapter 10

He didn't even know what he expected, but this wasn't it.

He'd been wary of Sara staying the week at first, thinking that she would have been clingy, or maybe a little demanding. She was none of those things; if anything, it was *he* who sought her out, not the other way round.

She was independent. She didn't seem to need anything from him and because he didn't do clingy, that should have pleased him, but it didn't. Strangely for him, he wanted her to need him.

At forty-one, he was very much set in his ways and for much of his adult life he'd lived on his own. His relationships extended only as far as him spending the night and then he left. Briefly, Amy had lived with him, but he refused to dwell on that part of his life, their love—their relationship—had been short. One moment he planned to spend a life with her, and the next—she was gone.

Sara respected his space, and kept out of his way, thinking that was what he needed. Before she moved in, he'd have said it was. But for some reason, the fact that he hardly saw her in the mansion irritated him.

The size of his residence was a factor; it was not an estate like his mother's or as large as David's, but his home was vast, all the same. The rooms were huge and numerous—five bedrooms on the first floor, his bedroom and a further three bedrooms on the second floor, and several reception rooms.

The majority of his time was spent in his office on the ground floor, and with three staircases to either floors, it was possible not to see each other if they really wanted. But he didn't want that. He gravitated toward her and found he had to seek her out. He was coming home early and leaving late in the mornings for the office, and he never did that.

She often worked from home and, occasionally, so did he. He'd be in his office and she would be in her room. He didn't see her.

She worked out every day. He remembered she'd told him she exercised to keep her weight down, but he couldn't see it, she was slim, her body hard and soft in all the right places. He'd told her she could work out at his gym on the ground floor. And she did. But never with him.

That first night he and Sara spent together, he told himself she was vulnerable and that she needed his comfort. She did, but it turned out to be much more than that. He felt complete, contented for the very first time.

She'd held on to him the whole night. If he shifted to give her room, she moved closer, as if she never wanted to let him go. A couple of times during the night, she whispered his name, as if to check that he was still there and he'd pull her close. It felt good to hold her, it felt comfortable—*right*.

He never felt this way with a woman—not even with Amy. With Amy, part of him always felt she wasn't really his; it was as if he had a sense that she would leave him, and at the time he'd wanted them to be married quickly, so she could be his for good.

But with Sara it was different, he felt content. And he slept, really slept. He couldn't remember the last time he'd slept that soundly. He was used to travelling, and taking naps on the plane. He never got used to unfamiliar hotel rooms, which meant sleep was slow in coming. After that first night with her, he wanted more. As far as he was concerned, it had to be a fluke. And when he awoke and found she was no longer beside him, for some reason he'd felt somehow abandoned—which was crazy.

But truthfully, maybe not so crazy.

Amy used to leave him at night. He used to wake, expecting her to be beside him and she'd be gone. Maybe deep down, he was afraid that would happen again. He'd finally connected with another human being on a level that he'd kept hidden since Amy. He loved Sara, but it was a love he'd never experienced before.

Amy had broken his heart, he'd loved her. They were together for five months before all was revealed. He fell for her and looking back—as he rarely did, not wanting to relive the pain—if he was truly honest with himself, she loved him. He'd been disgusted, hurt and angry after discovering what she'd done—lied to him, used him, made him believe that the babies growing inside her were his—made out of their love, and that hurt the most.

But on reflection, his love for her outweighed all sense, and the thought of a life without her was unbearable. He'd told her to leave and then reconsidered, and when he returned with the intention to beg her, like a fool, to leave her husband and marry him, she had gone, walked out of his life.

Their love was new. In a way, he was infatuated with her and the babies she carried, and he clearly hadn't known the person she really was.

The love he felt for Sara was totally different. He'd fallen for her so hard, so deep, it confused him. The very first moment he'd set eyes on her, it hit him. He'd been intensely attracted to her, and it was her beautiful hazel eyes that drew him—revealing an intelligence with a hint of mischievousness that he later discovered matched his own. Full lush lips, her hair long, loose in waves to her waist and the dress she'd worn that night fit her body to perfection. She was tall and shapely, a stunning woman—exotic, someone who was not ashamed of her looks and knew the impact she had on men—*had on him*.

He couldn't even remember the film they had gone to see. They'd talked and laughed throughout the whole night—a whispered conversation that every time she'd leaned over to say something to him, the feel of her warm breath brushing against his skin had enticed him and made him think of other things they could be doing. Yet he'd fought what he felt, knowing that if he let it, he'd lose all control.

At the beginning he'd foolishly thought sex would alleviate the longing that tore at him, but he'd later realised that delving deeper in that regard would cause him to lose himself—he had no defence against her and he was in no way prepared for that.

When all was said and done, the fight within himself was to no avail, as it happened anyway. With every touch, every look, even the way she teased him and made him laugh. The way she came alive when he held her and kissed her. She never once hid her feelings from him. The love he saw every time she looked at him, as if she couldn't help herself. It felt so good that she loved him.

He discovered that he needed it—*needed her*. And more than anything, he wanted a life with her—he wanted the life God had shown him, he wanted to make two lives out of their love—their twin girls.

So why hadn't he told her? Why did he find it so hard to tell her how he felt?

Because he was afraid; afraid he'd end up with a broken heart again.

This time he doubted he would ever recover from it.

He was discovering more and more things about her. For one, there was the singing. Like that morning, he'd heard her singing in the shower. She did that a lot. Why hadn't he noticed that about her before? With her, there was music and angels. Most afternoons after she'd collected Arianna from school, Sara prepared dinner, Arianna would be seated at the kitchen table, and they would be singing, usually to a worship CD. His music system was wired throughout his home and he found for the first time ever, he'd felt peace. God's presence—she'd brought that with her.

On two occasions, he'd overheard Arianna ask Sara about her piano lessons. He hadn't been aware she was taking lessons and felt he should have known. Then later, discovered that Sara was teaching her, but without a piano that wasn't a possibility. He remedied that straight away and had a white baby grand piano delivered. She'd told him she used to own one, but was unable to take it with her after her divorce. When she told him about it she'd become wistful, as if it had meant something to her and it hurt to leave it behind.

Her ex had hurt her, and Daniel still felt guilty that he hadn't stopped it sooner. He wanted to please her and see her eyes light up with joy, and give her more than her ex had ever given her.

"Oh Daniel! A baby grand!" Sara exclaimed when she arrived home to find it in the far end of the living area, where he'd asked the delivery men to place it. She stared at it for a moment. "It's beautiful, how did you do this? *When* did you do this?" She turned to him then, with tears in her eyes and hugged him, clinging to him. He closed his eyes for a moment savouring the feel of her, taking in her scent.

She pulled away, looking deep into his eyes and touched his face. "I don't know what to say... Thank you."

For a moment, there was a look in her eyes that he'd never seen before and it touched him. A silent communication was shared between them that he couldn't deny anymore. The words that he wanted to say—the same love he felt for her that he could see in her eyes for him— became lodged in his throat. He couldn't say it.

Then she smiled her beautiful smile and took his hand and led him to the piano. He sat with her on the bench and she played for him.

She was different with him after that—it was subtle, but it was there. She was freer with her affection toward him. Although she had never pulled away or rejected his affection, she always responded with complete abandonment—uncontrolled. But before, she would ask him to stop or run away, fighting a battle within. He understood that battle; it was one he was struggling with. But now, she touched him often—when she wasn't hiding in another part of the house. She touched his chest, caressed his face, even ran her fingers through his hair. He loved it when she touched him—she had awakened feelings within him he could no longer control, along with a deep need to possess.

She would come close and step into his arms, or when he was in his office working, she would distract him by sitting on his lap and fitting her body against his, resting her head on his shoulder to talk to him for a while. He had a longing for her that never went away, embedded deep within him. No other woman had ever made him feel this way, he wanted more—he wanted her, and it was time he did something about it.

There was one thing he was certain of. It was the knowledge that she needed him at night. The last six nights he'd gone to her room. He tried with everything within him to stay away, but it was impossible. He couldn't stay away and all he did was hold her, talk to her, and laugh—they did that a lot, too.

He wanted her there beside him and he liked waking up with her. He held her tight, close to him, so she couldn't leave again, as she had the first morning. She had to wake him first if she wanted to leave his side.

He noticed she was much more comfortable with him. Maybe it was because he was a Christian now, which came with the responsibility that they could not have sex outside of marriage, and she now felt unrestrained as he would no longer pressure her in that way.

And then there was Arianna—he discovered new things about her, too. He was a neat freak. Not many people knew that about him—not that he was OCD about it—but he liked his home a certain way. And with a woman and a child, he'd expected mess.

Wrong again. His home remained immaculate.

He'd seen it at Sara's home, but he wasn't sure what would be revealed after they'd lived together. But with Arianna, he would say she was the perfect child. Mature for her age, she was quiet, well behaved, and understated. At dinner and breakfast she was very chatty; she talked about school, her friends, her homework. She was a very intelligent child.

But then she would become pensive as if she was downloading information and knowledge. She would be quiet and he rarely heard her most of the time. She was often reading or sometimes watching TV, drawing or writing; she was very creative. She wasn't into games consoles as most children of her age nowadays, and he realised it was Sara's influence.

Deep down, he considered her as his own. Witnessing what he'd seen with her father confirmed what he'd always felt about her, and she clearly felt about him. He was overprotective of her and he didn't want that man near her anymore.

One afternoon he'd come home early. Sara and Arianna were both at the kitchen table, drinking milk and munching cookies, with paper scattered about. TV off, music playing in the background, they were singing and drawing. He didn't know that Sara had such a skilful hand. It seemed she could draw anything, and he'd been impressed.

Sara asked him to describe the angels he'd seen.

"You want me to describe them?" he asked, curiously surprised.

"Yes. Please?"

"Okay." He slipped off his jacket and tie, placing them on the sofa, and then joined them at the table.

Sara reached for a new sheet of paper, pencil at the ready.

"You're going to draw it?"

"I'll try..."

He began describing one with a brilliant white robe-like tunic and large beautiful wings. This particular angel had sparkling blue eyes and a pleasant face. Daniel couldn't quite make out the colour of his hair, as there was a bright white light that permeated from him.

Sara listened as he described the angel and closed her eyes, picturing it. Then she began to draw, her skilful hand using wide, long strokes across the page. He was fascinated. Arianna copied her mother's movements, and he looked over her shoulder. She was pretty good for a five-year-old and had captured his angel perfectly. She clearly had her mother's creative talents. He praised her and gave her a hug, and he was rewarded with a huge grin that lit up her face and her honey brown eyes.

But it was what Sara produced that captivated him. She'd sketched it just as he'd described, everything as if she could see into his mind—as if she'd been there. It was amazing. He was astounded. And then she smiled as if she had a hidden secret which he knew nothing about, and in a way, she did. And he wanted to discover more.

There were other aspects to the description which he'd left out, like the note pad in the angel's hands. The fact the robe was not long, but short, and the angel had sandals on his feet. How did she know that? He realised that God must have given her insight; somehow; she had to have seen it.

"How did you know? You've captured everything, even parts I didn't tell you."

"I had a vision just as you described it. It's amazing, Daniel. I'm finding my spiritual gifts are heightened when I'm around you."

The following day she had it framed, along with Arianna's sketch and placed in his office. When he looked at it, it warmed his heart.

They had even been to church together. He could easily pretend they were a family as they walked in holding Arianna's hand. Sara's church was different to David and Rachel's; it was very modern, larger and lively. There was praise, worship, prayer—and dancing. He felt God's presence straight away.

The dancing was new to him. It wasn't what he was used to, but it felt good to dance in church. The music was good; it was a celebration of who God was and being thankful for all He had done for him. He could understand why Sara attended this church; it was very much who she was.

She celebrated God in the way she lived her life—she worshipped Him every day, throughout her day, and since she'd been staying with him, he'd joined in with her worship. They'd become closer spiritually.

Pastor Simon was animated, preaching with passion. "Jesus gave his life for us. Have you thought about how profound that is? How gracious He was to consider us? He died so we could live, the ultimate act of love..."

The pastor's words stayed with Daniel. It *was* profound, a love he'd experienced more and more. He'd never considered this, the peace he felt when in God's presence.

He never knew. He'd felt it through David, the joy and the love—it would fill him, and looking back, he didn't know why. He'd felt God's love—the Holy Spirit's presence, and it stayed with him. Although he fought it. The Holy Spirit would talk to him and he would listen, as he had no choice. He could not block what he picked up through David and it was even stronger since Rachel came into David's life. It drew him, and he discovered a love inside for God which, he realised now, had always been there.

A humbling of self and a yearning need to connect with his Heavenly Father, it overtook him powerfully. No sooner than he submitted to God, he could no longer hold back on what he felt, the love and adoration poured out of him, a need to worship Him, thank Him, to love Him.

Without God, he was nothing, and he regretted taking so long to fully understand the importance and his purpose on this earth. Jesus had touched his life and brought him to a place with Sara that he never would have thought possible; he was now spiritually connected to her.

The Holy Spirit had told him things about his future—that he had great plans for him, and these plans all included Sara and Arianna. His spiritual progression, his development, his future, and his ultimate obedience—all of these involved Sara.

One did not exist without the other and he'd finally accepted it. God's word was true, God's hand was on his life, and it was time to submit his future to Him.

*   *   *

"So how's it going with Sara?" David asked Daniel, heading for the fridge. He retrieved two bottles of water, and handed one to his brother.

It was early Saturday morning and they had just finished a workout in David's gym. Weekends were their chance to catch up, so more often than not, they would work out together at David's gym for convenience.

Daniel took a long swig and looked at his brother. "I think the term I would use is challenging."

David gave him a questioning look. "With Sara? She doesn't come across as the type of woman that would give you problems."

Daniel smiled. "Yes with Sara, but not in that way..."

"Oh..." David gave him a wry smile. "Enough said."

"I don't know how you managed to stay celibate for two years. This is torture."

David chuckled. "Marry her. I don't know why you're fighting it."

"Maybe I'm just not ready."

"When is anyone ever ready? Maybe you just need to take the plunge."

Daniel contemplated that for a moment. "I don't want to end up in a situation you found yourself in with Karen."

"Sara is nothing like Karen, Daniel." David took a seat at the kitchen table.

"True, but who knows what she might feel five years down the line—what I might feel, even."

"Rachel grew up with Sara, and they are very close. Sara is not that type of person, she's loyal. Since she is often at my home with Arianna, I've gotten to know her and I really like her, I think she's perfect for you. You suit each other—she's classy—and she's funny. She makes me laugh, and I see a difference in Rachel when she's around. They're always giggling like school kids. It's quite something to see." David poured water in a glass and put it to his lips, draining its contents. "Rachel only has good things to say about her. God has brought her into your life and He wants you to marry her. There is no question about this. She is far removed from anything Karen was."

"Tell me about it. Karen was quite unique, to say the least. I don't know why you married her." Daniel took another sip of water, leaning back against the counter.

"She made promises to me and I believed her, I've always been a family man and that was what I wanted. Anyway, the first five years, weren't too bad."

Daniel shook his head in disgust.

David narrowed his eyes. "What?"

"You don't want to know, brother."

David sensed something within him. Daniel found it difficult to hide his feelings from David, as he would sense his moods straight away. It was a wonder he'd been able to keep the truth from David over the years. Deep down, he knew that David probably didn't really want to know the truth about Karen.

David stared at him for a moment, assessing Daniel. "What aren't you telling me?"

Daniel sat beside his brother, splaying his hands across the surface of the table. "Karen wasn't truthful about what happened between us," he began reluctantly. "What you saw that night wasn't me kissing her—it was Karen who kissed me. I did not pretend to be you, she knew exactly who I was and what she was trying to do."

"What?" He saw anger flare in David's eyes. "Why didn't you tell me?"

"I tried to warn you about her before you married her, and you refused to listen. She wanted both of us and had no morals whatsoever. I was careful over the years not to be alone with her. It wasn't the first time she tried, David."

"All this time, you never thought to tell me?" David responded angrily.

"What good would it have done if I had told you? The girls were young, and I didn't want to cause problems. Nothing happened between us, David, because I wouldn't let it. I would never have done that to you. I respected your marriage, and it did not benefit you or me to tell you. You would have been angry, and nothing actually happened. I kept well away, and the times she flirted with me, I kept my distance."

"When she told me that you instigated it, why didn't you say something then?"

"She begged me not to. She said if you were to find out, your marriage would be over. Keira and Sophie would have a broken home and I didn't want that for them. Karen made me feel guilty. I couldn't do it. I'm sorry I didn't tell you the truth, but I had good intentions."

David looked at him incredulously. "I can't believe you didn't tell me. I was so angry at you for years..."

Daniel gave him a wry look. "Yes, even now. You believed the worst, and you don't trust me around Rachel." He eyed David knowingly. "Rachel was never a consideration, David. Before you got married, yes, I'll admit that, I pursued her. But not after you got married. It was open competition. You know that has always been the rule between us."

"Yes, and Rachel chose me. It was hardly open competition, Daniel." David gave his brother a smug smile.

Daniel laughed. "Okay, okay—" he held up his hands, "—I accept defeat on that one. But I think Rachel understands that I'm the better-looking twin."

David chuckled, shaking his head. "I've always said you should have been a comedian. So what you're saying is that any misgivings I have about you and Rachel being alone are unfounded?"

"Yes. My heart is elsewhere, with Sara—as you keep reminding me." Daniel raised a brow.

David smiled. Then a real look of relief touched his face that made Daniel laugh. "I'm pleased the way things worked out. Sara is everything I could ever want in a woman. I just need a little time to get used to the idea."

David eyed him. "You're afraid she's going to hurt you like Amy did."

"Yes. I don't know how to get past that one. But I'm getting there."

"Have you told her you love her yet?" David asked.

"No, not yet. I want to...I need to."

"Don't leave it too long. She needs to hear it."

It was true; Sara *did* need to hear it. He no longer needed to guard his feelings as he used to. He'd come a long way these last few months.

He and David had come to an understanding that day. Years of resentment, gone in a moment, and he realised it was time to let go and let God.

* * *

She'd awoke that morning and Daniel wasn't beside her, as he'd been every morning since he'd asked her to stay with him. He was gone. She'd felt deserted and a lump formed in her chest.

Where is he?

She made her way up to his room on the second floor. She opened the door, expecting to find him asleep in bed, but it was neatly made up, untouched. Maybe he'd gone for a run, as he did most mornings.

It had been wonderful being with him here at his home, and she didn't ever want to leave. She'd worried they might not get on and she had taken pains to deliberately give him the space he needed.

Adam had been moody and did not want her or Arianna under his feet, so she and Arianna were used to keeping to their space and not encroaching beyond. But Daniel was not content with that—which was a surprise—and would seek her out, slipping his arms around her and kissing her. For no reason, he would just hug her, and he gave her so much affection she was revelling in it. She'd been starved of affection for so long.

So if he wasn't hugging and kissing her, he was touching her in some way, holding her hand. An arm around her waist, on her shoulders, even his hands in her hair. He liked to caress her face, too, and just look into her eyes.

She loved him so much.

It was so evident that he loved her, too—his actions demonstrated what she'd been missing all these years and confirmed what she'd discovered too late; that Adam never loved her. What she experienced with Daniel was true love. He made her heart soar and her spirits lift when he was here. As soon as he pulled up outside, her heart leapt with joy at him being home and all she wanted to do was please him.

He clamped her close to him in bed at night. She suspected it was to ensure she didn't leave him like she had the first morning. She'd tried a couple of times to extricate herself from his arms, but his hold would tighten around her waist, drawing her closer to him. She had no choice but to remain with him, watching him sleep. Then she'd pray for him, and God would talk to her about him.

The Holy Spirit would tell her about Daniel's past, his hurts, his pain, and she would pray for healing and restoration. Every morning she would have quiet prayer time with the Holy Spirit while he slept and it drew her closer, spiritually connected.

This was what she'd needed for so long, which Adam had never given her. He'd showered her with gifts, trips abroad—things, which in the end meant nothing, and she'd resented his wealth. It became a bitter pill in her mouth. This short time she'd spent with Daniel filled her with such joy and contentment that she would forego all wealth for this.

They prayed together every day, and worshipped God in the mornings. They'd become close—spiritually close—which had heightened her spirituality. When she was with him, God allowed her to see visions. She'd been so amazed. And in the mornings before they got up, they would share their dreams, and she would explain how to interpret them. Often he would have a message for her, and she would have a message for him. Their relationship had grown and developed, and Daniel had become her spiritual partner.

She recalled the morning before. She opened her eyes and looked at him; he was still asleep, and they were sharing the same pillow. She shifted slightly and his hold on her tightened.

"Where are you going?" he mumbled, his eyes still closed.

"I've got to get to work early today."

He groaned and pulled her closer to him. "No, don't go. I need you to interpret my dream."

"What did you dream?" she asked, studying him, his eyes were still closed. From experience, just the slightest movement of your head or a thought on something else could cause you to lose the dream and it would disappear—totally erased from memory. She suspected this was the reason he remained still.

"I dreamt about Arianna. I was...I can't remember where I was...we were outside, in a park maybe." He paused, trying to remember. "I was holding Arianna's hand and we were walking along a path." He opened his eyes and looked at her. "Then Adam turned up and took her away from me and continued down the path holding her hand. And I just stood there watching them walk away from me and I didn't stop them." Daniel stared into her eyes

Sara frowned, a little concerned by the dream. "Maybe you should have gone after her—didn't you want to?"

"I don't know...I felt he had the authority—the right as a father to have Arianna, and I didn't."

Sara was silent for moment, contemplating. *What does it mean?*

"I don't know why I didn't stop him—why I didn't go after them."

What does it mean, Lord?

"Daniel needs to make a decision about your situation. He is aware."

Do I need to be concerned?

"He needs to make the right decision. Pray, Sara."

She wondered why she wasn't in the dream. Did this mean that Adam might take Arianna—but why from Daniel and not her?

They prayed together that morning asking for the full interpretation of the dream, as it confused her. There was a look in Daniel's eyes that told her he knew the interpretation of the dream, but he did not want to reveal it. She wondered what it was. Surely, if it was something she needed to be worried about, God would reveal it to her and so would Daniel. So she didn't push and instead waited for him to tell her.

She looked at her watch. It was still early. She headed to Arianna's room, only to find her still asleep. Deciding not to wake Arianna, she made her way downstairs to start breakfast.

Daniel always had a healthy appetite following his run, so she looked in the fridge and prepared breakfast for them.

A little later, the sound of Daniel's car told her he'd returned, then he appeared through the front door, armed with groceries and flowers.

"Morning," he said.

"Morning," she replied, then smiled.

He handed her the flowers. "For the beautiful lady."

She grinned. "Thank you, Daniel. They're lovely." She brought them to her nose to take in the scent. They were carnations and he'd picked them especially for her; they were her favourite flowers. He was so sweet to her, and considerate.

She sighed wistfully, she loved him so much. *Oh please, Lord, I want him to be mine...*

"How are you today?" Daniel asked, and placed the groceries on the counter. Her bruises still looked quite painful, but she was no longer stiff in her movements. It concerned him and made him feel helpless—guilty, a stark reminder of how he'd failed to protect her from Adam. He would never let anyone hurt her again.

"I'm okay." Sara looked away for a moment. He asked her every day. The night before, she'd worn a sleeveless vest top to bed, which exposed her arms, reminding them both of the situation with Adam.

Daniel held her gaze, both not knowing what to say, but she could see the emotion in his eyes—the love, the tenderness—and then he kissed her gently, not demanding of her. He kissed a path to her neck, her shoulders and further, where Adam viciously sought to hurt her. Daniel kissed her there on the curve of her arms, which were now, a reddish purple colour. Gently and lovingly he took his time, kissing her along her forearms to the palm of her hands, and she couldn't help the tears that sprang to her eyes.

He drew her close then. "I'm sorry, Sara," he whispered as he held her in his arms.

"You have nothing to be sorry for, Daniel," she mumbled into his neck.

"I shouldn't have let him hurt you."

She looked up at him, seeing the guilt and regret in his eyes. She touched his face and ran a finger along his jaw to his lips. "No, you weren't to blame."

She brushed her lips against his and kissed him gently, allowing him to deepen the kiss, and when he drew away, he held her close until they both fell asleep.

He made her feel loved and cherished, and she didn't want to be reminded of Adam today. She still found it unsettling.

She placed the flowers on the counter and changed the subject swiftly. "You've arrived just in time. Your breakfast is ready."

Daniel smiled. "Thank you." He stepped closer to her and kissed her tenderly, holding her for a long moment caressing her back. She wrapped her arms around his neck pressing her body against him. She touched his face, her other hand slowly stroked his neck, and as her hands touched and explored him, she moaned and a possessiveness filled him and a great need coursed through him.

He drew away slowly, looking down at her. Her eyes were closed. She opened them after a moment and seemed just as dazed as he was. He gave a slow smile.

He could seriously get used to this—having her here permanently. He liked having her here and he loved the way she looked after him. She naturally did the womanly thing, which was to make breakfast for them every morning. He could easily prepare it, as he was used to making breakfast himself and was quite proud of his culinary skills. But when he had his workout in the mornings and took his early morning run, Sara would always have breakfast ready for him. She was spoiling him and he wasn't ready for her to leave yet.

"I thought I'd get a few groceries in as I wasn't sure how long you would be staying."

Sara met his gaze. *Was that his way of saying that he wanted her to leave?* The predicament Sara found herself in was that she didn't want to leave and had probably overstayed her welcome. "Thanks, for letting me stay here, Daniel. I wanted to talk to you about that..." She let her hands fall to her sides and stepped away from him. "I think it might be time that I went back home."

Daniel assessed her for a moment. He didn't want her to leave. "Why? I'm not really comfortable with you going back there."

Neither was she, but she couldn't stay here with him forever—how would that look? It had been over a week. They hadn't had sex, but they wanted to; it was the unspoken topic that seemed to hang in the air. Her staying with him, him coming to her room at night and holding her, was not conducive to no sex outside of marriage.

She was too comfortable with him. It had become almost natural, and she longed for it every night. She found she couldn't sleep without him beside her. And this morning was telling enough, that she'd felt somehow abandoned, because he'd left without waking her and she had no right to feel those things. "I think it might be best, Daniel."

He came and stood before her, resting his hands on her shoulders. "Don't you like it here? I hope I haven't made you feel unwelcome, I'm used to living on my own." A frown crossed his brow, a look of concern crossing his face. His touch sent a shiver up her spine as his hands lingered, caressing her arms.

"No, you haven't made me feel unwelcome." She reached up and caressed his jaw. "I just don't think it's a good idea and you know why..."

Daniel's heart sank, but he understood. He wanted her badly.

It took all of his will power to leave her that morning, and he felt a good workout at David's gym would ease his frustrations.

Tucked in close beside him, she had looked so beautiful, her hair splayed across the pillow, the quiet sound of her breathing. Her eyes were closed, framed by her long eyelashes. He chose not to wake her; if he had, he wouldn't have left. He was fighting a battle which he was afraid he might lose.

"I don't want you to go, but I understand." He stepped away from her and began unpacking the groceries. "When were you thinking of leaving?"

Sara picked up a bag to help. "Tomorrow. Is that okay?"

Daniel looked over at her. *No, it's not okay. I want you to stay.* "That's fine." He turned and said nothing further.

Sara felt his disappointment and it hurt. She went over to him, tucked herself to his side and slipped her arms around his waist. He brought her body closer to his and looked down at her with those beautiful green eyes of his, gently cupping her face. He touched his lips to hers and kissed her, slowly, lovingly. Her arms slipped up his back, holding on tightly as she felt the rush of sensations that seemed to want to carry her away with herself, leaving her feeling senseless and lightheaded.

He pulled away and looked deep into her eyes. She could see his love for her, so why didn't he ever tell her? She needed him to and now she had to leave and she didn't want to.

Feeling discontent at their situation, her heart constricted. She wanted to be his wife, but she doubted he would ever offer her that and she hurt inside at the thought of it. "Daniel, what are we doing? It's never going to be anything more than this, is it?"

His hands fell away and there was a look in his eyes she couldn't quite read. Then he stepped away from her again and she regretted saying anything at all. Even so, she couldn't help but continue. "I don't even know how you feel. You've never told me..."

At that point Arianna breezed into the room, looking cute in her fuzzy bear pyjamas, and the moment was lost.

But it was later, on their last night together, that he continued their interrupted conversation. Neither had wanted the night to end and he held her close in bed, quietly talking to her about family and how important it was to him and it made her wonder again as to why he never wanted a family of his own.

"Tell me again about how it would be if we lived together in the Caribbean?" she asked, reminding him of the story he told her of their life together when they were in Negril.

Daniel looked at her, amusement in his eyes. "We will be married and have twin girls—beautiful just like their mother. Arianna will be their overprotective older sister and we will be happy. There may be some ups and downs, but our love for each other will outweigh everything."

Sara's heart skipped a beat; he said the words as if it would actually happen. She held his gaze, wishing it could be so.

"I love you, Sara."

She blinked, not believing the words he'd just spoken. "You love me?" she whispered in response.

Daniel smiled. "Yes. I've always loved you, and you've known that. When I told you that story in Negril, it came from a place inside that I didn't even understand at the time. God has shown me confirmation of it through a series of dreams."

Tears came to her eyes, she couldn't speak. "Oh Daniel..." she whispered. Her tears spilled over and streamed down her face. "I've longed for so long to hear you say the words...I thought you never would."

Daniel caressed her face, then gently kissed her tears away. He wanted with all his heart to ask her to marry him; but his fears, as always, overwhelmed him. What was it that held him back? They were here, together, closer than they had ever been before. He didn't know; he didn't have the answer, but it would come soon.

His lips found hers and he kissed her passionately, wanting to show her what he hadn't been able to say until now. He slowly ended the kiss, drawing her close. She closed her eyes and so did he. Content at being with her, but a little poignant that this would be their last night together.

He'd finally told her how he felt, just as he would eventually marry her. There was no rush; they would have a life together, and he accepted that now. It was what he wanted more than anything, and he would finally have the family that his father had always wanted for him.

Chapter 11

"*What did you say?* You're joking?" Sara asked, not believing her ears. She sat down for a moment, shocked. "You're pregnant?"

"Yes, I'm still in shock. I can't believe it. It was one night, Sara, I gave in. I know I shouldn't have. I feel so condemned. I've been praying for forgiveness ever since, but now I'm reaping the consequences of my wrong deeds. I don't know what I'm going to do."

Even over the phone, she could hear the desperation in Samyra's voice. "Samyra, all children are gifts from God. This is not a punishment, regardless of how this baby came to be." Sara kept her tone soft and encouraging as her sister was clearly distraught. "How did this happen? You were a virgin—you said you were saving yourself for your husband."

"I know..."

Samyra began to cry, which tore at Sara's heart. "Myi...oh please don't cry. We'll do this together, I'll help you, don't worry. Even though this wasn't how God intended, being outside of marriage, this baby is a gift from him and you must see it as such. It's a blessing, Myi."

"I wanted to be happily married with a loving husband when I got pregnant. What am I going to do?"

"Does the father know? Who is the father?"

"Huh! You don't even want to know...and no, he doesn't know. I wasn't even in a relationship with him. It was one night. I can't even believe I lost all control like that. I've never done anything like this. You know me—I would never do a thing like this."

It was true. Samyra was truly committed—a new Christian, who upheld God's values to the letter. Their mother had brought them up as Christians and Samyra believed. She only committed fully within the last year, but had always been an outward rebel in the way she dressed. She supposed it was her lifestyle, travelling the world as a photographer on set, trendy and stylish. Samyra loved leather; jackets, high-heeled boots, ripped jeans and wore the latest fashion trends, due to her line of work, which did not conform to how their mother felt a good Christian woman should dress. It was a common argument between them, and one Samyra always won, as she would remind her mother that God does not look at the outward appearance, he looks at the heart.

As if to substantiate that, her lifestyle and moral standards were very much in line with God's ideals. At thirty-three, she was so righteous she often put Sara to shame, and both Samyra and her mother would often gang up on Sara over some of the choices she'd made in life that they felt did not conform to Christian principles. They probably would never approve of her staying over at Daniel's home, regardless of the circumstances.

Her mind drifted to him. She missed him. It was unbearable. She felt lost when she was separated from him, and she didn't know what she was going to do.

She'd been back home a week and everything within her wanted to pack her things and return to him. She hoped he would visit tonight. But his short visits were no longer enough.

He'd come over for dinner a few times and he'd been reluctant to leave. Neither did she want him to go, and had hugged him tightly before he left. Then she'd cried, big fat sobs. She was in such a state and her heart ached. The night he told her he loved her, he spoke as if they would be married and she wanted it more than anything.

Her thoughts drifted back to her sister's worrying situation. She was thankful she hadn't given in with Daniel—when everything within her wanted to—for reasons such as this.

"How am I going to face the church? This is so embarrassing. Mum is going to kill me!"

What a mess. Still, it was one Samyra would have to leave to God to resolve, and Sara realised now why she'd decided to return to the UK. "How far along are you?"

Samyra was silent for a moment. "Four months…I was afraid to tell you."

Four months?

"At first I kept myself busy with work and I ignored it, but I'm going to start to show soon. I won't be able to hide it for much longer." She paused for a moment. "I'm not sure I can have this baby, Sara. I will be the laughing-stock of the church."

"Now you get those thoughts out of your mind, Samyra," she began firmly. "You're going to have this baby, and I'll help you. We'll do this together, okay? It doesn't matter what anyone else thinks."

Samyra continued to cry. Sara looked at the clock over the fireplace in the living room. She needed to leave soon to collect Arianna. "God loves you, Samyra. Things will work out for the best, I promise you. Why don't you spend the weekend with me, and then we can talk. You don't need to tell Mum yet. We can do that together if you want."

Samyra gave a long sigh. "Okay, thanks, Sara. I can't do this on my own." Samyra's voice was quiet, filled with sadness.

The news was shocking, especially as Samyra had held her virginity as sacred. There was more to this story than Samyra was letting on. She didn't do one-night-stands; she had to have feelings for the man she lost her virginity to, and Joshua came to mind. If Joshua was the father, she suddenly felt very sorry for him, as Bradley would tear him apart. This was more than a mess.

At the sound of another call coming through, Sara looked down at her phone. It was Adam. *What did he want?* She groaned inwardly, she didn't need this right now. She ignored his call.

"We'll make a decision together, okay?"

"Okay."

"Dry your tears, hon."

Adam's face flashed through again—he was calling for a second time.

"Samyra, I've got to go. Adam keeps calling. I'm going to have to take the call. I'll see you later."

She disconnected her sister's call and switched to Adam's, not sure how to handle his call, as she'd promised to advise the police if he contacted her again. "Hello, Adam."

"I'm outside. Let me in."

Apprehension filled her. "What are you doing here?"

"We have a daughter together, and I have a right to be here. I would have let myself in if you hadn't changed the locks."

Which meant he'd tried to gain access to her home. Trepidation hit her. "I'm not sure that's a good idea, after what happened the last time you came." Her heart began to pound in her chest. "Anyway, I'm about to leave now. I'm going to collect Arianna from school."

"There's no need, as I have already done that. Open the door, Sara."

She dropped the mobile on the sofa and rushed to the door, swinging it open. "Where is Arianna?" Fear gripped her.

Adam filled the door frame, an imposing figure she found intimidating. She used to be enamoured by his good looks and tall frame, but not anymore. Now, all she saw was an arrogant, conceited man who only wanted to control her.

"She's at home with Mrs Krycher. It is also time for you to come home, Sara."

Sara stared at him in shock. "Adam, you need to bring her home. You'll unsettle her."

Adam closed the door. "Clearly you do not understand what I am saying to you." There was a gleam in his eyes, one of pure evil. "You belong to me and you will be packing your things—right now—and coming home with me. Arianna is with Mrs Krycher, where she is supposed to be."

A feeling of dread began to fill her. "Adam—"

"You will do as I say—otherwise you will never see Arianna again."

Sara's heart pounded hard in her chest as fear overwhelmed her, but she reasoned that Mrs Krycher—Adam's housekeeper—would take good care of Arianna as she'd done in the past. "You can't do this! You don't even want Arianna."

"True…but I want you, Sara. You had no right to walk out on me. You're my wife." He grabbed her, pulling her roughly against him. "I've allowed this to go on for long enough, and I will not let another man have what belongs to me."

Alarm filled her. She pushed against his chest. "Please don't do this, please bring her back." She begged desperately. "You'll scare her, please Adam."

His hold tightened and he began to kiss her along her neck. Sara stiffened, realising his intention to carry out his threat. "Please don't..." She pushed against him.

"Don't fight me. You belong to me! You will give me what I want. Otherwise, Arianna will end up being a distant memory to you." He grabbed her hair roughly, forcing her to keep still as he pressed his mouth to hers.

Oh Lord Jesus, please help me. Please, in the name of Jesus, help me!

Terrified, tears came to her eyes, as realisation dawned that he could rape her. He forcibly pushed her toward the sofa and she began to pray in tongues in her mind, pleading with God in her spirit to help her and to stop this.

The doorbell rang and he froze, still holding her tightly. "Let me go and see who it is." She pushed against his chest.

"No. Don't answer it."

The doorbell sounded again.

"They can see my car on the drive—they won't go away. Please let me answer the door," she pleaded. She needed to get away from him. If she could escape and lock herself in her room, she would be safe. But what about Arianna? She had to go to her. She had no choice but to ensure Arianna was safe. Her heart constricted, knowing she needed to keep Arianna safe from this evil man.

Resigned, she realised she had to do what he told her and pray that God would have mercy upon her.

Have faith, Sara, she told herself. God would not forsake her. He sent someone to the door and she would use that to her advantage. "Let me answer the door, and I'll tell whoever it is to leave. Please, Adam."

He narrowed his eyes at her. "Don't do anything foolish," he warned.

"I won't. You have Arianna." She held his gaze and he released her reluctantly.

Lord, please help me.

"I'm here, Sara. Have faith."

She held on to the Holy Spirit's words as she shakily opened the door. Relief filled her at the sight of Daniel at the threshold.

"Daniel... Hi." She tried not to let her voice sound desperate.

"I thought we could go and collect Arianna together today. My meeting got cancelled," Daniel said with a smile. He'd missed her and Arianna, and he wanted them back home with him. He'd gotten used to them waiting for him when he got home. He couldn't bear to live apart from Sara anymore. For the first time in a long time, he wanted to share a life with a woman—commitment, marriage. With Sara, it was what he wanted. He needed her.

It was with that thought he'd gone out that morning, and bought her a ring that was currently burning a hole in his pocket. He was nervous, his old wounds resurfacing. What if she said no...

Daniel looked at her. There was no smile in response and there was something in her eyes...

"There's no need today. Arianna's already been picked up from school." Sara looked at Daniel. She only needed to take a few steps and she would be in his arms. He would protect her.

But thoughts of Arianna held her at bay. She knew she could not ignore Adam's threat. He would have her tied up in court for years and she did not have the money to fight a legal battle with him. She would never see Arianna again.

"Are you okay?" Daniel could sense something was wrong. Was she angry with him?

Sara held his gaze. *No, I'm not—please help me, Daniel.*

Before she could mouth the words, Adam came to stand beside her. He slipped his arm around her waist. She stiffened, feeling cold at his touch.

"Sara is perfectly fine. It's Daniel, isn't it? Sara and I have decided to remarry, therefore, you no longer need to come and see Arianna anymore," Adam informed Daniel, a smug look on his face.

Daniel stared back in disbelief, his eyes drifting to the way Adam possessively slipped his arm around Sara's waist, pulling her against him.

Daniel looked at Sara, trying to understand what was going on. She didn't pull away from Adam, and he couldn't read the look in her eyes. Anger filled him to the core.

"Sara?"

She said nothing in response and looked away.

In that moment, he felt as if someone had ripped his heart out—*Sara had.*

Crushed—and very much defeated, Daniel said nothing more. He turned on his heel and made his way back to his car. With the sound of the door closing behind him came finality.

It was over between him and Sara. She'd made a fool of him. *And he'd let her…* All the signs were there; he should never have got involved.

Rage filling him, he got in his car. *"Sara and I have decided to remarry…"* Adam's words kept replaying in his mind. *Remarry?* Sara told him she loved *him*. And he believed her!

She was no different from all the other women he encountered in his life—deceptive, calculating and could not be trusted. Why did he think she would be any different…?

He needed to smash something—*anything*—to keep from going back to the house and beating Adam to a pulp. And *he* was going to ask her to marry him; he was such a fool. What made him think that marriage could ever be the way forward in any situation? He would never make that mistake again.

Through his rage, he heard a voice. A small, still voice that he'd sought comfort from recently—a voice that he no longer wanted to listen to.

"Daniel."

I listened to you, Lord, I listened to you. Sara never loved me. She was using me and you knew it! Why would you allow this to happen?

"Daniel." Holy Spirit's voice was insistent. *"Listen to me."*

Daniel did not want to listen. He'd listened to the Holy Spirit, who told him that marrying Sara was the right thing, and he believed Him.

Sara knew how he felt, when all the while she was doing the same thing to him that Amy had done. Playing him against another man, to see what she could get. Well, she got him to agree to buy her house outright, didn't she? Was this all a ploy to get her husband back?

Humiliation hit him like a wave. Feeling like a fool, Daniel pushed the key fob to his car, needing desperately to get away. But nothing happened. He tried again—nothing.

What was wrong with the car? There couldn't possibly be anything wrong; it was barely a year old.

His phone rang beside him; the familiar ring tone filled the car.

Daniel answered. *"What is it David?"* he barked, knowing his brother would say something he felt would be insightful, but not what Daniel would want to hear.

"Sara needs you, Daniel. Whatever has made you angry is not the reality. You need to listen to what God is trying to tell you."

"Well, that is some speech, brother, but Sara doesn't need me. She's remarrying her ex-husband. I've been a fool again!"

David was silent for a moment, then said, "That doesn't sound right. Sara has always said she would never go back to her ex and you told me just last week what he did to her. Something's not right, Daniel. What is your spirit telling you? You're allowing your mind and your emotions to take over, what has God been trying to show you? Your inner man—your spirit—is what you should be listening to. You're being deceived, Daniel."

"Yes! *By Sara!* She's just like Amy! And I was a fool not to see her for what she was!"

"Daniel! Will you listen! God is trying to tell you something, wait...I need to tell you...listen." He paused for a moment. "Sara needs your help, Daniel. She's frightened, and I will not let you leave until you see clearly. Pray, Daniel, and I will instruct you..."

After he disconnected his brother's call, Daniel waited as he was instructed. He had no choice; his car would not start, which he realised had to be God's divine intervention. God did not want him to leave.

He prayed in tongues, not fully understanding what was happening. He felt his anger leave, but he still had a feeling of trepidation within him. *What's wrong, Lord? Why is Sara frightened?*

"Continue to pray, Daniel."

He began to worry, remembering the words he overheard Adam use to threaten Sara. If Adam hurt her, he'd tear him apart.

None the wiser as to what was going on, Daniel continued to pray in tongues, trying not to think about what was now becoming so glaringly obvious. Apprehension hit the pit of his stomach like lead, as realisation dawned that she could be in danger.

Then, just as he decided to go back and face Adam, he looked up and saw Sara leaving the house, carrying a suitcase. Adam followed behind also carrying a suitcase; he put both in the boot of his car.

Unable to find a space near to Sara's home, Daniel had parked down the street. He could still see them clearly, without them knowing he was there.

She's moving back with him. Daniel felt his anger rise again.

Then he heard the Holy Spirit's voice within. *"Things are not as they seem, Daniel. Pray."*

Daniel took in a breath and did as he was told, taking note of Sara's clothes. She was wearing jeans. He'd never seen her in jeans, wearing flat shoes with her hair tied in a bun. That was odd; Sara never dressed that way. He couldn't see her expression from where he was parked, but she got into Adam's car willingly. She did not look frightened.

"Follow, Daniel," Holy Spirit told him.

Miraculously, the engine roared to life, as if he hadn't been trying for the last half an hour to get the car to start. Daniel did as he was told and swung the car into action, following behind them realising for the first time that this was serious, and that things might not be as they were being portrayed.

A picture flashed before him of the way Adam had manhandled Sara and the bruises on her body. It crossed his mind to call the police, but he needed to be sure first. She'd gone with Adam willingly, and he had to be careful.

His mind in turmoil, he kept three cars away but continued to pray in tongues. He hoped for Adam's sake this wasn't what was becoming increasingly evident, as he would not be responsible for his actions.

Chapter 12

Frightened, Sara continued to pray in tongues, but she had faith that God would help her. She tried to push away thoughts of the many instances she'd heard in the news about domestic violence—stories of ex-partners who suddenly went crazy and took the lives of their wives and children. God would not let that happen to her; she still had too much to do on this earth. This was not her time, she told herself; God would protect her from this evil.

Without a doubt, evil was indeed what this was; she could feel it within Adam. It was unleashed.

She glanced over at Adam and did not recognise him. There was an edge to him; he held the steering wheel tightly, focused on the road, but she refused to look at him directly. She didn't like what she saw in his eyes, and she was afraid he might hurt her again.

She stared out the window, thinking about her baby, hoping Arianna was safe and that Adam had not harmed her in any way. *Lord, please protect Arianna, send your angels to look after her, please…*

"All is well, Sara. Be not concerned, I am with you. Do not fear, my word is always true. Hold firm to that. I will not forsake you."

Her fear eased slightly, as her mind began thinking of ways she could get out of this situation. She knew she couldn't do anything until she got to Arianna. She prayed that going with Adam to his home would not seal her fate as the mansion was gated—security sealed. Once inside, it was difficult to get out.

She hoped he hadn't changed the security code.

She'd dressed appropriately in jeans and flat shoes, her hair in a tight bun. She'd read once that you should never wear your hair loose or in a ponytail when in a compromising situation, as it provided an easy grip for an attacker. She'd been on the receiving end of that when Adam had grabbed her hair back at the house. Her clothes were not easy to remove, as she had no intention of sleeping with him tonight.

Her thoughts returned to her near-escape at the house after Daniel had left.

As Daniel walked away, Adam slammed the door shut and grabbed her tightly by the arms. "You've been sleeping with him, haven't you?" Adam demanded. He shook her when she did not respond straight away. "Tell me the truth!"

"N-no, I haven't. Adam, you're hurting me!"

"You belong to me, do you understand?" He grabbed her hair, forcing her to look at him. "Do you understand?"

Tears came to her eyes as he pressed his mouth hard against hers. Instinctively, she tried to push against him and turned her face away. He held her still, his fingers digging tightly into her flesh, and his other hand pulled hard on her hair, causing her to yelp with pain.

He released her. "Get upstairs, Sara. I want you now."

Her heart pounded hard in her chest, fear gripping her. *Lord, please help me!* Her mind racing, wishing she'd said something when Daniel had come to the door. But she was too afraid of losing Arianna, and now it was too late, Daniel was gone. She'd seen the hurt and anger in his eyes. She would never see him again—he was lost to her.

Her heart was filled with pain. She ached for Daniel and she also ached for Arianna. Whatever happened, she needed to ensure that Arianna was safe.

"No, Adam, not here. I will do as you have asked. I will go home with you, but I need to pack some clothes for Arianna and a few things for me. Let me do that." She kept her voice calm and measured, hoping to keep him at bay, even though her heart hammered so hard now she could hear it.

He assessed her for a moment. "Don't do anything stupid. Give me your phone."

She walked over to the sofa and handed him her mobile. "I won't. You have Arianna. I need to see that she is safe."

"Fine. I'll wait. Prepare yourself, Sara, you will be sleeping in my bed tonight." His words sent a cold shiver up her spine, and she tried desperately to swallow her fear.

She quickly changed her clothes and threw some items into suitcases. When she stepped outside, she gave a quick scan of the cars and noticed Daniel's DB9 still parked on the road. Was he still there? Why hadn't he left?

Not wanting to alert Adam, she didn't look in that direction for too long to see if Daniel was still in the car. She hoped he was.

When Adam got in and pulled off, she kept her eyes focused on the wing mirror, trying to see if Daniel was following, but he wasn't, why would he? Adam had told him that they would remarry, and she was afraid of what Daniel must think of her now. It all seemed bleak, but she knew her God would never fail her. He had said all is well, so she had to have faith and hold on to that; be thankful that he loved her and that he always took care of her.

She was reminded of her dream, where God had shown her of an attack and realised it was a warning of this moment. In the dream she sang and the spider disappeared; she knew then what she needed to do.

She began to sing in praise to God, which brought tears to her eyes, but she blinked them back so Adam would not see. Adam looked over at her, but did not say anything at first. She continued, feeling God's presence fill the car.

She could feel Adam become agitated as he always did when they were married and she used to sing.

"Do you have to do that?"

She ignored him and continued singing. She would not stop; whatever happened, she would give praise and thanksgiving—in all things, give thanks.

"Will you stop."

She paused and looked at him then, knowing God's presence was affecting him. "I won't ever stop singing to our Lord, no matter how you feel about it."

"And it's exactly that attitude that ended our marriage," he responded harshly, his hands tightening on the steering wheel.

She averted her eyes from his gaze, but did not respond to his accusation. What was the point? Maybe if she hadn't been so weak and responded to the unreasonable stance he imposed so often throughout their marriage, then she wouldn't be in this position now.

When the traffic lights changed and they turned left, that's when she saw it—*Daniel's car!*—following three cars behind.

Her heart leapt. *God had a plan!* All *was* well; she needed to have faith and be smart. She glanced periodically at the wing mirror, to make sure Daniel was following as they drove, praying Adam wouldn't notice.

When they finally arrived, she looked up at the mansion that had been her home for ten years. A huge, imposing estate, far too large for Adam on his own, so he filled his rooms with antiques. It had become more like a museum than a home.

She'd loved this place once, but the novelty of it waned after a while. It was so vast and she was always on her own. Adam travelled for weeks, sometimes months, at a time. The only thing that kept her sane was her marketing work. Organising women's lunches, charity events, and business dinners, in the end, felt meaningless to her and she wanted more out of life.

Adam retrieved the remote that he kept in his sun-visor.

She watched as he punched in the code and noted it was the same code she remembered; he hadn't changed it. The gates opened and her mind spun frantically. *How am I going to get the remote and open the gates for Daniel?*

She glanced out the window as they drove up the long driveway, which was devoid of any greenery. She always felt it was in disparity to the back where the gardens were endless.

Adam pulled up and parked, just as his mobile rang. He answered, and she could tell he was speaking with a client.

Sara watched him as he walked around to the boot and took the opportunity that presented itself, grabbing the remote from the sun-visor. She kept an eye on Adam to ensure he could not see her, and quickly punched in the code for the gates to open.

She hoped the gates were far enough away that Adam would not hear or see them open.

*   *   *

Great.

Daniel looked up, exasperated. He hadn't expected a gated mansion. He pulled up and parked outside. He doubted he could climb over the walls.

What now, Lord?

"Have faith, Daniel."

No sooner had the Holy Spirit said the words, the gates opened again, as if just for him. He frowned for a moment, not believing it had opened, then swerved the car in. He stopped at the end of the long driveway, not wanting to be seen. Then he reconsidered; he was not some cowering fool. He could take Adam on—it wasn't even a consideration.

He continued along the drive and pulled up beside Adam's black BMWi8, noting the private plate—4DAM—it made Adam easy to find, if necessary.

As Daniel stepped out of his car, and scanned the estate, he tried to push the thought from his mind that he could be making an error; that Sara was indeed planning to remarry Adam and he was making a dreadful mistake.

*   *   *

"Where's Arianna?" Sara asked as she followed Adam inside, her only thoughts on her child.

"She's upstairs."

"Arianna! Arianna! It's Mummy, come here!" she called; she needed to see her baby.

"Mummy!" She looked up as Arianna shouted down from the top of the curved staircase. Sara waited as Arianna ran down the long flight of stairs and straight into Sara's arms. Relief filled Sara, and tears came to her eyes as she stooped and hugged Arianna tightly.

"Are you okay, baby?" Sara cupped Arianna's face, and kissed her.

"Why are you crying, Mummy?"

Not wanting to alarm Arianna, she stood, picking her up and holding her close. "Because I missed you so much."

"I would not have hurt her, she's my daughter," Adam remarked, a look of annoyance crossing his features.

Mrs Krycher made her way downstairs. "Hello, Mrs Mason."

Sara held back the urge to say, *Ms Mason*. She was no longer Adam's wife, which he apparently failed to grasp.

"Hello, Mrs Krycher," she responded, but the housekeeper had already looked away, turning to Adam.

"Did you want me to do anything, Mr Mason?"

"Yes, we'll eat in the dining room this evening."

Sara placed Arianna at her feet, holding her hand. Sara tried to catch Mrs Krycher's eyes, but she kept them averted, refusing to look at Sara. She was dressed in the gray uniform that Adam insisted his staff wear—a portly woman with greying dark hair. She suspected that Adam had given her strict instructions.

She'd always found Mrs Krycher to be a pleasant woman, with a caring, motherly nature that had appealed to her, and who had always been supportive to Sara. Mrs Krycher had expressed her regret when she'd divorced Adam and had always been good with Arianna, but she understood her boundaries and her loyalties were always with Adam—he was her employer, after all.

"Adam, we're not staying."

"You agreed to stay."

"Well, I've changed my mind."

His eyes narrowed in anger. "Let's go and talk in private."

"No, I'll be leaving now. I won't be staying for dinner."

"What are you going to do? Walk?" he asked her mockingly.

She remembered he had her mobile; she couldn't even call a taxi. She hoped Daniel had made it in through the gates—otherwise, she was stuck. "If I have to, I will."

She made her way to the door. Adam blocked her path, grabbing her arm. He leaned in, close to her ear so only she could hear. "You're being foolish. Don't test me, Sara. *Get upstairs!*"

She broke away from him, heading for the door, but he grabbed her again, holding her in a firm grip. "Let me go!" she hissed in a quiet voice, not wanting to alarm Arianna.

"You're not going anywhere! I told you what I wanted."

Sara struggled against him, but his hold was too strong.

"Mr Mason, was there anything else that you needed from me?" Mrs Krycher's voice sounded wary, and she looked alarmed as she witnessed the scuffle between them.

"Yes, take Arianna and get her ready for bed."

"No! Arianna stays with me!" Sara exclaimed. She pushed him, hard, and somehow managed to break free. Tightening her hold on Arianna, she headed for the door once again, pulling it open.

"If you walk out of that door, I'll cut you off and file for full custody of Arianna."

"I'll see you in court," she replied defiantly, hastily making her way out and colliding into a solid chest.

"Oh, Daniel!" She flung her arms around his neck and hugged him fiercely, tears coming to her eyes. She looked at him, touching his face. "I was so scared...he took Arianna...I'm not going to marry him."

Daniel pulled her close, relieved he'd got it wrong, that she still wanted him. It meant he had to finish what Adam had started, once and for all, and this time he would not hesitate.

"If you have any sense, you will."

Sara broke apart from Daniel at the sound of Adam's menacing voice. Instinctively she drew Arianna close to her, in case they needed to run.

"You will not be taking Arianna. I am her father and she stays with me."

A flash of Daniel's dream came forth in his mind; of Adam taking Arianna down the path. He would not let that happen. It was what God had warned him.

Adam moved as if to grab Arianna.

Daniel blocked him. "No, she won't be staying here. Her place is with her mother."

"And who do you think you are? You're trespassing on my property, and you have no right to be anywhere near my daughter or my wife!"

"Sara, go to my car, and take Arianna," Daniel said. He threw her his keys, not taking his eyes off Adam, still blocking him.

"Get out of my way!" Adam shouted angrily, shoving Daniel hard.

Daniel grabbed his arm, pushing Adam against the wall.

Worried that the two men would come to blows, Sara didn't need to be told twice and headed to the car with Arianna. Daniel and Adam were both big, physically fit men and she didn't know who would be the victor in an actual fist fight.

Reaching Daniel's car, she helped Arianna into the back and Sara climbed in the driver's side, in case she needed to get away quickly.

"Mummy, why was Daddy shouting at Uncle Daniel?"

Sara reached over and caressed her cheek, wanting to calm her. "Well, they both love you and want what is best for you. But your daddy needs to understand that you should stay with me." She chatted to Arianna for a while about the sky and the birds in the trees, anything to keep her mind off the unpleasant scenes she'd witnessed.

Sara began to grow apprehensive. Daniel had been inside the house for some time. *What is taking so long?* She prayed that God would keep Daniel safe.

Then she saw something out of her peripheral vision and turned, seeing Daniel approaching the car looking no worse for wear. Relief and pride filled her. She slid over to the passenger side, allowing him to get in the car.

"Did he hurt you?" Daniel asked, looking over at her as concern crossed his features. "So help me, God, I'll go back in there and finish what I started."

"I'm fine, we're both fine." She paused, unease filling her. "What did you do to him?"

"Nothing he didn't deserve," Daniel stated angrily. "He won't touch you again."

Sara couldn't help the smile that came to her lips. She touched his arm, wanting to calm him. "Thank you for coming to my rescue..." She reached up and caressed his face, looking into the depth of his green eyes and she kissed him, a tender kiss which spoke of love and future promises.

"...and not damaging this beautiful face."

*   *   *

Not wanting to go back to her house for fear that Adam would turn up again, Sara gratefully agreed to spend the next few days with Daniel at his home. As before, it was glorious; she felt at home with him and she felt safe. It was where she wanted to be.

She said a prayer, hoping Daniel would change his mind about marriage—that some part of him would change his mind about them. He'd rescued her, and brought her here to be with him and he'd virtually implied they would be married…hadn't he? Or was she reading more into things than was there?

She'd seen the look on Daniel's face when Adam had told him they would remarry. He'd been hurt and angry; he believed Adam, which was understandable after his past experiences with women. Daniel found it difficult to trust and his distrust was something that was deep-rooted.

So what made him change his mind?

She knew it had to be God. He had been with her every step of the way. Tears came to her eyes as she thought back at how differently things could have turned out and she was so thankful to Him for saving her. He sent Daniel to help her and Daniel had been obedient, going against what she suspected he instinctively wanted to do, which was to never see her again, if the situation which had presented itself was to be believed.

She looked out through the open sliding glass doors at Arianna, happily playing in the gardens. Her heart ached as she remembered the turmoil she'd felt at nearly losing Arianna. There was no way she would allow Adam to take Arianna away from her. She would fight him with her last breath.

She pushed her unpleasant thoughts from her mind and thought about Daniel instead. How much he cared for Arianna, and she wanted more than anything for him to be a father to her.

She recalled the events of the day before.

Sara looked out the window on the drive; Daniel was washing his two cars, his Jaguar F-Type and his Aston Martin. She watched as he lovingly handled the cars with care, preferring to do this rather than asking his staff, as he didn't trust anyone near his cars. Yet he happily allowed Arianna to "help" him, which was an exaggeration, as she was playing in the water rather than actually washing the cars. Sara walked out to them.

Daniel loved his cars, and she teased him, asking if he named them.

"Yes."

"You're joking?"

"Nope."

She grinned. "Okay, what are they called?"

"Sara One and Sara Two."

She dipped her hand in the bucket and splashed him. "I don't know whether I should be offended or take that as a compliment."

He flinched as the water hit his face and laughed. "Definitely a compliment. I love my cars, I ensure they receive the customary premium valet, and I regularly maintain and service them. I take them out, and no one else is allowed to drive or take ownership of my cars."

"Mmmm, so I interpret that to mean that you love me, you will take care of me and take me out, but no other man is allowed to come near?"

"You would be correct in your assessment." He grabbed her, pulling her close. "I won't ever let another man have what is mine…"

"Oh yeah…?" She raised her eyebrows questioningly.

"Yeah…get used to it…."

And before she could turn away, he dowsed her face with the huge orange sponge. She screamed, and then burst into giggles. They then proceeded to have a water fight, which Arianna loved, amid laughter and screeches from them both as Daniel chased them.

She smiled as she remembered. She loved the way he included Arianna in everything. Since they had been staying with him, he'd got Arianna involved in his work, showing her ad campaigns and asking her opinion. Arianna's little face would light up; he made her feel important. He even gave her an official title as his ad campaign consultant and had regular meetings with her. Daniel loved Arianna and treated her as if she were his own daughter, and she loved him for it.

It was Saturday morning. She didn't have any plans other than opening the official letter that Daniel had presented to her after he'd picked up her mail from her house. She couldn't put it off any longer.

With trembling fingers, she tore through the envelope, knowing Adam had indeed gone ahead with his threat of taking her to court.

Daniel entered the room. He'd just taken a shower after his morning workout and had even gotten a few hours work in early at dawn. Although he was content that Sara was staying with him, he now found he couldn't sleep when she was here, his needs overwhelmed him. He craved her like no other woman he'd ever known. Frustrated, he'd finally given up on sleep, spent some time in prayer, and eventually gone into the office. He'd passed by Sara's house on the way back to pick up her post; no doubt the large white envelope was from Adam's solicitor.

She was seated at the kitchen table. Tears were in her eyes and a distraught expression on her face.

"What's wrong, Sara?"

Sara looked at him. "Adam's taking me to court...he's applying for full custody of Arianna." Her tears spilled over. "It's a letter from his solicitor. Adam said he won't do it on one condition—if I agree to marry him again. I have until Wednesday to make a decision. If I don't do as he asks, he'll tie me up in court and he'll use my relationship with you against me."

She felt fear fill her heart, realising in that moment that she could lose Arianna. She didn't have the money to fight Adam in court and she was sharing the home of a man to whom she was not married. It would not look good to a judge.

She began to fret. She had to go home. *But what if Adam turned up again?* She brushed absently at her tears and stood on shaky legs.

"What are you doing? Where are you going? What decision?" Daniel rushed over to her, pulling her into his arms. "There's no decision to make, Sara. You're not going back to him, are you?"

"I don't know what to do..." She looked at him, her eyes bleak. "I can't stay here, he'll use it against me."

"I don't want you going back to that house. He could turn up again."

"Then what am I supposed to do? I can't stay at my mother's— she wants me to get back with Adam. My sister is going through a situation of her own. And I don't want to burden Rachel and David with this, they've only just gotten married."

As her thoughts raced through her head, she thought of Bradley; maybe he could help.

She pulled away from Daniel's embrace. She was trying hard to be strong, but she wasn't sure she had it in her to fight anymore. She wanted to be married again—she hated being on her own and she desperately wanted another child. Maybe her fate was sealed, maybe her mother was right—she shouldn't have divorced Adam. She had broken God's law which said she should not get divorced unless there was adultery, and she couldn't prove that Adam had, in fact, committed the act.

What options did she have? She couldn't lose Arianna. Adam was wealthy and powerful; she would no doubt lose the court battle, before she even began. And for Arianna's sake, maybe she needed to do what was right.

Her heart filled with dread. She forced herself to move farther away from the wonderful shelter of Daniel's arms, wishing with all her heart that things could be different between them. She realised if she made this decision, she would never see Daniel again.

Daniel didn't like the look he saw in her eyes and panicked, suddenly feeling helpless. He didn't want her to leave.

What should I do, Lord?

"Help her, Daniel."

How?

"You know how. It is what I have been showing you. Daniel, it is time."

Daniel closed his eyes for a moment, finally acknowledging what he'd been desperately trying to suppress. He loved Sara and there was no way he was going to let her walk out of his life.

He gently pulled her toward him again, enveloping her in his arms. "Will you marry me? Be my wife and have those beautiful twin girls I told you about?"

Tears filled her eyes again, but this time they were tears of joy. "Oh Daniel... *Yes,* I love you."

"I want a life with you, Sara. I want to commit to you, commit to our love for a lifetime. That way he can't ever hurt you again."

Chapter 13

"We're choosing the cake this afternoon. Your mother is scary. She had the caterers whipped into shape, wedding planner all frazzled, she even had Pastor Simon wrapped around her little finger." Sara laughed, a happy sound that warmed Daniel's heart. "She's quite a lady."

Daniel chuckled. "That she is."

"How long are you going to be away?" Sara asked.

Her voice sounded sad, with a longing that pulled at him, as he felt exactly the same way. He didn't want to leave her. "A week, maybe two. I'm not quite sure." Daniel distractedly scanned the crowded airport as he waited in the queue to check in.

"I'm going to miss you, Daniel."

"I miss you already, Sara, but I have to go. I'll call you when I get to the hotel." He stepped away from the queue and waited until a couple pulling their luggage behind them walked by him and were out of earshot. "I love you, Sara."

"I love you, too, Daniel. Safe journey, my love."

He disconnected, concern filling him over the situation with Adam. He'd given David strict instructions to keep an eye on things while he was away. He'd fly to the ends of the earth and seriously do some damage if Adam hurt Sara again.

He loved Sara, and had become overprotective these last few weeks. He said a silent prayer of protection over Sara and Arianna, and he realized there was no point in trying to rationalise his feelings. All he knew was that he wanted to marry Sara before it all went wrong.

He'd been here before, engaged to be married, and it was taken from him. He couldn't cope if it happened again.

They were in the middle of their wedding plans, but he couldn't tell her the real reason for his unexpected trip to Miami. It had come at the worst possible time and he hated to think what Sara's reaction was going to be when he explained what he'd discovered. It changed everything.

His mind returned to the week before, and the tension and unease that hadn't left. In fact he felt sick about it and wondered if God was playing a cruel trick on him. *Why now, Lord?*

Silence.

He sighed, returning to his thoughts.

"You have two interviews," Barbara began, handing him the recruitment packs. "One at three o'clock, the other at four."

"And the reason I'm doing this is because…"

"You're a wonderful employer and are filling in because I have an emergency at home, Shannon and Jane are on leave, and Paul called in sick this morning." Barbara smiled sweetly. "Everything is prepared for you, the questions and details are in the pack. I've booked room five-o-one."

"Fine, I hope your daughter is okay." Barbara was a good worker and when she'd called to say that her daughter had taken a fall and broken an ankle, he agreed to interview the last two candidates for their recent recruitment campaign for junior level staff in admin.

He made his way down to the fifth floor, squeezing into the packed lift, and ending up next to Bernice. He groaned inwardly.

"How are you, Daniel?" Bernice asked, her eyes lighting up and a smile forming on her lips.

"I'm good, Bernice, how are you?" He glanced at her, then looked up at the display counting down the floors.

Bernice was in her late fifties and managed his events team. She was looking for a toy boy, and that toy boy certainly wasn't going to be him, no matter how many times she tried to corner him.

She shifted closer to him. "You cancelled our meeting last week." She made an attempt to pout.

On a fifty-something-year-old woman, pouting did not flatter her features. She had short spiky hair with red and blonde highlights, and her skin was leathered from too much sun. Huge breasts and a matching behind, she was hardly his type and he'd been avoiding her like the plague. Her eyes drifted over him—he felt like a piece of meat.

"I'll be here until late tonight. Why don't you stop by...?" she said, touching his arm suggestively.

When is this woman going to get the message? He heard a snigger from behind him—Mark from finance. Daniel narrowed his eyes, giving Mark a pointed look.

Mark averted his gaze, pretending to check the floor they were on. Mark had had his run-ins with Bernice himself, which was probably why he found this so amusing. *The woman is a predator.*

The lift opened on the fifth floor, as he stepped off with Mark, he promised to email Bernice.

"You know she wants you."

Daniel smiled. "Yeah, she wants you too. I could take a bet that she'll have you in her hooks very soon."

"You've got to be joking. I'll leave her to you, who am I to stand in the way of true love!" Mark grinned, making kissing noises as he headed to his office.

Daniel laughed, shaking his head. He made his way in the opposite direction and scanned the reception area for the candidates.

Both were already there, waiting for him; a man, who looked the part in a suit. The other, a young woman that for some reason, his senses seemed to become alert at her presence. He gave her a second look. There was something about her....it pulled at him and seemed oddly familiar.

She was looking down, leafing through a magazine, her long legs crossed. She was dressed in a grey tailored suit—attractive, her shoulder length dark hair sweeping across her face, obscured his vision so he couldn't quite see her whole face.

He entered the room already set up for the interview. Two folders were placed on the table, along with a bottle of water and three glasses.

He took a seat, leafing through the pack. Her name was Daniella Anderson. *Good name,* he thought, chuckling. A female version of himself.

He looked at her credentials. Her CV was sparse, listing her current job in retail, and before that, four years admin in a property management company, and she was....*sixteen?* She was far too young and couldn't possibly have the experience; she would have had to have started work when she was twelve.

Barbara was slacking; why she'd agreed to interview her was beyond him. Sixteen-year-olds should be at home studying. He looked at his watch, Two-fifty-six, this shouldn't take too long. At least he'd be able to get back to the pile of work he had on his desk sooner than anticipated.

He buzzed through to the receptionist asking her to send in the first candidate.

She entered after knocking, and he stood to greet her, but was taken aback, totally astounded. *She was beautiful, and...*

She stared back at him. Her features reminded him of someone; the lips, the nose, the arch of her brow and her *green eyes...*

"Hello, I was told I was being interviewed by Barbara Hemple."

Daniel was flabbergasted. "There was a change at the last minute," he heard himself say. He stared at her for a moment and she stared back at him, seeming to make her own assessment of him. Then he realised he hadn't told her she could sit. "Take a seat," he said, gesturing with his hand. He noted she had an American accent. "I'm Daniel Anderson."

He took a seat himself and with trembling fingers, he leafed through her application again. *She was sixteen...* He looked at her date of birth, and his heart began to pound.

"I know. Before you start, I wanted to point out that I have four years of experience in business administration. I was employed by my mother."

"And the company is?"

"AMDC Property Management."

"So, you're saying you started your career at the age of twelve?"

"Yes," she replied with a chuckle. "My mother was a hard taskmaster. When she started the company, she couldn't afford to employ staff so my sister and I were her employees for a while." She smiled. "I can tell you anything you want to know about the property business. Current market trends, house prices, potential profits..."

She had a sister? His heart lurched. "Do you have a reference from your mother?"

"I included it in my application, but I have another copy—" she rummaged into her handbag and stood, handing it to him, "—here. My mother's name is Amy Carling."

The words slammed into his chest. He stared back at the young woman; it was clearly obvious from the moment she walked into the room she was his daughter. After the initial shock, he became numb.

Daniella—clearly named after him—watched him for a moment. He didn't know what to say.

"My mother doesn't know anything about this. She doesn't know I applied for a position in your company. I haven't told her. I wanted to meet you."

"You know who I am?"

"Yes, she named me after you. My sister—Maya—she has your name, too. Maya Danielle. Mum said it means *God is my judge*. Would you say that was right?"

Maya... Daniel stared back at his daughter. For the first time in his life, he was dumbfounded. *Amy...?* He swallowed; his mouth had gone dry, his throat tightening. He reached for the water and poured some into a glass. He took a long sip.

"Did God judge her because of what happened between you?"

He didn't know the answer to that, he didn't know what to think. Daniel frowned. "Where is your mother?"

"We live in Florida, but I'm staying with my grandparents on holiday."

"Is your sister here?"

"No, I wanted to do this on my own." She paused, staring at him again. "I look like you...."

He held her gaze for a long moment, and then looked away, not knowing what to say. It all came flooding back, the feelings he'd suppressed over the years. He remembered the last time he'd seen Amy, nearly seventeen years ago.

It was a day he would never forget.

When Daniel arrived, he suspected she sensed something was wrong, as she was hesitant with him. She was usually exuberant at seeing him.

After the surprise visit he received from Charlie—her husband, Daniel was thankful she kept her distance. He was so angry he couldn't think straight.

It was a warm day, yet she was dressed in a long sleeved top and jeans, which wasn't her usual attire. But he didn't dwell on it. He wanted her out.

He *threw down his keys and mobile on the table at the door. His briefcase went next.*

Amy looked at him cautiously. "Hi baby," *she began tentatively.* "I cooked dinner, your favourite..."

She went to hug him as she always did, but he stiffened and stepped away. "I want you out."

Her eyes flew to his; he could see the shock, then the realisation cross her face. She backed away. "What?" *she whispered.*

Daniel was still, anger and pain, choking him. "I want you out," *he said again, emphasising every word,* "and I don't ever want to see you again."

Amy stared at him, and he watched as the reality of the situation hit her. "What's wrong, Daniel?"

"You're married! How dare you come into my home—meet my family—under this pretence to con me out of money!" *Daniel didn't know what to expect when he confronted her, but he could see the guilt written on her face. He fought with everything within him not to break down and cry. His heart was broken.*

Amy shook her head, backing away from him even further, hitting the kitchen counter. "I'm sorry, I never intended to con you, please let me explain—"

"I don't wish to hear any more of your lies! Take your things and get out!" *Daniel shouted. His chest was tight, and he felt as if Amy had literally ripped his heart apart. Did she really think he would allow her to continue to lie to him?*

He looked at her, the woman he loved. Not only did he feel pain and hurt—so excruciating he wasn't sure he could survive it. Anger and disappointment at the loss of the babies he thought were his. But he still felt the love, the intense, all-consuming love that had overtaken him, made him into a fool. It had also caused him to lose all sense of judgement, and he vowed never to feel love for a woman like this ever again.

Tears came to Amy's eyes. Her hand rested, almost protectively—on her tummy. "What about our babies?" *Amy asked quietly.*

He gave a humourless laugh. "Our babies? You mean his, your husband's?" *His voice faltered then, tears coming to his eyes, the pain searing through him.* "Just leave."

Tears streamed down her face. "I'll go, but I want you to know, that I love you, Daniel, and I never meant to hurt you, I'm so sorry....but these babies are yours—"

"Don't insult my intelligence! At least your husband was honest, it is more than I can say about you."

She gave him one last look, and left the room to pack.

He left shortly afterward. He couldn't bear to stay in his apartment with her. Although he was angry, a part of him wanted to beg her to stay; a life without her would be unbearable. But he wasn't going to reduce himself to that level.

When he returned later that evening, after deliberating with himself for hours, his need for her outweighing all sense, he'd decided to ask her to stay.

But she was gone. His bedroom was devoid of her presence, leaving the two Moses baskets he'd bought for their babies—the babies he'd thought they'd made out of their love. The babies he'd wanted, and—most important—of which his father had been so proud.

She'd lied to him and he was crushed; it was a short-lived dream that had finally come to an end. His heart was broken.

He stood and went over to Daniella, emotions he could not name overtaking him.

She rose from her chair and opened her arms as he pulled her close. He didn't notice the tears that rolled down his cheeks as he held his daughter. His chest was tight with a release of emotions he'd suppressed for years.

Amy didn't lie to him. She'd told him the truth about his babies, but at the time he'd refused to listen. As a result, he'd missed out on sixteen years with his daughters.

He'd also missed out on a life with Amy.

He closed his eyes, feeling a weight ease away, replaced by a sharp pang of regret.

That was a week ago. Daniella told him where Amy would be; they lived in Fort Lauderdale, but Amy was working, attending a conference in Miami. He'd booked the next flight over there.

He couldn't bring himself to tell Sara; she was going through her own situation with her ex and he didn't want to add to her uncertainty and worry. Besides, she and his mother were both involved in wedding preparations and Sara seemed focused and happy. He didn't want to rock the boat.

So when he told David, he wasn't surprised by his twin's reaction of shock and disbelief.

"But you said that she was pregnant for her husband...?"

Daniel paced the length of David's office. Frustration, anger, fear, and guilt were only some of the emotions sweeping through him. "Yes, that was her husband's story and I was so angry at the time, when she tried to assure me that they were mine, I refused to listen." Daniel continued to pace, back and forth.

David stared at him. Daniel already knew what he was thinking as he attempted to defend his actions. "All I knew was that she'd lied to me. She was a married woman, why would I believe anything else that came from her lips?"

David still said nothing, raising a querying brow, his silent communication very clear.

"I don't know." Daniel stopped pacing and closed his eyes for a moment. When he opened them again, he felt tears sting his eyes and he ran a hand through his hair. "My feelings are all over the place. I just found out I have sixteen-year-old twin daughters, and I feel like someone just punched me in the gut. I don't know what I feel about Amy."

"And if you still love her, what then?"

Daniel sunk to the sofa in the room, his head in his hands. "I don't know..."

The tears came, totally overwhelmed by the situation. He tried to hold them back—tried to be strong enough and hold it in, but it was all too much. *Why, Lord? Why?*

He did not get a response to his plea, but David agreed when Daniel said that he had to go and see Amy. He needed to be sure how he felt.

When he arrived at the hotel where the conference was being held, he searched the crowd for her. Images flashed through his mind of her beautiful body and her long shapely legs, attributes that had enticed him from the very beginning. He didn't know what he was looking for; he didn't know what she looked like now—it had been years. Had she aged? Let herself go? Part of him wished that was the case—it would make things easier for him.

He scanned the crowd. Some were milling about in the foyer, others were in the conference room. People were talking in huddles, and others walking in and out. He searched everywhere he even focused his attention on the organisers on the stage delivering a presentation. Daniella had told him Amy was giving a presentation and was involved in the organisation of the conference. Maybe she wasn't here. Maybe Daniella was mistaken.

Just as the thought crossed his mind, he saw her.

She was standing at reception, her back to him. It was her stance, the way she stood at the counter; he instantly knew it was her. He knew every inch of her. Her hair, now worn long, with soft waves that fell to her shoulders.

She wore a formal black sleeveless pencil dress that had a splash of colour where it dipped in at the waist, emphasising her slim curves. Matching high-heeled sandals adorned her feet, and her heavenly legs—legs that had always captivated him—were exposed to mid-thigh. As always, they were bare, long and shapely. No one had legs like Amy. With her handbag on her shoulder and a briefcase she held in her hand, she appeared the consummate businesswoman. Although she looked professional, it did little to change his overall impression of Amy; she was a very desirable woman. Memories of her filtered through his mind, along with a rush of emotions.

He walked over to her, afraid this was a dream or that his eyes were playing tricks on him, that she was actually a mirage. "Amy?"

She turned. He saw the shock register on her face, but what struck him first was that she was still so beautiful. Then everything else hit him like a tonne of bricks—everything he'd ever felt came rushing back. He took in a breath at the magnitude of it all. The attraction, the need—the love—*everything*. His heart racing, he just stared at her, and she, in turn, stared back at him. *She's so beautiful...* At forty-one she looked amazing; the years had clearly been good to her.

Her hair had been short years ago. Now worn long, it gave her a softer appearance which made her look even more beautiful, if that was possible.

Unbidden, his mind flashed back to when they'd first met at the Dorchester Hotel in London. Her gorgeous, golden-brown legs had drawn his gaze, and in a striking red dress, he would never forget the day they'd met. They had spent the evening talking and getting to know each other. He remembered their first kiss, and the passionate night of lovemaking that followed. It had been love at first sight for him.

Her brown eyes took him in, then welled with tears. "Daniel?" Her hand came up and covered her heart. She seemed to be having difficulty breathing and she reached up and held on to the counter as if to steady herself. "I can't believe it's you..."

He didn't know what to say; he was totally blown away. He'd played this scene over and over in his mind, but he didn't expect this.

Their gazes locked, her eyes watery and bright, then she looked away as a man approached the reception counter.

Daniel hedged closer and reached out to touch her, but stopped himself, knowing that if he did that, he'd be lost. "Let's go and sit and talk for a while." He nodded toward the seating area.

Hesitant, she slowly raised her eyes to his again. She nodded and headed toward the comfy chairs.

Again, he went to touch the small of her back, but let his hand fall away. He was overwhelmed by the way he was feeling—he was drawn to her as he'd always been. It was as if they had never been apart, and he wanted to touch her and hold her. His mind was a fog; he was trying to think rationally, but he didn't feel rational. He didn't know what he felt, as a tailspin of emotions rocketed through him.

They both took a seat, Daniel's eyes lingering on her long legs for a moment. Her dress was just the right length that he was able to see a good portion of her thighs. When his gaze returned to hers, her tears had spilled over.

"I never thought I would ever see you again," she whispered, as her tears rolled down her cheeks. She brushed them away.

His heart clenched; he wanted to hold her, comfort her in some way. "Amy, I—"

She stood suddenly, picking up her briefcase and handbag. "I can't do this. Please..."

He stood, panicking. *Don't leave.* He took a step toward her, crowding her. "Amy, we need to talk."

She looked up at him. "I know," she said softly. She reached into her handbag and pulled out a card, handing it to him. "I can't talk here, I have to work. Call me later."

Her eyes begged him to understand and she waited for him to allow her to pass. He didn't move, wanting to pull her into his arms. He fought with everything within him not to reach out.

And even though she waited for him to move, her body leaned toward him as if she was going through a battle of her own not to touch him.

Her perfume hit his senses and images of intimate moments with her flashed through his mind; her beauty, her scent—her love. Lazy days spent together in bed, holding her, kissing her, making love.

His heart ached.

He finally allowed her to pass and she hurriedly walked away, heading for the ladies.

As he watched her walk away, he couldn't help but think about how much her eyes revealed her pain. He was reminded of her past and felt guilty for telling her to leave back then. He didn't look after her as he'd promised to do, never protected her.

The weight of that revelation hit him—he needed to do right by her and their children.

Along with the revelation that he was still in love with her.

Chapter 14

Daniel looked at his mobile as it rang for the third time, Sara's face flashing on the screen. It was a picture he'd taken one day when they were out at a park with Arianna. Sara was smiling, her hazel eyes bright, filled with amusement. Her beauty always astounded him, from the very first; much in the same way he felt about Amy, only different, and right now, he couldn't quantify it. He was confused and he wasn't ready to talk to Sara yet. He didn't know what to say to her, because he didn't understand himself.

He was restless and emotionally drained.

Throwing his mobile on the bed, he undressed and took a shower, allowing the hot, pulsating streams of water to hit his skin. He stood there for a long while, trying not to think about Amy and his daughters, but he couldn't get them out of his mind.

He still couldn't believe he was a father. When Amy told him about his daughters back then, he'd been ecstatic and excited at the prospect of two new lives they'd created. They were a part of him; he was going to be a dad. And when that didn't happen, he closed himself off; it hurt too much. There was an ache inside that never seemed to leave.

And now, knowing the years had gone by and he never had any input or say in his daughters' lives, never held them in his arms, never saw them grow up, wasn't there to see their first step or hear their first word, he was angry. Angry at Amy for keeping this from him, Angry at the situation—angry at himself. He could have had a life with Amy, a family.

How in the world had this happened? *How did I get this so wrong?*

He stepped out of the shower and dried off, dressing in trousers and a shirt while replaying moments with Amy over and over in his mind. But she was married at the time; he'd seen the guilt cross her face when he confronted her and she never denied it. She hadn't lied to him about the babies; she'd told him the truth in that regard.

So had her plan been to trap him? He thought about that for a moment, then shook his head. That didn't make sense. If her intention was to trap him, how could she do that if she was a married woman? He didn't understand it. Then he figured that her intention was to con money out of him. Twin daughters—his offspring were a goldmine to the Anderson fortune. But never once had she contacted him over the years, asking for money—so again, he was confused. He couldn't for the life of him understand what had happened.

He needed answers.

Why is this happening now, Lord? Why now? When I'm about to marry Sara?

"*You need to forgive, Daniel. For you to move forward with your life, you must forgive Amy.*"

"*Why didn't you tell me she had my babies?*

"*I sent you dreams, Daniel.*"

But I didn't understand what they meant. Why didn't you tell me?

"*I told you, Daniel. You chose not to listen. Your resentment and unforgiveness blocked anything I tried to tell you. It is time to forgive now, Daniel.*"

Daniel sighed, totally at a loss. He had to admit that he remembered the promptings from the Holy Spirit, the reminders. Little things that reminded him of how it had been with Amy—the love.

But over the years, any mention, any thought about Amy he would push to the back of his mind, refusing to think about her, but allowing the bitterness concerning what she'd done take over. So, if there was anyone to blame it was himself.

His heart and mind were in turmoil, and he didn't know what to do.

He went over to the window and looked out at the views on South Beach. The weather was hot and humid—typical Florida weather—and he thought maybe a walk along the beach would clear his head.

He wasn't surprised when his mobile rang beside him.

"Seriously, Daniel? I felt the anger, the resentment and the pain over the years, but love? You still love her?"

Trust David to pick up on my feelings.

"Yes, I still have feelings for her. I thought I'd dealt with it, but it all came flooding back when I saw her. I guess I must have suppressed what I felt and not addressed it."

If he'd addressed it as the Holy Spirit had prompted him over the years, he would have found her and would have discovered his daughters sooner, and he wouldn't be in this predicament now.

"Have you told Sara about your daughters?"

"No." *I'd been afraid to.*

"You have to be honest with her, Daniel."

"I know." *But what would I say?*

"It was because of Amy's dishonesty why you're in this situation, Daniel, remember that."

"Yes, I'm aware." It didn't change the situation that he didn't know what to say to Sara, and he was afraid he might lose her.

"What did Amy say?"

"We haven't really talked. I'm meeting her later."

David was silent for a moment. "Don't meet her alone."

"How else am I going to talk to her unless I meet with her alone?"

"Well, meet her in a public place then. You don't want to go and do something you'll regret later on."

"I think I can handle one meeting with her, David," Daniel responded, irritated at his brother's assumptions, even though he knew David was right. He'd met with her for all of fifteen minutes, and he'd been thinking and feeling things he shouldn't.

He disconnected with that thought in mind, then called Amy.

It was time to face the music.

* * *

Sara walked into the room slowly, music playing softly in the background. The white Cinderella wedding gown looked perfect on her, a fairy-tale dress, with a fitted bodice and full skirt. Sara spun around for effect, doing a twirl.

"What do you think?"

"Oh, Sara it's beautiful."

Sara put a hand on her hip. "You've said that for the last seven dresses I've tried on. That's not very helpful, Rachel."

Rachel laughed. "It's the truth. You do look beautiful, but if you decided to wear a dustbin bag as a wedding dress, you would still look beautiful."

Sara flopped down beside Rachel on the sofa. "I really don't like this one. It's too heavy, the material is too thick for the Caribbean, and I can't breathe—the corset is cutting off my circulation."

"But it's a Vera Wang, and it fits perfectly."

Sara looked over at her reflection in the floor-to-ceiling mirrors of the dressing room of a bridal boutique in London. They'd booked out the whole day, and had been there for hours. "I know."

"And we've been out all day and you've tried on every designer dress in the world!"

"I know."

Rachel sighed. "What about the Jenny Peckham one?"

"Nope, that's not the one."

"Sara," Rachel whined. "I'm tired..." She rested her head on Sara's shoulder. "I can't bear to look at another wedding dress!"

"Listen, girl, when you were getting married to David, I had to endure the search for two dresses! Two!" She held up two fingers. "Now suck it up..." Sara laughed trying to get up. "Help me!"

Rachel laughed, standing, then pulling her future sister-in-law up to stand. "Imagine trying to pee in this..."

Sara giggled. "Exactly. I'm going to try on the Carolina Herrera one, it's satin and quite thin, and it's pretty."

Rachel rolled her eyes and groaned. "You're torturing me..."

Sara grinned. "I think the bridal consultant has had enough of me. She's taking a break."

"Well, while she's out of the room, you can tell me what's wrong." Rachel eyed her knowingly.

Sara sighed. "My heart's not in this today..."

"Oh, I wouldn't have guessed," Rachel said dryly.

Sara poked her tongue out at her. "Daniel's gone away on business and we're supposed to be married in three weeks and he said he might be gone for two—"

"Hold on a minute"—Rachel held up a hand—"what do you mean 'supposed to be?' Katherine and I have been running around trying to get everything prepared, and the wedding planner is pulling her hair out!" A look of concern crossed her face. "You haven't changed your mind, have you?"

"I haven't, but I think Daniel might have. He's been acting strange. This trip came out of the blue and he seemed distracted, as if he was worried about something. He's arrived in Miami and he told me he would call and he hasn't. I've tried to call him, numerous times, and he's not answering, He always answers my calls."

"He may have got caught up in meetings. I'm sure he'll call."

"Something's wrong, I can feel it." Sara frowned. "What if he's changed his mind?"

"He loves you—of course, he hasn't changed his mind."

"Has David picked up on anything?"

Sara watched Rachel closely. Her friend looked away, returning to the sofa. "He hasn't said anything," Rachel replied, hesitantly.

Rachel looked at her for a moment, but there was something in her eyes... "You know something, tell me." Sara reached out and leaned against the wall as she removed the high-heeled sandals that were beginning to pinch her feet.

"Honestly, David hasn't said anything."

Sara hoisted up her skirts and sat beside Rachel again. "I didn't ask you what he told you, I want to know what *you* know. Please, Rachel, I'm worried."

Rachel sighed, resting a hand to her bump. She was showing now. A longing pulled at Sara.

"Well, he's arrived safely, David spoke to him yesterday. I couldn't hear the conversation, the girls were talking to me. But it was David's body language that stood out, he seemed tense over something. I did ask, but he smiled, one of his captivating smiles and then kissed me, and I forgot all else. I'm sorry," Rachel said apologetically, then she smiled.

Sara's unease increased; there was definitely something wrong. She'd sent Daniel three text messages too and received no response. He'd seen them, but chose not to respond and that just wasn't like Daniel. It didn't matter how busy he was or how many meetings he had, he always called, always responded to her messages. Especially after what happened with Adam—he'd been overly attentive, checking in on her at regular intervals during the day.

He was acting the way he did when he was fighting his commitment to their relationship; when he was unsure about things and tried to keep his distance. This was concerning. If he changed his mind, it would cause problems for her. They'd agreed on a quick wedding to pre-empt Adam's plans in court. She was feeling very insecure and desperately needed some kind of reassurance from him.

And what made it all the more concerning was the Holy Spirit waking her around three o'clock that morning and telling her to pray for Daniel. Something was seriously wrong.

"Something's wrong, Rachel—I know there is."

Rachel took her hand in hers. "Let's pray about it, and I'll talk to David later. I'll let you know."

Sara nodded, but didn't feel any better about the situation, wondering why Daniel had left so suddenly, and who he was meeting. Tension filled her and concern over Arianna. She needed to consider her options and ensure she had a plan B.

* * *

Amy was already in reception when Daniel arrived. She was staying at the same hotel where the conference was being held, overlooking Miami Beach.

She wore a long pale blue summer dress with thin straps and high-heeled sandals. He was relieved, as the dress covered her beautiful legs, but as she sashayed over to him—the silky material flowing with her body as her hips swayed seductively from side to side—he noticed the v-neckline hinted at her cleavage.

He averted his eyes, trying to keep his thoughts pure, focusing on her face. Her beautiful face seemed ageless; she looked exactly the same, apart from her hair. Her eyes told a different story, and he suddenly wanted to know everything.

She smiled. "Hi, Daniel."

"Hello Amy."

It seemed strange hearing her name on his lips after so many years. And there was a moment of awkwardness where he considered kissing her on her cheek, but he decided against it. "Have you had dinner? Did you want to have a meal in the restaurant?"

She searched his gaze. "No, I haven't. I was too nervous to eat. Yes, let's have something then."

You're not the only one, he thought, acknowledging the nervousness within.

He gestured for her to go ahead of him and that was a mistake. Her dress was backless, the contours of her back exposed. Images flashed through his mind of the many times he'd touched and stroked the smooth skin there and he realised then he was in trouble. He took in a deep breath as he followed behind, unable to take his eyes off her. Her hips swayed gently back and forth, back and forth.

Lord, please help me, he pleaded silently.

Moments later his phone pealed in his pocket. *Sara.*

He answered this time, needing to hear her voice. He stepped away as Amy spoke with the maître'd. "Hi Sara."

"Oh, Daniel, are you okay? I've been so worried, you didn't answer my calls..."

"I'm sorry," he said contritely, and then the words were out of his mouth before he could stop them. "I need you, Sara. I want you to come." He had to tell her the truth, before things got out of hand, and he needed to see her.

"Pardon? Where? To Miami?" she asked in disbelief.

"Yes, I need you. Please?"

"What's wrong? What's happened, Daniel?"

"I can't talk right now." He looked over at Amy, who was waiting patiently for him. "Please Sara, use my credit card, book the next flight here. You know where I'm staying."

"Daniel, you're scaring me..." She paused for a moment. "Okay I'll come, but Arianna's at school and I need to organise childcare. It will probably be tomorrow now."

"Okay, tomorrow then, she can stay with my mother or Rachel. I've got to go, Sara. I'll call you later."

He disconnected the call, the uneasy feeling in his chest lessening slightly as he approached Amy. He only needed to get through one night and then Sara would be here.

The maître'd led them through the busy restaurant to a table by the window overlooking the beach. It was warm and blindingly bright. Views were spectacular; palm trees, white sands, the ocean as far as the eye could see. Dedicated sunbathers dotted across the beach, children playing and running about, families in groups enjoying the sun, sea and sand. But he wasn't here for the views; he was here to reacquaint himself with the woman before him who was causing his heart to race out of control.

He looked at her, and she looked at him. For the life of him, he didn't know what to say to her.

A waitress appeared at their table. "Can I get you anything? Drinks?"

"Just water for me," Amy said.

"The same for me," he replied, and the waitress disappeared.

Amy looked around the crowded and noisy restaurant, his eyes followed her gaze. They were seated by glass sliding doors that led to the beach. Periodically, people were passing their table heading in and out of the restaurant; children, parents, couples. It was distracting.

"I guess Daniella called you?" Amy asked, her eyes searching his.

"Yes, she came to see me."

"She didn't tell me. Daniella can be...very bold at times." She fingered the tablecloth. "I thought about this moment so many times."

"Why didn't you tell me?" His eyes pierced hers.

She was silent for a moment, looking away. "I did tell you, Daniel."

"When did you do that?" He leaned forward, lowering his voice, conscious of the families at the other tables. "When did you give me the courtesy of contacting me and letting me know?"

The waitress chose that moment to appear with their drinks, placing them on the table. "Can I get you something else?"

Daniel looked up impatiently. "No, that's fine for now."

When the waitress disappeared again, he returned his gaze to Amy's, expecting an answer.

"You promised to look after me and protect me. I told you the truth about the babies." She glanced away as a young baby girl—a toddler—headed for their table. Soft brown curls bounced on her shoulders, a mischievous expression on her face.

Her mother looked frustrated. "Katy, come on. Come to Mummy."

Katy looked up at Amy, ignoring her mother's voice, and grinned. Amy smiled and held out her hand to steady her. She wore a pink summer dress and little pink sandals on her feet.

"I'm sorry," Katy's mother said, swooping Katy up into her arms. Katy giggled and waved at Amy.

Amy smiled and waved back, amusement filling her eyes as Katy disappeared with her mother out onto the beach. It made Daniel wonder what their daughters looked like at that age; were they just as mischievous? What kind of mother had Amy been?

He would never know. Guilt seared his chest. "So you've been punishing me all these years? Is that why you've kept my daughters away from me?"

"I guess I was afraid you might reject me again."

"That's an excuse and you know it!"

They received a few stares at his raised voice. He looked around the busy restaurant; he couldn't talk to her here. Maybe a walk along the beach? No, he needed to be alone with her. But when his gaze returned to hers, there were tears in her eyes and he regretted his harsh tone.

Nevertheless, he was angry. "We can't talk here." He stood. "Let's go to your room."

She blinked. "All right."

He allowed her to lead the way, being careful not to touch her. He glanced away, trying not to notice the bare skin of her back and the gentle sway of her hips.

They were silent in the lift going up to her room, but very much aware of each other. David's words crossed his mind and he said a silent prayer, asking God to give him the strength and wisdom to do what was right. The pull toward her was great. He wanted to hold her hand, but resisted the urge.

When they arrived at her door and Amy opened it, they entered the spacious room with walls of glass overlooking the beach. It was bright and airy, and a huge bed dominated the centre of the room.

She walked over to the windows, staring out. The sun cast a haze over her body, the light making her dress transparent, allowing him to see the contours of her body, her legs silhouetted, and her beautiful bare back tapering down to her waist.

He was beginning to think this wasn't such a good idea.

"I'm sorry, Daniel, I was hurting, and I went through a difficult time."

"Don't you think I was hurting too? Sixteen years, Amy? Sixteen years you've deprived me of a relationship with my daughters."

She turned and looked at him. "I'm sorry."

He held her gaze and the atmosphere seemed to change; everything they felt for each other could not be denied.

Amy walked over to him and stepped into his arms and he did nothing to stop her. He heard her soft sigh and he exhaled, too. His arms came up and held her close, one hand slipping into her hair.

In that moment, he felt healing and restoration wash over him, the ache—the pain that he'd held deep inside for years—melted away. He closed his eyes; he felt whole. As he held Amy, everything he'd suppressed over the years—every emotion, every need—the love.

Returned like a wave.

He was in trouble.

Chapter 15

Daniel awoke to the sound of his phone buzzing.

He looked beside him. Amy was still asleep. She was tucked in close next to him. He reached for his phone. Sara's face flashed up on the screen. He groaned inwardly. He'd overslept. He never intended on spending the night with Amy.

He eased away from her slowly, being careful not to wake her. He headed to the bathroom and brushed his teeth and washed his face, then stared at his reflection, wondering how he was going to explain this to Sara. He grabbed a towel and dried his face, muttering under his breath at his stupidity.

He scribbled a note for Amy and gave her one last look as she slept peacefully, her hair flowing over the pillow, her body curled toward the space where he'd lain. He sighed with regret and headed out of the hotel room.

In reception, he dialled Sara's number. "Hi Sara."

"Daniel, were you asleep? Reception have been calling your room."

"Are you at the hotel? I was going to pick you up at the airport."

"It's okay. I took a taxi. Should I come up? What floor are you on?"

He groaned. *How am I going to explain this one?*

"I'm on my way. I'm not far away."

Sara thought for a moment. It was eight o'clock in the morning. "Daniel, where are you?"

"I'll be there in five minutes." He disconnected.

Sara took a seat in the reception area. She was tired after an overnight flight and she didn't get much sleep on the plane. Eager to see him, she got a taxi and made her way to his hotel. She was surprised he wasn't in his room. Where had he spent the night? She didn't get a chance to dwell on that thought too long, as she saw a taxi pull up and his large frame stepped out.

Sara's heart leapt as he walked into reception. His eyes lit up when he saw her. Relief filled her. She was so worried he'd changed his mind about marrying her. Then she wondered what was wrong. She'd heard the desperation in his voice and this was the first time he'd ever said he needed her.

She smiled and stepped into his arms. Whatever it was, he needed her and she would be there for him. She wrapped her arms around his neck and he held her tightly for a long moment. She touched his face, searching his eyes. "What's wrong, Daniel?"

Daniel brought her hand to his lips and kissed her palm suddenly afraid that after he told her everything, he would lose her. "Let's go to my room and talk."

When they made it to his room, Sara was nervous again. She could feel the tension within him. He held her hand on the way up in the lift. His grasp was tight; something was clearly playing on his mind.

His room was pleasant enough, with expansive views of South Beach below. But her focus was on Daniel. Worry plagued her mind.

Daniel placed her suitcase beside the bed. "Are you hungry?" he asked, switching on the TV.

He stared at her, not knowing what to say. She looked classy in a short sleeveless, turquoise fitted dress. The thin satiny material moved with her body. His eyes drifted for a moment to her amazing legs and the high-heeled sandals she wore. She looked beautiful and glamorous.

He could see she was hot; her hair had corkscrewed slightly into wavy curls around her neck. He wanted to kiss her there.

"No, I'm fine, thanks."

She smiled, but her eyes were wary, making him hesitate for a moment. He needed to think, he didn't want to hurt her. "I'm going to take a shower. I won't be long."

Sara watched him head to the bathroom. She noted that his bed hadn't been slept in. He'd obviously spent all night out. She wondered why.

What's wrong, Lord?

"He needs you, Sara."

Why? What's happened?

"Give him the love that he needs."

Concerned, she called to him through the bathroom door. "Are you okay, Daniel?" She could hear the water running.

Daniel answered, "I'm okay now that you're here." It was the truth. He felt his unease lessen as soon as he held her in his arms. But he couldn't take away the guilt he felt at having spent the night with Amy.

Daniel stepped into the cool shower, trying to think of what he would say to Sara, his thoughts drifting to the evening spent with Amy.

They'd ordered pizza. It wasn't on the menu, but the chef had prepared it specially for them. They sat on the floor, catching up on their lives like old friends; it was as if time hadn't separated them.

Amy told him that after she left she went to live with her aunt in California. Once she was able to fend for herself—looking after twins was not easy—she got a job and with a steady income coming in, she saved enough money to move to Florida. She'd always loved Florida, its beaches and the boating canals of Fort Lauderdale.

He was desperate to know about his daughters, as he missed a lifetime with them. But he let her talk at her own pace and listened attentively.

She told him when her aunt died, Amy inherited some money and that helped her to start her property management business. Her interest piqued through conversations she'd had with his father. Her expression changed to one of sadness when he told her his father had passed away.

"I really liked your father. He gave me tips on what to look for when purchasing a property, and what would make an easy profit. It was because of him why I started my business. Maybe a part of me wanted to make him proud of me one day. We were going to work together..."

Daniel's father had taken her under his wing for a while, intending for her to work with him in the family business. That was before Daniel discovered the truth—that she was married.

"....I'm so sorry, Daniel."

She shifted a little closer and squeezed his hand. It was natural to talk to her about his father. She knew a part of his life that no other woman had the privilege of.

His heart was filled with regrets. He couldn't hold back any longer, he needed to know what happened.

"Why, Amy?" His eyes pierced hers. He didn't need to clarify his question; she knew what he was asking.

Why had she lied to him?

Why didn't she tell him about their daughters?

Why didn't she tell him she was married? There were so many unanswered questions...

She looked at him, regret in her eyes. "I never meant to lie to you. I always intended on telling you the truth about Charlie. But I was afraid you wouldn't want me anymore." She paused for a moment. "Charlie and I never had a relationship in that way."

His eyes narrowed. "But you were married."

"Yes, but in name only. He forced me to marry him." She sighed. "I never saw him as my husband."

Daniel shook his head in disgust. Regardless of the situation, she lied to him. She was a married woman, making him inadvertently commit adultery, something he'd vowed he would never do. She was never his. She deceived him.

"I'm not trying to make excuses. I just want you to understand from my point of view."

He looked at her and waited, wondering where she was going with this.

"When I met Charlie, we had a brief fling, and he got me pregnant. Back then, I was young and foolish. I'd cut myself off from my parents and had no one to turn to, and he promised to look after me and my baby, but insisted we get married. It didn't feel right at the time, but he gave me no choice. After we wed, he changed and insisted I abort the baby." She licked her lips drawing his attention there. "I wanted my baby, the gift that God gave me, so I refused...." She paused; looking away, and her eyes began to well with tears as she remembered. "He beat me that night, and kicked me repeatedly in the stomach. I lost my baby...." She brushed the tears from her cheeks, returning her gaze to his. "I'm sorry, I don't like to talk about Charlie. It upsets me. I should have told you before, but I was afraid you would reject me. But you did that anyway, so I should have just told you, and I'm sorry for that."

Shock and guilt hit him. He frowned, making an attempt to respond, but she held up her hand.

"I need to tell you from the beginning what I should have told you before." She sighed. "Charlie was an abuser. The scars on my body were made by him, a reminder of what he could do. I was terrified of him. He beat me almost every day."

He remembered the scars on her body; cigarette burns, cuts made with a knife. He'd asked her about it once, but she'd been vague, not wanting to discuss it, so he didn't push.

She slipped off her sandals. He was drawn to the movement, grateful for the distraction. Anything, but having to look at the pain in her eyes.

His chest tightened from the guilt he felt. He'd promised to look after her and protect her, and he failed in that regard.

His eyes remained glued to her feet. He always felt she had perfect feet, not one blemish or imperfection.

Her toes were painted light blue, to match her dress.

He remembered when she got busy with cooking, and cleaning his apartment, how he used to grab her, lifting her into his arms and taking her to the sofa. He would tickle her feet until she was in tears of laughter and she succumbed to him. Then he would kiss her. He would start with her feet, then her legs, then...

He pushed his unruly thoughts aside as his eyes drifted upward, grateful for the long fabric of her dress that covered her legs, as it had been her legs that had captivated him all those years ago.

He didn't need that kind of distraction right now.

He returned his gaze to hers and listened uncomfortably as she told him about all the things Charlie did to her, and he wanted to tell her to stop. He felt it pull at him, and it made him want to draw her in his arms and promise to make things right with her. But he resisted and continued to listen.

"I was terrified of him, Daniel, and forced to do the things he asked. My fear of him was real, I had the bruises and scars to prove it. But my fear also became irrational, where I thought he was waiting at every corner just to pounce. On some occasions, he did do that, as he used to follow me." Her eyes became distant as she remembered. "I would take time out sometimes and sit in a park and pray for hours, just to keep sane, and he would come and find me."

She closed her eyes for a moment and when she opened them again, her eyes were filled with tears. "He would be so angry and would use his fists when he got me home. But the irrational fear grew through the vicious cycle I found myself in. I saw no way out, when really, I should have gone home to my parents. Called the police—something. But I never did, too afraid to try. Until I met you."

She smiled through her tears. "I fell in love with you straight away. You took my breath away." She reached over and fingered the folds of his shirt. "I adored you, and I wanted to be your wife so much..."

"But you were married," he reminded her. This seemed to be his only defence to the mess he'd made of things.

"Yes—in name only, Daniel. We never once consummated our marriage. He wanted me for one purpose only, to fund his gambling debts. He wanted me to meet with wealthy men and prostitute myself to get as much money out of them as possible. I hated myself for doing what he told me. I wasn't brought up that way, but I drew the line at sex. I became skilled in getting men to part with their money before it got to that."

She shifted closer to him. They both at some point had somehow shifted closer to each other, their bodies nearly touching. Everything within him wanted to draw her close, but he resisted with difficulty. Her knees were touching his thigh now, and he felt the heat flow through him. "And you intended to do the same to me, too?"

"Yes, but I fell in love, I think from the very first, and when you kissed me, I was lost. You promised to love me, look after me and protect me, and I believed you. And I truly thought that God had forgiven me for my sins. I began to have hope for a future with you and our babies."

Daniel looked down, the guilt he felt turning to pain. He'd promised her, even when he was suspicious over the paternity of the babies. He vowed to protect her regardless; he was the one that was wrong and the pain of it seared his heart.

"Then that day, I went shopping to buy that dress, and Charlie turned up. He hurt me—he must have followed me—I had bruises all over my arms..."

Daniel looked up, remembering that day, the last time that he saw her and he'd told her to leave. He'd wondered why she was dressed the way she was; it was out of character for her.

"...I was afraid he would surely kill me and our babies. I managed to get away from him and when I got back, I changed my clothes. I didn't want you to see the bruises, but then he'd obviously already got to you...and the rest, as they say, is history."

She looked up at him then and tentatively touched his face. "It's been nearly seventeen years, Daniel, and I never stopped loving you. I've never allowed another man to touch me...you were the love of my life."

No man has touched her since me?

Daniel held her gaze, fighting with the turmoil within, the pain of the past, the years he'd wasted. He felt the pull and he wrestled with his emotions and when she drew closer and touched her lips to his, he responded. He closed his eyes as old and familiar feelings erupted within and for a moment he was drawn in, but it felt wrong—*it was wrong*. Then Sara's face drifted into his mind.

He opened his eyes and gently pulled away.

She stared at him, and he stared at her.

"Amy, I can't..."

"I'm still in love with you, Daniel."

He closed his eyes for a moment, knowing he needed to be honest with her, but not knowing how to. He felt guilty about everything; he was responsible for so much, he could never make amends. He opened his eyes again, his gaze drifting to her lips.

"I never stopped loving you, Daniel. And I hoped that this day would come that we could be together again." She smiled, gently caressing his face.

Daniel knew he needed to say something—anything—to stop this from spiralling out of control. He needed to get a handle on his emotions.

"Amy...I'm with someone..."

Her smile faded, a look of bewilderment crossed her features. "I-I thought...Daniel..." Her eyes filled with tears. "But you still have feelings for me, I know you do."

He looked away. He was so sorry, for everything. He'd hurt her. For years he'd resented her for what she did to him, when in reality, he hurt her. He was responsible for their daughters growing up without their father's love and support.

He got up, needing some distance from her, because right now, all he wanted was to hold her and comfort her, to try in some futile way to make things right.

But the reality was, he was going to hurt her again.

She stood too, coming to stand in front of him. "You still love me." Her eyes searched his as they filled with tears. "Oh please, Daniel. I want to be with you..." Her tears spilled over and rolled down her cheeks. "I've waited so long...please, Daniel. I love you."

Tears came to his eyes, the pain of it too much to bear. "Why, did you wait? Why didn't you contact me?" If only she'd reached out to him sooner, he would have married her, and they could have had a life together.

"I was afraid you would reject me again. I've spent most of my life afraid, I guess it's something I need to work on. Please, Daniel, please don't reject me again," she begged, tears streaming down her cheeks, her eyes pleading with him.

His own tears spilled over as she stepped into his arms. She clung to him, her head resting against his chest as she sobbed.

He tried to offer comforting words, but what could he say? His heart belonged to Sara and he couldn't change that, and he didn't want to.

He didn't think it was possible to love two women, but he did—in different ways. Amy represented his past, a woman who had found her way into his heart when he was young and open, a woman whom he'd wanted to protect and would have given the world. She was childlike in some ways, yet wise in others, through the abuse she suffered, which compelled him to love and shield her. She was also the mother of his daughters, and for that alone, he loved her as he did back then. He *knew* Amy—the wonder of being with her intimately and he would never forget those moments of joy. He was grateful that out of their love they had created two beautiful daughters he was eager to get to know.

The hurt and resentment he'd held onto over the years thinking she'd deceived him were gone; he was restored. Ultimately, he knew he had to somehow bring restoration to Amy. He had to make things right for her and his daughters. He also admitted to himself that there would be a part of him that would always love Amy.

So he lifted her and carried her to the bed and held her for hours, and comforted her until she quietened and shed a few tears of regret of his own.

He offered her a tissue to wipe her runny nose. She took it from him and gave an embarrassed smile. "So, I'm too late...?"

They were both lying on their sides on the bed, their heads resting on the soft white pillows. He held her gaze. He didn't want to hurt her, but he had to be honest. "I'm getting married in three weeks."

She lowered her gaze. "But you're still in love with me," she whispered, touching his chest.

He covered her hand with his own. "Yes, I am, but with Sara it's different, I can't explain it, but it's different." Guilt churned within him.

"Do you have children together?"

"No, but she has a daughter I'm close to."

She searched his gaze. "So Daniella and Maya are your only children?"

"Yes, and I ache with regret."

"I'm the mother of your children, Daniel..."

Yes, he'd considered this. He planned to start a family with Sara, and ideally only one woman should mother his children, but he couldn't change the past, nor would he change his plans for the future—a future with Sara.

"Yes, you are and I love you for that. I'm sorry I didn't believe you. I'm sorry I didn't protect and look after you as I promised. I wish you had called me when you had the girls, sixteen years is a long time Amy, you could have contacted me at any point."

"Would you have believed me if I contacted you? You would have assumed that I was trying to get money out of you and that the girls were not yours."

She was right, of course; he'd been so angry at life, at his father, at Amy, he probably would have rejected her. The guilt he felt about the situation twisted into a tight knot of discontent that he needed to resolve.

So they talked into the early hours of the morning. She told him about the girls—his daughters. She tried to update him on their whole lives, but sleep won out, and she tucked herself close to him, her arm curled around his waist and drifted off like she used to all those years ago.

Daniel stepped out of the shower, none the wiser as to what he would say to Sara. He needed to be honest with her, but how honest could he be without hurting her?

He dressed quickly, in jeans and a T-shirt, taking a deep breath and he headed back to the living room.

Sara was sat on the sofa, flicking through the TV channels, obvious disinterest on her face. Her eyes lit up when he entered.

He wondered whether the love he could see so plainly in her eyes would continue to be so after what he had to tell her.

He sat opposite her.

Her eyes grew wary.

She came and sat beside him and took his hand in hers. "Daniel, what's wrong?"

He squeezed her hand, linking his fingers through hers, and he told her about Daniella coming for the interview, then meeting Amy. He saw her eyes change—she was hurt. Guilt hit him again.

"But you told me she was pregnant for her husband, and that she tried to con you out of money."

"Yes, that was what her husband told me, and when I confronted her at the time, I was so angry I didn't give her a chance to explain. I saw the guilt on her face. She didn't deny she was married, so I believed his story. I didn't believe her."

Sara searched his eyes, not believing what she was hearing. *He has twin daughters? Where does it leave us? Does he still love her?*

Her heart constricted, suddenly afraid. She wanted to be happy for him, that he'd discovered he had daughters, but she wasn't. She heard the note in his voice, she could see it on his face, he felt guilty—responsible. Which meant he would want to be a part of their lives. But where did that leave them?

"Do you still love her?" Her question was barely a whisper.

Daniel looked away, not knowing what to say. He didn't want to lie, but how could he tell her the truth without hurting her? So he did what he knew best, he deflected.

"It was all a shock, seeing my daughter in front of me, someone who looks so much like me. Then I felt anger, as Amy had kept them from me. It's been nearly seventeen years and she didn't tell me, never contacted me. If Daniella hadn't have come to see me, I still wouldn't have known."

Sara watched him and held his gaze when he returned his to hers. A knot tightened in her chest.

He deflected.

"So, what did Amy say about that?"

"She said she was afraid I would reject her again. I felt that was an excuse, there was nothing stopping her from contacting me, but then she asked the question—would I have believed her if she contacted me. She said I would probably assume that she was trying to get money out of me and I wouldn't have wanted anything to do with her. And when I think about it, she's probably right, I've been living with so much anger and resentment over the years, thinking she deceived me that I wouldn't have listened to anything."

But do you still love her? "How do you feel?"

"Guilty. My daughters have grown up not knowing their father. They are Andersons, they should know their family—their heritage. I have so many regrets. They never got the chance to meet my father, he'd been so happy about it at the time..."

Her apprehension increased. "Your family knew about the babies?"

"Yes, my father had been ecstatic, and I was happy, because it meant I had finally done something right in his eyes, they would have been his first grandchildren and he liked Amy and wanted us to get married."

Sara pulled her hand from his. *His father met Amy?* Daniel had never told her this. In fact he'd hardly told her anything about Amy. A pang of jealousy filled her. "So you were engaged?"

"Yes, when it transpired that she was already married and I thought she was trying to con me out of money. My father was so angry and we argued over it—our relationship went even further downhill after that."

Daniel watched her closely. He didn't like the way she pulled her hand away from his. He shifted closer so his thigh was touching hers.

"So, she's your ex-fiancée then?" Sara didn't like where this was going. It meant that Amy was more important to Daniel than she'd originally thought.

"I suppose she is."

"How does she feel about you?"

"What do you mean?" Daniel asked. He was stalling, he knew exactly what she meant.

"The fact that she had your babies—she never lied to you, presumably she was in love with you, so is she *still* in love with you?"

He hesitated before answering. "Yes."

"I take it she's single, too?"

"Yes."

Sara would have loved to be a fly on the wall when they were having *that* conversation. Alarm bells were ringing and the uneasiness she felt deepened. "Why did you call me here, Daniel? What does this mean?"

"I wanted to tell you in person."

"You could have done that when you returned home." She eyed him suspiciously. *He's still in love with Amy—he wants her.* She could see the look in his eyes, and a feeling of doom filled her.

"I needed you here."

She looked at him noting the way he was avoiding her eyes, and the look of guilt on his face. Her heart began to pound, afraid to push this, but knowing she had to.

"You're still in love with her, and you wanted me here because you're afraid you might do something you shouldn't."

Daniel didn't know what to say. He didn't want her to misunderstand. "Sara—"

Sara stood then; his pause was too long. "Did you sleep with her?" She felt tears sting her eyes.

He stood as well. "No, I didn't." He took a step toward her, but halted when she took a step back.

"But you spent the night with her?" she asked, watching him carefully. *He's hiding something.*

"Yes, but we only talked. I needed to know about my daughters. Sara, please, I—"

"You want to cancel the wedding..."

"No, I don't." He rushed over to her, his hands on her shoulders, drawing her close. "I still want us to get married, I love you. This doesn't change anything."

Relief should have filled her at his words, but it didn't. Instead, she felt apprehensive. "This changes everything, Daniel, and we can't move forward if you can't be honest with me."

"I have been—I am."

Sara stepped away from him, shaking her head. "You're still in love with her. How can we get married if you're in love with another woman?"

Daniel panicked. He needed to make her understand he didn't want to lose her. He went over to her and caught her by the waist, pulling her against him. She put her hand to his chest to stop him, but he wasn't going to be deterred. He cupped her face, holding her still when she tried to pull away.

Sara fought to stay in control, but he moved so fast she didn't have time to think. She had no defence against him, regardless of the situation.

His touch was gentle and he had a look of tenderness in his eyes when his mouth captured hers. She was lost in the heat and wonder of his kiss as it always was with him. He immobilised her and she felt weak, her eyes fluttered shut and she gave in, slipping her arms around his waist as he kissed her senseless.

Daniel groaned, closing his eyes. Everything he felt for Sara coursed through him; the love, the intense, uncontrollable desire that always rocked him. He drew her closer, wanting more.

This was the difference. With Amy, it was familiar—feelings of his past that had never left, but with Sara, it was intoxicating, an uncontainable need that consumed him. Even though they had not been intimate as he'd been with Amy, he knew with everything within him that when they joined as husband and wife it would be potent, explosive, and powerful.

He couldn't lose her now. Sara was his. When he thought about the years he'd lost with Amy, there was no way that he would lose Sara, too.

He opened his eyes, slowly drawing away, kissing a trail along her cheek and then on to the delicate curve of her neck.

"Sara, when I kiss you and hold you, do I leave you with any doubt that I could ever want to be with another woman?" He looked at her, her eyes still closed, her luscious lips slightly parted, tempting him to kiss her again.

Sara slowly opened her eyes. She felt faint and grateful that he held her close in his arms. She gave a slight shake of her head because she couldn't speak.

"I love you, Sara, and I want you to be my wife. My past can't change how I feel about you."

She reached up and caressed his face. "Then why do I feel as if you're not being honest with me?"

"I'm trying, Sara. I wanted you here because I need your support. I want you with me. You're going to be my wife and this affects you, too."

The uneasiness she felt returned. She didn't like this situation at all.

"I want you to meet her."

Sara pulled away; she couldn't think when she was in his arms and meeting his ex-fiancée wasn't something she wanted to do. She took a seat on the sofa. "Why do I need to meet her?"

He sat beside her. "Because she's the mother of my children, and I want you to meet them, too."

Sara looked away from his intense gaze. She wasn't certain about that. All she felt was jealousy. She'd felt it before with Daniel, when virtually every woman he was in contact with would fawn all over him. But this was different; those women meant nothing to him. Amy was his ex-fiancée, his first love—and this concerned her.

Amy was also the mother of his children, twin girls that he now would need to get to know and would mean many visits away to see them, and the visits would include Amy. She suddenly felt very insecure. Although he loved her, he had feelings for Amy. Selfishly, Sara wanted all his love; she didn't want to share him.

She tried to muster some happiness for him, but she couldn't find it within herself. Why was this happening now? Hadn't she been through enough?

Lord, why is this happening now? You brought Daniel into my life, for me and Arianna. Why is my happiness being threatened now?

"Daniel needs to forgive and right what was wrong."

Right what was wrong? What did that mean?

But before she could ask for clarification, Daniel was talking again.

"Sara..." He caught her chin, forcing her to look at him. "This doesn't change anything."

Her eyes welled with tears. "It changes everything, Daniel."

"No, it doesn't—"

"You're still in love with her! How can we possibly have a future?"

It was his turn to look away. At a loss for words, his hand fell away.

She eyed him intently. She suspected that he was debating as to what he should tell her. "Are you going to deflect again, Daniel?"

Daniel returned his gaze to hers. "No, I want to be honest with you..." He sighed. "I'm not sure of what I feel about Amy, all I know is that I love you and want to be with you. You're everything to me, Sara."

"But she means something to you, you just spent the night with her...were you only talking? Did you want to sleep with her?"

Daniel said nothing, guilt plaguing him.

Sara's tears spilled over and rolled down her cheeks. "Amy has known you in ways I haven't, and I'm not sure I can compete with that."

He cupped her face. "Sara, I want you—"

"Do you?" She took his hands in hers bringing them to her lap. "If the scenario was different, and you hadn't met me, would you marry Amy?"

He looked away.

She leaned into his line of vision. "Would you have made love to her last night?" She looked at him, seeing the answer in his eyes and her heart constricted with pain.

She stood and brushed at her tears. "I'm going to book into my own room."

Daniel stood, panicking. "Please, Sara, I wanted us to talk this through, I thought you would stay here...?"

Sara shook her head. "I'm going to book another flight and leave in the morning—"

"Sara, please, let's talk about this," he begged, his eyes pleading.

"Something happened between you and Amy. I can see it in your eyes, Daniel."

"I didn't sleep with her."

Clearly she was asking the wrong questions. "What *did* you do?"

Daniel stared at her, suddenly very afraid that he could lose Sara. Just because of a moment—he'd lost his head, his emotions were in turmoil. But ultimately he knew he had to be honest with her.

Ever since his breakup with Amy, he'd always ensured he was honest with the women he dated and he expected the same from them. With Sara it hadn't been any different. He was a Christian now and with God, there could only be truth, so the truth was what he told her.

"We shared a kiss—that's all. I pulled away."

They kissed? She stared at him in shock for a moment, trying to digest what he'd told her. Sara was crushed, her heart breaking.

"I'm sorry, it just happened…. Please, Sara, let's talk about this?"

"I don't want to talk anymore." She took in a breath as tears streamed down her face, evading his arms as he tried to draw her to him. "I think we should put the wedding on hold."

"*No!* I want the wedding to go ahead as planned. Please, Sara…"

"I don't think you know what you want, Daniel."

"Sara, don't do this. I'm coming back with you, we'll leave together."

"No, I think you should stay. You have a family here, and you need to get to know them. It's right that you should stay."

She walked over to her suitcase and extended the handle, pulling it along as she headed for the door. But Daniel blocked her way.

"Don't do this, Sara. Please?"

"Daniel, just take some time. Think things through and make a decision."

"I've already made my decision, Sara."

"No, you haven't, not really…" She looked away. "I'll be at home, we'll talk when you return." She stepped passed him and opened the door.

She didn't look back, and he let her go.

Chapter 16

"You left? Why would you go and do a thing like that?" Rachel looked at Sara with disbelief.

"He let me go, Rachel. If he loved me, he would have come home with me, but he didn't." Sara looked over at Rachel. Sadness filled her as she remembered when she walked out of Daniel's hotel room expecting him to stop her, call her back—say something—but he let her go and she was hurting.

It was Saturday and they'd spent the day shopping for the twins. Rachel was five months along now, all belly and huge. To look at her from behind, you would never know she was pregnant; it was only when she turned that it was obvious. She was still so slim, dressed in black leggings and an oversized cream jumper, she looked beautiful, her long dark hair twisted to the side.

Pregnancy suited her; she was glowing and rested a protective hand to her tummy as she rocked slowly back and forth in the huge rocking chair in the twins' nursery.

Sara sat on the sofa opposite. She'd hoped that she would be in the same position in a few months, when she and Daniel were married. Now, she wasn't so sure.

"But you told him not to."

"Yes, and he didn't."

Rachel gave her an incredulous look. "So you were testing him? That's a dangerous game, Sara. He called you because he needed your support and you left him high and dry. You shouldn't have left him."

Why is she fighting me on this? Sara needed Rachel's support. She contemplated her friend's response. Rachel and Daniel had become close, especially since he became a Christian; clearly she was protective of him. But Rachel was *her* friend and should be on her side.

"Why shouldn't I have left? Because he might end up in the arms of his ex? Well, if there is a risk of that, then I would prefer it happens now and not when we're married. And besides, if that is a possibility, then it wouldn't be right for us to get married at all."

"You should have fought for him. You should have gone with him to meet Amy."

"Why? To make me feel worse? I feel so insecure..." Her eyes filled with tears yet again.

It had been five days since she flew back and she'd spent the majority of it in tears. There had been no sign of Daniel, and she'd hoped that Daniel would have returned home by now.

Maybe she'd pushed things too far, but she needed to be sure that he loved her and really wanted to be with her, and not secretly wanting his ex while they got married. Scenarios flashed through her mind of Daniel having secret trysts with Amy, and their marriage ending over his love for her. It was essential that Daniel made a choice now; either her or Amy. She needed to be sure and she allowed him the space to make that decision on his own.

"Why don't you go back? Tell him you've changed your mind."

"No, Rachel, don't you understand? I need to be certain that he loves me and is not marrying me out of obligation after everything that happened with Adam."

"I know, hon, but you need to consider this. You said Amy is still in love with him and she's single, what if she decides she wants Daniel back?" Rachel rubbed her back and shifted to a more comfortable position. "Some women can be manipulative."

Sara looked away, not wanting to think about the number one topic that had kept her awake the last few nights. Fear that Daniel had gone back to Amy, that they'd made love, and he decided to marry Amy instead. She was so afraid—fretful and anxious, and she couldn't stop the tears. Part of her regretted walking away, but what else could she have done?

"The same applies, if he is that weak for her, then we shouldn't be together."

"You are very gracious, Sara. My claws would have been out by now."

"Would they? When David was having issues with Karen, did your claws come out then? Or did you back off?" It was a rhetorical question; she already knew the answer.

"Okay, okay, you're right. I backed off. I didn't want any part in it and I guess, deep down, I was testing David. I gave him an easy get out, and I even told him that maybe he should try again with his wife." Rachel smiled, thinking back. "He didn't like that suggestion very much." She stifled a yawn and gently stroked her tummy.

Rachel was tired, soon she wouldn't have the energy to go shopping, so they'd literally bought everything needed for the coming months. Clothes, nappies, nursing equipment, bottles, toys, nursery furniture, the works. Numerous shopping bags littered the floor. The larger nursery furniture they'd arranged to be delivered. They'd finally headed back when Rachel had enough and had become too tired—and hungry. She seemed to be continually munching on something. Even now, she rummaged in one of the bags and pulled out a packet of crisps.

The room was large, with powder blue walls. Twin cots, a white chest of drawers, soft toys galore—a huge, light brown stuffed bear sat in the corner, so cuddly she wanted to take it home with her. Bunny rabbits, puppy dogs, kittens, every farm animal ever made, and toys filled the play area of the room.

Rachel had given Sara the task of creating a hand-painted mural. Calligraphy-styled strokes adorned one wall with the babies' names and the meaning, including a scripture;

Nathan—Gift of God. Victorious...
1 Corinthians 15:57; But thanks be to God! He gives us the victory through our Lord Jesus Christ.
Joshua—God is my salvation. Bringer of truth...
James 1:25; But whoever looks intently into the perfect law that gives freedom, and continues in it—not forgetting what they have heard, but doing it—they will be blessed in what they do.

Rachel had also requested angels; she wanted the room to glorify God and the things of him. Sara had skilfully painted them on the wall, and the effect was beautiful—peaceful, serene, and evident that God's presence filled the room.

"Then you know how I feel." Sara sighed. She'd had enough of crying; part of her wanted to go away and never come back. This endless uncertainty was becoming unbearable.

Rachel munched on her crisps. "I hear what you're saying and I understand it, but I just feel you should be with him right now. What if he finds himself in a situation he can't handle?"

Sara returned her gaze to Rachel's, her mind pondering on Rachel's words.

Daniel hadn't called. She waited every evening, apprehension filling her, for him to call and say the words and end it with her, advising her that he loved Amy and had decided to marry her instead. She went to bed with it on her mind and awoke with it in the mornings and carried it throughout her day. She felt so out of control and she missed him terribly. She missed him holding her at night. She missed the way his arm would curl and tighten, drawing her closer to him if she moved. She longed for his whispered words of love through the night. His laugh, his beautiful smile, his gorgeous green eyes—she missed *him* and this was so unfair.

She prayed continually, but her fears did not allow her to have peace over the situation. "Yes, and I'm worried. But all I can do is pray and trust that Daniel will do what is right. If he doesn't, then we weren't ever meant to be." She brushed away the tears that fell to her cheeks. "Daniel will always be travelling and there will always be other women. Just a few months ago it was Emma, and I can't follow him everywhere, Rachel, I've never been the obsessive, jealous type."

"So how do you feel now?"

"Obsessive and jealous."

Rachel smiled. "So what are you going to do?"

"I'm scared I'm going to lose him, Rachel." She looked away, her tears rolling freely again down her cheeks. She reached in her handbag for a tissue and wiped her face.

"Ahh, Sara, please don't cry..." Rachel made an attempt to get up, but flopped back down again. "I would come over there, but I'm so fat and tired..."

Sara smiled through her tears and shook her head.

"...You won't lose him, he loves you Sara. He calls David every day and asks how you and Arianna are. He's given David strict instructions to make sure you're safe."

Sara blinked. "So why hasn't he called *me?*"

"I don't know...David said he's a little angry."

Angry? He's the one that is in the wrong here. "Is that what Daniel said?"

"I don't know what he said, not really. David always speaks to him when I'm not around or when I'm otherwise occupied. It was just a comment David made the other night."

Sara thought for a moment, wondering what Daniel could possibly be angry at her about, when he was the one who ended up kissing his ex.

"He spent the night with her," Sara blurted. She needed to talk about this; surely her reaction wasn't wrong. Rachel was making her feel as if she was the one that was irrational.

Rachel looked shocked. "Did he sleep with her?"

"He said he didn't, but it was only when I pushed that he finally admitted to a kiss—they *shared* a kiss, he said, whatever that means..."

Rachel stared at her for a moment. "*Shared a kiss?*"

Sara shrugged. "I don't know what it means, did *he* kiss her, or did *she* kiss him? Whatever it is, as each day passes and he still hasn't come home, I know he's going to end it between us."

"You don't know that for sure."

"He *kissed* her, Rachel!"

"Okay, that's bad," Rachel popped a few more crisps in her mouth and chewed thoughtfully. "Does this mean that you don't want to be with him?"

"I don't know..."

"He loves you, Sara."

"And he loves Amy, who was his first love, who has been intimate with him and is the mother of his twin daughters. How can I even begin to compete with that? And right now I'm not sure if I want to..." She paused for a moment. "I think I should put the wedding on hold."

"Sara, no. This is what God had always intended for you. He's shown you dreams and visions..."

"Yes, but as you know, we all have free will, and I think Daniel's will is elsewhere."

"Are you sure you want to do that? When God sends us dreams and visions, it's to prepare our hearts, so when something unexpected like this happens, it helps you to remain focused on his divine purpose."

"Yes and look at how many dreams and visions God sent you before you got married. Did you listen?"

"Okay, so I was a little reluctant, but I got there in the end. This is meant to be."

"Why waste everyone's time? Katherine has put a lot of work into the preparations, and I just think it would be best for everyone. What's the point in pretending anymore?"

"This isn't God's will."

Sara didn't respond.

"What has Holy Spirit said?"

"I haven't asked."

"Don't you think you should?"

"Maybe," Sara whispered, despondence filling her. She was silent for a moment, deep in thought. "I think I might go away for a while."

"*What?* Go where?" Rachel asked. Her expression was filled with concern.

"Somewhere where Adam can't find me."

"Sara, you're talking as if you and Daniel are over."

"You haven't been listening to me, Rachel, he's in love with Amy. It's already over. Which means I'm faced with a custody battle with Adam. I have nowhere to live and there is no way I'm going to allow Adam to take Arianna away again. I don't have the money to fight him in court."

"But Daniel will help you."

"That was before, and everything has changed now. I have to do something. Arianna means more to me than anything, and I refuse to allow Adam to control me again."

So with her resolve set, she decided to pack her things and leave. She needed to get on with her life. She told Katherine to put the wedding on hold. Katherine hadn't been pleased and had tried to convince her otherwise, but Sara didn't explain her reasons, and Katherine didn't ask. Sara figured that Katherine must know the cause.

It was early, and Arianna was still asleep. She'd already loaded the car with their suitcases; all that was left was her suit carriers and her small suitcase with her essentials. Being Sunday morning, there would hardly be any traffic on the motorway and she wanted to get an early start. She had enough money to tide her over for a few months, and she could easily find another job with her qualifications and experience.

She sipped her tea, deciding she'd give Arianna another half an hour before she woke her.

Sara wondered what God had in store for her. Going back to Adam was not an option for her. She had Arianna's welfare to think about and her daughter came first before anything. Her mind was set—she would never go back to Adam, no matter how he might force this. And if he took her back to court again, as he threatened he would, then she would have to battle it out in court when he eventually found her. But she would make it difficult for him to find her, as not even Rachel knew where she was going.

She headed over to the piano, sat at the bench and played, singing a song of worship. She felt low and needed the Holy Spirit's strength, his presence, to get her through this day. She closed her eyes taking in his presence.

"Forgive him, Sara."

She opened her eyes, her fingers stilling on the keys.

But he kissed her, Lord...

Tears came to her eyes. She didn't realise how much it hurt that he'd betrayed her this way.

"Forgive him."

She sighed. It wasn't what she wanted to hear. Daniel had pursued her for months, made her fall in love with him, and when she'd finally given in, moved in with him and handed him her heart, he strayed. Maybe she just wasn't good enough.

Sadness filled her heart, becoming tearful as she thought about Daniel. Last week she'd been so happy, finally planning to be with the man she loved and now everything had fallen apart. Her heart ached at the thought of never seeing Daniel again, but the thought of working in the same company and seeing him every day as he made a life with another woman was too much to bear. This way, at least she could cope somehow.

She ran her fingers along the piano, enjoying the feel of the smooth polished surface. She closed the lid regretfully, making her way to the kitchen. She wouldn't get another chance to play for a while.

She blinked back her tears, she was going to miss Rachel. They'd been together all their lives, but if she told her friend where she was going, Rachel would tell David, who would in turn tell Daniel, and she didn't want Daniel to come after her out of obligation. He loved Arianna, and he would make a sacrifice for her and Sara, and she didn't want to embroil him further in her life over fears of what Adam might do.

It was better this way. Later on, when she was settled, she would contact Rachel.

*   *   *

Daniel pulled up on the drive. He was tired and emotionally drained. He felt like he'd been through the wars. He said a silent prayer; he needed God's strength to get him through this.

Sara had cancelled the wedding. She hadn't even had the courtesy to call him and let him know, he had to hear it from his mother. It hurt him deeply, and fear filled his heart; he couldn't lose Sara now.

His mother had chewed his ear off. She'd been angry, and his mother rarely got angry. She'd turned up at his hotel in Miami that morning. He'd planned to spend the day with Amy and the girls, and had just showered and dressed when his mobile rang. His mother's face flashed up on the screen, it was unusual for her to call so early in the morning.

"Mother? Are you okay?" he asked, a little worried.

"I'm in reception. What floor are you on?"

His heart lurched. *What is she doing here?* "Pardon?"

"You heard me, Daniel," she replied, annoyance filling her tone.

"Twelfth floor, I'll meet you by the lifts."

He kissed her on the cheek when she stepped out of the lift. He was concerned. For his mother to get on a plane and fly over to see him, it had to be important. "Is everything okay?"

"No, Daniel it's not," she replied, her expression one of displeasure, her eyes glaring at him intently.

Great, I don't need this. She followed him into his room, closing the door.

"Sara has put the wedding on hold. Why is that, Daniel? What have you done?" She gave him a disapproving glare.

He blinked. It felt as if someone had taken a sledgehammer and hit him on his head with it. "What do you mean, she's cancelled the wedding?"

"You heard me. She called yesterday and told me to stop everything. What's going on, Daniel? Why are you still here? And why isn't Sara with you?"

He hated when his mother was angry at him. He'd told her about everything before he travelled, but he'd not told her what had transpired since. He'd been too afraid to share his feelings. "I'm still in love with Amy, Mum."

Katherine stared at him for a moment, then walked over to the sofa and took a seat.

Not sure of her reaction, he remained standing.

"I've always known that you were, Daniel. Your emotions were too strong, you never dealt with the pain of losing her, you internalised it and became angry. You've been angry for too many years..." She patted the space beside her. "Talk to me, tell me about my granddaughters."

He couldn't help the smile that came to his lips at the mention of his daughters. Although his heart ached at the thought of losing Sara and he wanted to call her—but would she listen? He doubted it; he tried before and she walked away when he needed her the most. The situation had spiralled out of control.

Still, he found he needed to talk about his daughters. Sara hadn't allowed him to and he needed someone to be happy about them, just as he was.

He sat beside his mother and pulled out his phone, scrolling through his photos until he got to the one he'd taken the day before. Maya and Daniella were hugging each other as they posed for the photo. They were smiling and had been since he'd made an appearance in their lives.

They were full of questions, wanting to know about their cousins—how many? What were their ages? Could they meet them? Wanting to know everything about their grandmother, their uncles and aunts, what he did for a living, and then the ultimate question; why he never married. He found with his daughters, they did not hold back, they said what was on their mind—*was it because of Mom?*

And what could he say in response? He could only be honest. "Yes, I've been hurting for a long time. I didn't understand what happened with your mother, I didn't give her a chance to explain and never knew about you all these years."

"Yes, we know. Mom was afraid. We're all she has," Maya said. She was just as beautiful as her sister, although with slightly shorter hair. She smiled. "But Daniella found you." She leaned over and hugged him. They did that a lot—hugged and smiled, they were very affectionate.

Amy had always been that way, too. He was surprised at how easily he loved them. It was virtually instant; they were a part of him, he was their father, and it still amazed him. They were his family, one that included Amy.

With every visit Amy was there, and she smiled a lot, too, seemingly happy he was there.

The conference had lasted a couple of days, so then afterward he'd returned with Amy to Fort Lauderdale. He stayed in a hotel nearby and spent most of the week with them at their home, located in a quiet residential area.

After the night they'd spent together, it had healed his hurts and had also healed some of hers. Her words played on his mind: *"...You promised to love me, look after me and protect me, and I believed you. And I truly thought that God had forgiven me for my sins. I began to have hope for a future with you and our babies."* Although she didn't say it, he knew she resented him for not living up to the promises he'd made to her.

While he understood she was afraid—and after what she experienced it was understandable—nevertheless, she could have reached out to him, but she didn't, and their lives would have been so different.

During the days that followed, she welcomed him into her home and cooked for him, reminiscent of old times, and they talked, really talked, like old friends. Daniel realised he missed their friendship over the years and hoped they could remain friends. He acknowledged the love he still felt for her and the longing he sometimes saw in her eyes when she looked at him. They both had regrets, but it was too late for them now; that chapter in their life could no longer be. It was time to heal that which was broken and renew their relationship. They were parents and he wanted them to be united in that.

Her home was a fair size and had everything she needed, he supposed, but he wanted more for her and his daughters. He vowed to change that, and had already contacted his lawyer to set up a trust fund for both Maya and Daniella, and to pay back payments of maintenance to Amy. Her house, her car, her lifestyle would change; he wanted her to have everything he would have given her if they'd been together. He wanted her to be happy, and if he could give her a glimpse of that through his generosity, then so be it. It was what he needed to do.

He looked over at his mother; her eyes alight with approval, for which he was grateful.

"They look just like you, and your father, there's a hint of Amy, but there is no mistaking they are your daughters." Katherine smiled. "Your father was so excited about the babies back then, they would have been our first grandchildren. He had been so disappointed when Amy left and regretted the arguments with you afterward. He would have been so proud, Daniel." Tears came to her eyes. "Our choices in life can either be a blessing or a curse, and the effects can outlast a lifetime."

Yes, his choice that day had been a curse that had made him bitter over the years. He'd wasted years running away from situations in a hopeless bid to protect his heart from further pain, when in actuality, he'd caused the pain, he'd cultivated it and made it worse by his anger and resentments.

His mother's eyes shone with joy. "I want to meet them."

"They want to meet you, too." Daniel showed her a picture of Amy and the girls.

"Amy is still very beautiful." She raised her eyes to his, looking at him intently. "So, Daniel, what are you going to do? You can't have them both. Who will you choose?"

"I know that, Mum. It's complicated, but I have no doubts as to who I intend to marry."

"I have no doubts, too, which is why I'm annoyed you allowed this to happen. Especially with the wedding preparations underway."

"I guess I could have handled things a little better, but I needed some space to get to know my daughters. I have sixteen years to make up for."

"But you could lose Sara, Daniel."

Yes, he was aware. He'd taken a risk in staying away so long and consequently, Sara had cancelled the wedding. He'd hoped that they could have visited the girls together. She was going to be his wife—regardless of the cancelled wedding. He would convince her, beg her even—it was what God intended and it was important that she loved his daughters, too.

But what if she never accepted them? What then? It was something they needed to discuss, it was important—*they* were important. But from what he'd known of Sara over the months, deep down he knew she would grow to care for his daughters, despite the situation.

"I know, I tried to talk to her, but she walked away. I needed her, Mum. I've tried to be there for her, but when the tables were turned, she walked away. I guess I was a little angry."

"So why did she walk away?" Her eyes assessed him, wanting the truth.

Daniel contemplated what he should say to her. It was obvious from her questions that Sara had not told her about his night with Amy, and he didn't feel comfortable telling her about the kiss. He wasn't sure his mother would understand. Besides, he was a coward when it came to her, and he did not want to be on the receiving end of his mother's wrath. "I've never lied to her, I told her the truth about Amy. Obviously she got upset."

Realisation dawned on Katherine's face at his words, and a frown formed on her brow. "Of course she would be upset, any woman would be. How would you feel if she told you she was still in love with an ex-boyfriend?"

"I'd break his face." A tightness hit his chest at the thought. "I had a glimpse of that with her ex-husband. For a moment there I thought she'd gone back to him, so I know exactly how it feels."

"She's hurting, Daniel."

Daniel sighed. "I just needed her here. This is an important time for me..."

"You were testing her, and I think you pushed too hard, Daniel."

Daniel looked at his mother. In a way, he supposed he *was* testing Sara, testing their love for each other. The kiss was a test for him, which made him realise that he loved Sara more than he could ever contain. When Amy's lips touched his, everything shifted, it was no longer about Amy, it was about his need for Sara. No matter the overwhelming guilt he felt about the situation with Amy, his need for Sara outweighed everything.

When Sara came to see him, he knew she would be upset, but he needed a friend that day, and he needed her unconditional love—not a jealous fiancée. It had been asking a lot, he knew, but in moments like this when they were married—when situations beyond their control transpired—if she couldn't be there for him, how would their marriage ever last?

He needed her; he still needed her. He'd hated being away from her, and this last week had been difficult at best. He ached to be with her. He missed her, missed holding her, missed talking to her into the early hours of the morning and her falling asleep in his arms.

On numerous occasions, he'd reached for his mobile to call, but he decided against it. What could he say? He was angry; she should have been there for him, and now she'd cancelled the wedding.

He took in a breath. It hurt; the pain of it caused a knot in his chest. "Maybe. But we're planning to spend the rest of our lives together—a life, and they are my daughters, they're important to me, and they're not going to go away because Sara is upset about the situation. I've already lost a lifetime with them and, I'm not prepared to lose any more."

"Did you explain this to her?"

"She didn't give me a chance. Her focus had been on Amy. This isn't about Amy, although she is a part of this—I didn't do what was right by her, Mum. I need to make it right."

They talked some more and then he took her to see his daughters. He would never forget his mother's joy when she hugged them; tears streamed down her face. She held them for a long time and then she drew Amy into the hug, and it pulled at his heart.

He'd left his mother there in Florida. She decided to spend a few days with them and he got on the next flight back.

He and Sara needed to thrash things out once and for all. He wanted a life with her, but he didn't know if she wanted a life with him.

The first thing he noticed when he walked in was her suitcase and suit carriers slung over the sofa. He frowned.

She's leaving me? He took in a breath as apprehension and fear hit, threatening to choke him.

She sat at the kitchen island, a cup in her hand. It was six-thirty in the morning, she was dressed and clearly getting ready to leave.

She'd agreed to marry him and now she intended to sneak away without telling him—it angered him.

With trembling fingers, Sara placed the cup on the counter as she met his gaze. He was angry.

"You're leaving me?"

"I thought it would be the best thing for both of us with the situation as it is," Sara replied, unsure. She'd hoped to have left before he came back. Now that he'd returned, it complicated things.

"Without even a *discussion?* You were going leave without even the respect of a conversation?" Daniel was outraged; he couldn't believe this.

Guilt seared Sara's chest, but she suppressed it. "I didn't think you cared anymore, Daniel." Her heart began to pound. *Don't cry, Sara,* she told herself as she felt tears sting her eyes. There had been too many tears over the last week; now she needed to be strong.

"Do you really think I'm going to let you leave?" Daniel threw his keys on the sofa and told himself to calm down. He was angry and hurt, a bad combination that had got him into trouble before. His mother's words crossed his mind. *"Our choices in life can either be a blessing or a curse, and the effects can outlast a lifetime..."*

He had a choice to make here. Nevertheless, all he knew without a doubt was that he wouldn't let her go.

Sara blinked. She hadn't been sure what his reaction would be. He was angrier than she'd expected him to be. Was his reaction because of his love for her or was it because of his ego?

"You don't really have a choice, Daniel. I've thought about this and I don't think things are going to work between us. You have an already-made family, I'm just getting in the way, so I'm making things easy for you." Her movements nervous, she got off the stool and placed the cup in the sink.

Already made family? Daniel stared at her, incredulous. Sara and Arianna were his family; they had been for a while now. "Where's Arianna?"

"She's in bed. I need to wake her soon so we can leave."

"No, you won't. You're not going anywhere." His tone was harsher than he'd intended and he tried to swallow the anger burning in his chest.

Frustration filled Sara then. After years of living with Adam and being under his thumb she refused to allow another man to dictate to her the way Adam did, regardless of how much she loved Daniel. "You can't stop me!"

"I can, and I will!"

Anger and frustration filled him. Part of him wanted to grab her and shake some sense into her, and the other part of him wanted to pull her into his arms and kiss her. He took a step toward her, but did neither, and took in a breath, running a hand through his hair. "Let me get this right, just for clarity. You're leaving me because you're upset over Amy?"

"You've made your choice, haven't you?" Sara watched him—waiting, afraid of what his answer would be.

"And as far as you're concerned, my choice is Amy?"

Why won't he say it and put me out of my turmoil? "It is, isn't it?"

"Would I be here if it was?"

"I don't know why you're here, Daniel. You've only come back because your mother must have called you."

Daniel sighed and shook his head. "You're a stunningly beautiful woman, Sara, with a loving and generous spirit. Most men would trip over themselves to be with you, yet you're still so very insecure. I don't understand, what is it about me that makes you feel that way?"

His words touched her heart, but she wasn't going to be distracted. "Oh, I don't know... You make plans to spend a week away with Emma and now, your ex-fiancée turns up on the scene, which you didn't bother to tell me about, and suddenly it's about me? *I'm* the one with the issues?"

"I never lied to you, Sara. I told you about Amy."

"You told me you planned to marry her, but you *didn't* tell me you got engaged and she'd met your family—that's totally different."

"What difference does it make? I told you that I wanted *you*, that I still wanted us to get married, but you refused to listen. You were going to just disappear and leave without bothering to tell me? I deserve better than that, Sara!"

Sara stared at him, unable to believe he was twisting things. She folded her arms defensively.

Okay, so he had a point about her leaving, and he did deserve to be treated better than that. All he'd done since they'd met was treat her with love, kindness, and generosity—she couldn't fault him on that.

But she was frightened. Her life was up in the air, she was so insecure. She didn't even have a home she could call her own. Adam owned the house she'd lived in, even though they were no longer married. Her former husband still had some control over her life and yet here she was, happily going to do it again—get married, become barefoot and pregnant for another man who would pull all the strings. Where was her self-respect?

She'd become Adam's wife, doted on him, and given up who she was to be his obedient, dutiful wife. She had no say, and lived her life how he wanted her to live it, in the prison he called a home, even though at the end she'd become strong and empowered through God. She'd always be eternally grateful for that. God had shown her that her life with Adam was wrong; he'd emotionally abused her. Now she'd grown into a strong Christian woman, and she didn't want to lose that.

Maybe it was wrong to want to do it again, to submit to another man and put herself in yet another situation. She'd moved in with Daniel—although temporarily—until they got married. Another man who would again control her, and if it didn't work out, what then?

She would be back to square one.

This was an untenable situation; Adam threatening to take custody of Arianna, and Daniel discovering he had twin daughters from his first love. Was marriage really the right way to deal with this?

Maybe walking away and taking some time out to really understand who she was, would be the best approach. And maybe over time, her heart wouldn't ache so much.

But then she thought what was so wrong in becoming a wife and mother and submitting to the man she loved with all her heart? Being independent and alone wasn't all roses and sunshine; she'd lived it over the last two years. She'd also spent ten years feeling alone in a loveless marriage, and her past was a clear example that marriage wasn't the answer either.

She was so confused.

She sighed. "Okay, I'm sorry, you do deserve better from me, but you've been away, spending time with your ex, the woman you admit you still love, who you *kissed*. How am I supposed to feel? I can't just pretend that it didn't happen, Daniel."

Daniel assessed her, trying to ascertain what was behind her actions. Did she cancel the wedding because she was angry? Or did she really want to end things with him and go back to her ex? The thought of it made his heart race with fear. "So you're punishing me? You called off our wedding to spite me?"

"No..."

"Which I had to find out from my mother, I might add. You didn't even give me the courtesy of a phone call to let me know."

"I know, I'm sorry." Sara gave him a contrite look and stepped a little closer to him. She was wrong. She should have called him, but she knew he would talk her out of it.

"Why, then? Don't you want to be with me?"

I don't know what I want. She didn't respond, looking away.

"You're just going to walk out and leave me?"

"Isn't that what you did to me?"

"Oh come on, Sara! I begged you to come out to see me, begged you to stay, and you refused!"

"Because you wanted to be with your ex. Who was I to stand in your way?"

"My wife to be, that's who you are."

"Am I?"

"Yes."

"So you haven't changed your mind, then?" She searched his face looking for a sign.

He sighed, losing his patience. "Why don't you tell me what you're really upset about so we can resolve this like adults, instead of you behaving like a child and running away?"·

That angered her. "So now I'm childish?"

"Well, if the shoe fits..."

She wanted to throw something at him. She saw amusement flicker in his eyes for a moment.

"Do it," Daniel challenged. "Throw something at me if it will make you talk to me instead of hiding behind the real issue here."

She said nothing in response.

He waited. Still nothing. "I'm sorry Amy and I shared a kiss. It shouldn't have happened."

"You *shared* a kiss? What does that actually mean? Did *you* kiss her? Or did *she* kiss you? Which is it, Daniel?" Sara blinked back the tears that stung her eyes. His kissing Amy had hurt. The pain of it stabbed her chest. Anger and jealousy flooded through her.

"So this is about the kiss, then?"

"Of course it's about the kiss! It's about everything! Amy—you loving her, your twins, everything, Daniel!"

He said nothing for a moment.

"Well?" she prompted.

"It was both. She kissed me and I didn't pull away, not straight away, anyway. We shared a moment, a moment where we remembered. And then I pulled away, because it felt wrong, she wasn't you."

He held her gaze. "I need you to forgive me for that. For wanting to remember, she's a part of my life that I'd suppressed over the years. I never really dealt with my feelings and I allowed the hurt and pain of it to fester into resentment and bitterness. Seeing her again, realising that she never lied to me, that the situation that she found herself in was forced upon her, knocked me for six. God had given me a gift and I threw it away. And the *guilt*, Sara, was difficult, because I'd made promises...that she believed, and trusted."

He sighed. "I promised to protect her and look after her and I didn't. So for a moment, we remembered, and I can't take it back. I'm sorry, I'm only human." He took a step toward her. "What I needed from you was your support. I needed you to understand. I know it's difficult for you, too. But I need this from you, Sara. I need your forgiveness, just as I need Amy's forgiveness for what I did to her."

Tears came to Sara's eyes and rolled down her cheeks. She wanted to go to him, because for the first time the love and compassion she should have felt for Daniel—the man who had become a precious and valued friend—hit her, the selfless love she should have felt in the beginning.

"We cried that night, and we talked, and then we cried some more. But I didn't sleep with her. I didn't want to. There is only one woman that I want, and that's you, Sara."

Sara saw the pain in his eyes, and she also saw the love. The fear and apprehension she felt disappeared.

"I love you, Sara."

"But you're in love with *her,* how can we get married if you're in love with someone else?"

"Do you think that the love I feel for Amy negates what I feel for you? It doesn't, Sara. We were created to love—God *is* love.

Do you think that love should only be restricted to one person? The love you feel for Arianna…does that limit the love you feel for me?"

"No, but that's different."

"Why is it different? God never intended for us to limit the love we feel for others and it's something I had to learn the hard way. I never explored the love I felt for my father, or should have felt, because I suppressed it through anger, resentment and unforgiveness. The closest person to me—my brother—I resented him, too. I resented his relationship with my father. I love my brother, but the love I should have shown him over the years was suppressed through unforgiveness, resentment, and anger. And then I met Amy and the cycle repeated itself."

He stepped a little nearer, now standing close enough that they could touch. He reached out and took her hand in his. "Since becoming a Christian—since falling in love with you, I've realised I can't be that person anymore. I cannot live with unforgiveness and resentments in my heart. I've let it go, and all that is left is love. I can't suppress it. So, yes, I love Amy, and there will always be a part of me that loves her. She's the mother of my children and I have to do what is right by her. But that does not change what I feel for you. You're everything to me, Sara. I love you more, my love for you is limitless. I want you, Sara. I choose *you*, not Amy. If I wanted Amy, I could have had Amy, but I don't, I want you."

He reached out and caressed her cheek. "You're my first choice, not my second, please understand that. I love you, and I want a life with you. I want you to have my babies, and I want to grow old with you." He pulled her into his arms. "I need you, Sara. Marry me, I want you to be my wife."

"Oh… Yes. I want to, so much. I love you, Daniel." Sara reached up and touched his face, then slipped her arms around his neck and hugged him close.

She closed her eyes when his arms circled her waist, realising for the first time how true his words were. God's love was limitless, and no one should limit the love they felt for others. Although the love he felt for Amy was still a little unsettling to her, she knew this was God's divine hand. The Holy Spirit had told her from the beginning that Daniel needed to forgive Amy, and He had asked her to help Daniel to do that. At the time she hadn't known God's divine purpose, and now that she did, how could she want to take that from him?

Her love for Daniel was not selfish; she wanted him to be happy and fulfilled just as much as she wanted that for herself. God's purpose all along had been for Daniel to re-unite with his daughters and she was reminded of 1 Corinthians 13—*Love is patient, love is kind. It does not envy, it does not boast, it is not proud. It does not dishonour others, it is not self-seeking, it is not easily angered, it keeps no record of wrongs. Love does not delight in evil but rejoices with the truth. It always protects, always trusts, always hopes, always perseveres.*

Daniel protected her, honoured her, had always been honest with her and ever so kind and giving.

He loved her, and she loved him, and ultimately, their love had—without a doubt—only ever been, a resolute love.

Epilogue

Sara nervously waited, willing the pregnancy indicator to change colour, although she already knew she was pregnant, the Holy Spirit had confirmed it.

Excitement filled her as the tiny cross turned blue and she screamed with delight. "Thank you, Lord!" she shouted, tears coming to her eyes.

Thank you so much.

"I love you, Sara."

She loved God so much; He had been there throughout her life, even when she ignored Him and decided she wanted the things of this life and not Him, and He showed her that without Him, there was nothing. It was then, when she realised this, that He gave back in abundance, rewarding and showering her with blessings. He gave her Arianna, and brought Daniel into her life.

She smiled as she thought of her husband. They decided not to wait any longer and had gotten married in Jamaica, just as she'd wanted. If it had been up to Daniel, it would have been sooner.

God truly loved her. He had shown her by bringing a man like Daniel into her life, so caring, loving, and considerate. A man who not only loved her how she needed to be loved, but also loved Arianna and gave her all the love she needed too.

And now she was pregnant.

She wanted to sing and shout to the whole world.

Needing desperately to share the news with someone, she dialled Rachel's number.

"You're on your honeymoon, why are you calling me?" Rachel asked, then laughed, "You can't be bored already?"

Hardly. Boredom is the furthest thing on my mind.

They were staying at David's villa in Negril; it was glorious, surrounded by floor-to-ceiling glass overlooking the Caribbean Sea. The beach was wonderful and they spent the majority of their time there. The family were at a hotel nearby; Maya and Daniella had joined them, too. Sara and Daniel had been there a week and rarely left their room.

"Daniel's popped out to get something for our lunch." Then she remembered something. "Do you remember when I told you we would meet two rich men and get married in the Caribbean? And you said, and I quote—'keep dreaming, Sara?'"

"Yes, how could I forget? You were right, I didn't take you seriously. You've always had the gift to speak things into being."

"Well, I've got some other news," Sara couldn't contain her excitement. "I'm pregnant!"

Rachel screamed into the phone.

"You can't say anything to David I haven't told Daniel yet, but I needed to tell someone. I'm so happy!"

Rachel laughed. "I think Daniel already knows, Sara."

"How do you know that?" Silly question, *David.* "Okay, what did David say?"

"He didn't come out and say it exactly, he had a dream and they often share dreams, don't they."

"Oh," she said, disappointment filling her. "I wanted to surprise him. How did Daniel react in the dream?"

Rachel laughed again. "I don't know, David didn't go into details. I'm sure Daniel will be pleased, he loves children."

Yes, and he loved Arianna; she had no doubts there. "I hope so."

"You do realise that you'll have twins, right?"

"Yes! I'm so excited... My two will grow up with your two!" Sara grinned. "I feel so blessed."

"We'll have this conversation again in six months. My tummy is huge!"

Sara didn't care; she was too happy to care about anything right now. She looked up at the sound of the door opening and Daniel's return. "Daniel's back, I've got to go, bye."

She disconnected the call and went to relieve her husband of the many shopping bags he carried in his hands. "What did you do, buy out the shop?" She placed them on the sofa.

He chuckled. "I wanted to have a special lunch today."

She smiled as he pulled her into his arms. "Every moment with you is special, Daniel."

He cupped her face and kissed her.

She would never get used to his kisses; they seemed to send her to another time and place, and every moment they kissed it was different, a discovery that took her to another level, rocking her senses.

He slowly pulled away, his eyes alight with something, and she couldn't quite work out what it was.

"I love you, Sara."

"I love you, too, Daniel, so very much."

He pulled away and took her by the hand, leading her to the sofa. He searched in one of the bags and took out a light brown stuffed bear, with huge soft eyes. "Do you have some news for me?" He smiled expectantly.

Sara grinned. "It was supposed to be a surprise!"

"No surprises with me, unfortunately for you. Holy Spirit told me yesterday and I dreamt about it last night. Well?"

"I'm pregnant. I'm so happy!" She flung her arms around his neck, hugging him tightly. Then a thought crossed her mind.

She pulled back and stared at him. "You're happy about this, right?"

"Yes, more than I ever thought possible."

The End

If you enjoyed *Resolute Love*, I would be so grateful if you could spare five minutes and leave a review. Your support really means a lot.

The Vision of Love Series
Find out what happens between Rachel and David

When Two Love As One
&
When Two Become One

Coming soon...

Circumstances push Samyra and Joshua together, forcing them both to re-evaluate their plans, their goals, their everything...

Discover how their love develops in Book 5 of The Vision of Love series, **HEAVEN'S GIFT.**

Shauna hates storms. Brandon rescues her one dark night and she sweeps him off his feet, turning his life upside down. He isn't prepared for Shauna—and he isn't prepared for the storm she creates within him...

Discover how Brandon rides the storm in Book 1 of The Unmerited Grace series, **A STORMY CONCEPTION**

Christine never stopped loving Andrew, but he is her past and she isn't prepared to open old wounds. She has moved on and she wants things to remain that way.

Will Andrew remain in her past? Find out in Book 2 of The Unmerited Grace series, **A LOVE LOST**

"I am yours, and you are mine..." It has always been that way between them, from the very first moment of love.

Kyle thinks his dreams have come true when he marries Faye. But soon they discover that their wants—never mind their needs—are the least of the challenges that lie ahead for them. Will her love remain his for always? Find out in Book 3 of the Howard Family series, **MINE FOR ALWAYS.**

Join my mailing list for updates and the release dates.
www.dionnegrace.com

The Prequel

The Vision of Love Series

Excerpt from My Heart Whispers

How it all began...

Four stories of love, hate, and deceit—a snippet of their lives, before their relationships ended. The scars that formed—and later healed by God through his love—are all revealed in this series.

Ben

Chapter One

"You had no right to do that!" Rachel's voice faltered and became a whisper. "I loved that dress..." She flopped on the bed in tears, clutching the remnants of one of her favourite dresses that he'd cut to shreds.

Her husband, Benjamin Brenner, was towering over her—angry and unrelenting. He wore a black suit, tie undone around the collar of his shirt. Average height and slim, yet conversely, his jacket hid his slightly rounded belly, which protruded over the waistband of his trousers.

"You're a hussy. I've told you that I don't want you wearing clothes like this. You're my wife and you will do as I say!" Ben paced angrily, irritated by her waterworks.

Lyndsey was waiting, and he was desperate to be in her arms. He hadn't seen her for a few days; she'd been away on business. He needed her, and he certainly didn't need *this*.

There was a Bar Association dinner at the Marriott tonight, and as a prominent lawyer at McIntyre and Porter, he was comfortable, experienced, and very much at the top of his game. He'd made a tonne of money over the years from rich clients—mainly in divorce cases—who hid money from their wives, property, mistresses, you name it, they hid it. Anything to get out of sharing half with their now-tedious plaything, itching to move on to the next woman they'd been sleeping with behind their wives' backs.

He'd picked up a few tricks himself, and had become quite cunning. He owned properties across London, making a fortune managing his rental income with limited effort on his part. He'd employed staff to run his businesses on his behalf.

Rachel didn't have a clue.

She was the Christian dutiful wife who always did as she was told. Well, it hadn't always been that way; he'd managed to manipulate her into his way of thinking through emotional exploitation. He focused on her weaknesses, and her strengths—he made her think even those were inadequate. He was skilled in the courtroom and apt at winning cases, resulting in him becoming top in his firm and highly respected.

And on Rachel, his manipulative skill served its purpose.

He'd never loved her, but it looked good to the firm to be married. It elevated his status. He fooled her into thinking he was a Christian man when they'd met, made her believe that he loved everything about the church, when his only intention was to get her into his bed.

He succeeded—she trusted him. They got married soon after, and lived a comfortable life; then he got her pregnant. Which again was deliberate, he wanted children—no, that wasn't altogether the truth, his status looked good if he appeared to be the loving family man, and perversely, it kept her on lockdown, he knew where she was at all times. He never let her go anywhere other than when it was convenient to him.

He took her virginity and she belonged to him. He would not let another man have what was his, even if he didn't want it himself.

Sex with her had been uninspiring and routine over the years and he left her alone to be the unresponsive ice queen *virgin* that she was. He'd shattered her ideals and beliefs, and it felt good to have that power over her.

He'd enjoyed himself over the years, as there were many willing females who satisfied his needs. He didn't need her in that way, and it suited him.

Rachel fulfilled her purpose. She was a very beautiful woman who turned heads when she walked into a room. She seemed unaware of this, and—given her somehow regal presence—one couldn't help but notice.

Again, this fed his power. All his associates at the office were jealous of what he had—it suited his intentions. He didn't mind if they looked a little, but not too much.

There had been an occasion where they'd gone out to dinner with his colleagues and their wives—did Rachel know her rightful place, to socialise with the women? No, that would have been asking for too much, wouldn't it?

He found her talking to some man in the foyer of the restaurant on the pretence of going to the ladies'. He'd been livid and suspected that, given the opportunity, she would leave him.

This happened often, more often than he liked. Men were drawn to her beauty like a magnet, but he wasn't having that. Thus, over the years, he put her on lockdown.

They had two children and they kept her busy. He'd contemplated getting her pregnant again, just to shut up her whining. But he couldn't bring himself to touch her.

He'd fallen in love with Lyndsey, and she was where he wanted to be—he just didn't care anymore. He looked at his watch; Lyndsey was meeting him at the hotel. His heart began to race in anticipation.

His thoughts drifted to the last time he saw her. They were staying at Claridges, their usual place when they were too desperate for each other to drive to their home in Kent. Their daughter was staying with her grandmother, so they had the night together.

Having three children; two with Rachel—Rebecca and Matthew. The other, Angelica. He should have been a proud father, but it was Angelica who was his pride and joy, only a year-old and made out of his love with Lyndsey. Angelica was his favourite and he felt no guilt about that.

He was stretched out in bed, and Lyndsey was dressing.

"I thought we were spending the night together?" He frowned, sitting up and leaning back against the headboard. His dark hair an unruly mess where she'd gently teased and stroked it. *God, he loved her.*

He watched her dress, admiring her, captivated by her beauty. Soft, porcelain skin, with delicate freckles across her shoulders that he loved to kiss. An hourglass figure—perfection. Her auburn hair was a curtain of fire that drifted and fell over her brow. She was a delight to him—his love.

"I haven't seen Angelica in three days. I need to see her, and so do you." She continued to dress, and he could see she was beginning to get upset. He wanted to hold her; he'd missed her while she was away.

He moved to the edge of the bed. "Come here, my love."

She loved it when he called her by that endearment, her smile a testament of this as she sauntered over to him. He pulled her close, wrapping his arms around her waist, resting his head against her tummy as she stood before him. She lightly fingered his hair, her other hand stoking his face lovingly.

He rested his hand on her tummy, lightly stroking the place where their baby was growing inside her, barely four weeks along. He kissed her tummy, then looked up at her, pulling her onto his lap. "Don't be angry," he gently coaxed. "I'll leave her, I promise—soon."

"You keep saying that and you're not doing anything about it." She pouted and caressed his face. "I thought you loved me?"

He looked deep into her eyes. "Soon, sweetheart, I promise, I just need a little more time to move some funds around. I don't want Rachel to have anything that belongs to us when we get divorced."

Lyndsey seemed content with that and she kissed him, gently, lovingly…

His mind returned to the present. Impatience filled him. He needed to see Lyndsey.

He looked down at Rachel; in tears over the dress she thought she would wear tonight to accompany him. Her long dark hair a loose array of curls, gold earrings dangling from her ears, big brown doleful eyes—a window to a broken spirit. She licked her full luscious lips as she took a breath in between sobs.

She nervously clutched her cream silk dressing gown closed. Mid-length, exposing shapely legs sheathed in sheer tights and heels she'd intended to wear tonight until he tore the dress off her, and slashed it with a knife. It felt good to use the knife—he saw the fear in her eyes.

He felt it rise up inside him, the power within…

His eyes drifted over her legs again—she looked beautiful, but he would never tell her that.

Evenings out with him? Those days were over; her place was in his home, looking after his children. He would do everything in his power to ensure she would never leave him, as he would never leave her.

Dominance and supremacy filled his soul. She was weak and broken—he'd done what he'd intended.

It felt good.

My Heart Whispers

The Vision of Love Series

Book 1

The Vision of Love Series

Excerpt from When Two Love As One

Rachel is not interested in another relationship and David wants a wife. She is the answer to his prayers, and being an impatient man, used to getting what he wants, he won't let her go.

She returned her gaze to his. "What did the Holy Spirit tell you about me...about us?"

David averted his eyes, taken aback by her question. What could he say without revealing what the Holy Spirit had told him?

"You want more than just friendship, don't you?" she asked, pressing him.

He returned his gaze to hers. He wanted a whole lot more than he'd realised—the attraction between them was too strong. "Yes."

Rachel guessed as much. She could feel it. "David...I can't be anything more than your friend." Her voice was gentle; she didn't want to hurt his feelings. "I'm sorry." She felt a nudge inside her from the Holy Spirit. She ignored it.

"Why can't we be more than that? We are very much attracted to each other, there is no denying that, and you are a very beautiful woman, Rachel."

His eyes darkened and became intense, making it difficult to keep eye contact. Her heart began to pound under the heat of his gaze, and she looked away for a moment, glancing around the busy restaurant at the other couples enjoying romantic interludes, and she wanted to keep well away from anything near romance. Yes, the attraction was strong, but it wasn't something she would entertain or consider. "Because I'm not looking for a relationship right now."

"When will you be?"

She laughed. "Never!"

He raised a brow, but did not join in with her laughter.

Her smile faded and she sighed. He was clearly irked by her response, hence the reason why she did not encourage friendships with men. It always resulted in her letting them down, their egos so bruised that she never saw them again. It was a shame, because she really liked David and knew she could learn a lot from him. "I'm sorry. I don't mean to make light of your interest in me. You're a very attractive man. I'm sure there are many women out there who would want your attention."

"Ahh, but they're not you, Rachel."

"Oh, I'm nothing special, believe me. I already have a failed marriage under my belt and have no intention of ever going down that road again." She paused for a moment. "And you strike me as a man who does not have casual relationships."

"And you do?"

She chuckled. "I don't have those either!" She looked over at him guiltily, as he clearly did not see the humorous side of this and wanted her to take him seriously. "Look, David, I don't want there to be any misconceptions between us, so I'll be as honest with you as I can." She paused, lifting her glass to sip her water. "I had a very unhappy marriage—nineteen long years. I did the right thing as a Christian woman and remained in a loveless marriage, feeling trapped and suffocated. When we got divorced, I was so relieved, happy for the first time in years. I'm free and at peace, and I want to stay this way." She held his gaze, ensuring he clearly understood her. "I'm damaged goods. I'm very much scarred. I could never trust you."

When Two Love As One

The Vision of Love Series

Book 2

The Vision of Love Series

Excerpt from When Two Become One

Rachel never thought she would find a love like this, but David wants more than she is willing to give.

When he arrived home, Rachel was waiting for him.

"You're late," she said, stating the obvious and quirking an eyebrow.

He placed his keys and mobile on the table beside the door. "I'm sorry, things became difficult." He pulled her into his arms and went to kiss her, but he did not get his usual response. She averted her mouth from his and gave him a half hearted hug instead, then pulled away abruptly. "Are you okay?" He wondered what was wrong.

"Yes, I'm fine. Are you ready for dinner?" Rachel asked heading for the kitchen. She was annoyed. *Why had he taken so long?* She could smell another woman's perfume on him. No doubt Karen's perfume. *Did he have sex with her?* She felt pain stab her heart as her mind ran riot thinking of what he must have been doing why he was so late and reeking of her perfume. He offered no explanation. *"I'm sorry, things became difficult."* What was that supposed mean? She remembered he'd told her that Karen wanted him back and would dress provocatively for him and make advances towards him when he went to pick up the girls. Something had happened between them, she was convinced of it.

David felt guilty for keeping her so long, knowing she had to get home. "Let me go and see the girls first."

"They're getting ready for bed. I need to leave soon too," she informed him as he made his way upstairs.

"Okay, I won't be long." He regretted staying out so long. He'd wasted a whole evening and had not achieved anything, and he wanted to spend some time with Rachel. He headed into the girls' room.

"Daddy!" they exclaimed at the same time, rushing into his arms.

"We waited for you, but Rachel said we had to get washed for bed," Sophie said.

"You smell like Mummy, Daddy. Did you go to see her?" Keira asked.

Oh no. No wonder Rachel reacted they way she did. *Oh Lord...!* How was he going to explain how Karen's perfume came to be on him? He hadn't intended on telling her that part. It did not look good at all. *He was in trouble.*

When Two Become One

The Vision of Love Series

Book 3

The Vision of Love Series

Excerpt from Committed to Love

Sara wants love and marriage. Daniel doesn't. Commitment is not on his list of priorities, but somehow he is drawn to her, and he wants more than she is willing to give.

Sara watched her best friend Rachel dancing with her new husband, David. She couldn't help but be a little envious as she watched them; the love between them was evident as they swayed to the music on the dance floor. Sara had been praying for a husband for so long that she wondered if God had forgotten her—or maybe this was it for her. Maybe she would never find love again.

She sighed, suppressing a deep need inside. Only one man held her attention, and her gaze drifted to him. He was standing by the bar with a drink in his hand. He was the most beautiful man she had ever seen. No, he was the second most beautiful man she had ever seen. He was David's twin—they were identical, two men who were positively divine. Rachel was a blessed woman.

Sara had known Daniel for three months now, and he fascinated her. He was a confirmed bachelor and intended on staying that way. He'd asked her out many times, but she never took him seriously, as she was one of a long list of women he pursued. So they'd remained friends, and she enjoyed just looking at him as she did now. Gorgeous green eyes, perfect nose, a moustache that accentuated his full lips and a short, neatly trimmed beard that shadowed his face. He was perfect, but a man she could not have.

She made her way to him, her dress flowing around her, clinging to her curves; as maid of honour, her dress matched the bride's—cool ivory satin, so perfect for the hot Caribbean weather. She'd completed the look with matching delicate high-heeled sandals. She stood beside him and followed his gaze as he watched his brother and his now sister-in-law kiss each other lovingly. Rachel reached up and caressed her husband's face and laughed at something David whispered in her ear.

"The one that got away, huh?" Sara asked, giving Daniel a knowing look. He tore his gaze away for a moment, and she saw something flicker in his eyes, but then it was gone, and she didn't quite work out what it was.

"What would make you say a thing like that, Sara?"

"Because I believe you're secretly in love with Rachel." She smiled, knowing it was the truth, not really expecting an answer. "Let me buy you a drink so you can drown your sorrows," she teased.

"It's an open bar, Sara." He smiled with her.

"Well, the thought was there. I'm a kind-hearted lass." She loved to tease him. "What are you having?"

"Fruit juice—the perfect tipple to drown my sorrows in."

She looked at him. Was he finally admitting that he had a thing for Rachel?

"No, I'm not admitting to anything. Get that thought out of your head."

She chuckled and busied herself with ordering their drinks. As she turned away, she could feel the heat of his gaze on her. Her dress was backless, with crisscross straps; she knew what would come next before she turned to him.

"You're a very beautiful woman, Sara. When are you going to stop fighting this thing between us?"

She turned to face him again, handing him his drink. "What thing? We don't have a thing." She sipped from her juice and avoided his gaze. His eyes travelled over her body, and his slow perusal felt like a caress. Her heart began to race. "Will you stop…" She met his gaze and saw amusement dance in his eyes, desire within their depths.

He leaned in close and whispered in her ear, and she felt the brush of his breath against the nape of her neck. "I don't want to stop. You outshine every woman here."

She stepped away from him, taking in a breath as butterflies fluttered in her stomach. She wondered if he had this effect on every woman he pursued. He made her weak, a temptation she could not afford to entertain. "Is that a line you use often?"

"Sara…stop fighting this."

His eyes darkened; they were almost blue, beautiful, holding her captive. She forced herself to look away, anywhere but in his incredibly beautiful green, blue, sometimes grey eyes. Then she said the words that she knew would keep him at bay, almost guaranteed; "If I didn't know better, Daniel, I would think that you were falling in love with me." His whole persona changed in response. He straightened and looked away from her. It works every time.

"What's love got to do with it?"

She laughed and sang a note from the Tina Turner song. He laughed with her, shaking his head. "You are so predictable, Daniel. You really ought to get over this thing you have against love and marriage."

"I have nothing against it. It's just not for me. I prefer other pursuits."

Committed to Love

The Vision of Love Series

Also by Dionne Grace

The Vision of Love Series.

MY HEART WHISPERS
WHEN TWO LOVE AS ONE
WHEN TWO BECOME ONE
COMMITTED TO LOVE
RESOLUTE LOVE

Howard Family Series

GIFTED LOVE
IF ONLY...

The Faith Series

FAITHFULLY AGAIN
FAITHFUL SURRENDER

God's Perfect Timing Series

TIME TO NEED

Individual Titles

MAYBE NOW
MAYBE FOREVER
A CHRISTMAS PRAYER
FOR ETERNITY
FOREVER IN MY HEART

Social Media Links

goodreads.com/dionnegrace

facebook.com/dionnegraceauthor7

instagram.com/authordionnegrace7

twitter.com/Dionnegrace8

pinterest.co.uk/dionnegrace7

Join her mailing list
www.dionnegrace.com

About the Author

Dionne Grace is a romantic at heart. She loves reading books, which in her early teenage years enhanced her vivid imagination. She would often invent fascinating love stories to entertain her school friends involving famous pop stars. She used to scribble notes on the back of school books while her teacher's backs were turned! Her friends loved it, and remind her of it to this day!

She loves to write and when she is not writing, she is reading and juggles this with her full-time job.

She writes sweet romances, about couples in relationships who have a passion for each other. Sometimes this passion leads them into situations where they lose themselves, taking them down a path which possibly they should not have gone down, or in contrast, through life's experiences; they reject the love that is offered, not having the faith or forgiveness to trust it.

Her books are intentionally thought provoking, and real life. A message about a discovery of how the scars of life can be healed, no matter how difficult this sometimes seems in this imperfect world. And ultimately, through God's divine intervention he imparts a revelation of what his purpose was all along.

As you must have guessed, she has a love for God and everything spiritual; she hopes this shines through in her books.

www.dionnegrace.com